SARAH GOODWIN
STRANDED

avon.

Published by AVON
A division of HarperCollins*Publishers* Ltd
1 London Bridge Street
London SE1 9GF

www.harpercollins.co.uk

HarperCollins*Publishers*
1st Floor, Watermarque Building, Ringsend Road
Dublin 4, Ireland

A Paperback Original 2021

1

First published in Great Britain by HarperCollins*Publishers* 2021

A catalogue copy of this book is available from the British Library.

ISBN: 978-0-00-846736-4

This novel is entirely a work of fiction. The names, characters
and incidents portrayed in it are the work of the author's
imagination. Any resemblance to actual persons, living
or dead, events or localities is entirely coincidental.

Typeset in Sabon MT Std by
Palimpsest Book Production Ltd, Falkirk, Stirlingshire

Printed and Bound in the UK using 100% Renewable Electricity
at CPI Group (UK) Ltd

MIX
Paper from
responsible sources
FSC™ C007454

This book is produced from independently certified FSC™ paper
to ensure responsible forest management.

For more information visit: www.harpercollins.co.uk/green

Sarah Goodwin is a debut author who completed the BA and MA in Creative Writing at Bath Spa. She also runs a book review podcast, called Witchfix. She lives in rural Hertfordshire.

To my parents, for believing I could do anything.
Even (especially) when I didn't agree.

Prologue

Frozen to the bone, I stumble from the boat and look around me at the village. It's not Creel, but some place exactly like it; houses tumbling like rocks down towards the hungry sea. Fishing boats and cracked concrete. I stand there, swaying slightly with the motion of the boat I've left behind. There's no sound or movement from the houses.

Somehow, despite coming so far, through so much, the idea of going up to one of the doors and knocking, being confronted by a stranger, has me frozen. What is waiting in those houses? Is there even anyone there?

'Are you all right, Poppet?'

I turn so fast I nearly fall over. On the doorstep of a tiny cottage is an old woman in a wool skirt and fluffy slippers. Her eyes are wide and she has a wire cage of milk bottles in one hand, her back still half stooped to put it on the doorstep.

As I turn, her eyes fall to the strap of the rifle and she drops the bottles. They smash, throwing glass over the concrete step. Fear is etched on her face as I remove the rifle and lay it on the ground.

I rise and glance down at my ripped and muddy clothing, hanging off my skeletal body. With effort I part my sticky, salt-crusted lips.

'*I need the police.*'

Chapter 1

'Maddy?'

I blinked, suddenly aware of how long it must have been since they'd asked the question I was fumbling to answer. I adjusted the laptop on my knees and looked at my image on screen. The fluorescent kitchen light made me look greenish on the rubbish webcam. My hair was ratty even though I'd brushed it out before the video call. My recent weight gain bloated my face like a toad. Had I not been blinking I might have looked dead.

'Yes, sorry,' I said. 'What got me into botany, uh . . . Well, it was my dad really. He was a gardener. Not as his job. We had a garden – a vegetable garden.' I was babbling, and I hated myself for it. On screen the woman interviewing me, Sasha, had a fixed smile on her face. She was in a glass cube of an office, crisp black suit jacket standing out against the white wall.

I forced myself to take a breath. 'My dad, he and Mum taught me at home. So everything I learned about

3

biology, about plants, that came from him. He was very involved in his garden.'

'So you were home-schooled? That's quite unusual – were you ever at a . . . traditional school?' she said, skipping over the word 'normal'.

I bit my lip. 'Um, yes. I wasn't home-schooled until I was eleven. Before then I went to the village primary school. After that everyone moved on to the secondary in town.'

I remembered in vivid detail my first day at the big secondary school. The laughter at my cartoon-dog lunchbox, playmates melting away into the crowds, abandoning me in the new, bigger pond we found ourselves in. Girls much older than me with lipstick and cigarettes chasing me out of the toilets. I'd cried in the car all the way home. Mum had taken one look at me and gathered me up in floury arms.

'There, what did I tell you?' she'd said to Dad. 'That place is far too rough for her.'

Within a few weeks it was all arranged and I never went to school again. At the time I was glad, but later I wished I'd hidden my feelings better. Whenever I wanted to do something new, away from the house – Brownies, ballet, horse riding – Mum was quick to remind me what had happened 'last time'. That incident gave her the last word in every argument.

Sasha cocked her sleek blonde head to one side and frowned, designer glasses slipping down her nose. 'Was there any specific reason? I think our viewers would be very interested to find out more about your background.'

4

'Nothing specific,' I said, mustering a smile. 'They just didn't like the school nearest us. Out that far in the country there aren't many options.'

'That must have made it hard, finding friends?'

I sensed the danger I was in. To be chosen I had to be a joiner, an adventurous optimist with an 'openness to new experiences and ideas'. It was on the website. I'd memorised it. This was not 'joiner' talk. This was too close to the truth.

'Not really,' I breezed, 'it wasn't that long until I went off to university and that was all very different. Exciting.'

She smiled and I cringed internally. Yes, university had been different. I'd been on my own. No cosy night-time reading by the fire with Mum. No long walks with Dad and the dogs. Just music and celebrities I'd never heard of, wearing clothes decades too old for me and thinking nine at night was for bed and books, not shots and a staggering run for the bus to town.

'You must be really close with your family,' she said, as if she could see into my mind and read every one of those lonely nights on the phone to Mum. 'Will you miss them, while you're away?'

'No . . . I mean, obviously I will, but . . . it's fine.' I forced myself not to look at the lone card on my bookshelf. The one drooping lily on it and the slightly cross-eyed dove conveying the deepest sympathies of my manager and a handful of colleagues. 'The, uh, website said the show is about the end of the world – how does it end in the version you've dreamt up?

Does the country get bombed or is there a famine, a war?'

Sasha smiled. 'That's actually one of the questions I was going to ask you. We're deliberately leaving it open-ended, to provoke discussion amongst the contestants. There are so many things happening in the world right now. Everyone has their own theories about the end of the world. What do you think it will look like?'

At the back of my throat was a sour taste. My world, such as it was, had already ended.

'I don't know. Maybe . . . Well, I did one of my dissertations on the dangers of monocultures. If we grow exclusively one type of plant and a pest arises that decimates it, that could spell disaster for our food supply.' I saw her eyebrows go up and immediately wished I'd said something less textbook. 'But I'd have to go with zombies,' I added, hastily, with a little laugh. 'I think most people would be disappointed if the apocalypse came and it didn't somehow feature zombies.'

She laughed and I breathed a sigh of relief, slowly, so it wouldn't be obvious on camera.

'So, what are you most looking forward to, should you get chosen to take part in *The Last Refuge*?'

This time my answer was genuine, unconsidered. 'The escape.'

From my life, my grief, from myself.

I just had to get away.

*

When the email came to tell me I'd been accepted my first reaction was disbelief. When that wore off I cried even as my heart raced with excitement. I was getting what I wanted. What I needed. I was getting away.

I went to a new doctor for a letter to say I was healthy enough to take part in the show. I was, aside from the therapy I was avoiding and the tablets I had to take, but she didn't have to know about that. Then I was up to London for official interviews, the kind that would be on television when the rest of the show aired. They had someone do my hair and makeup. Sasha asked me questions; apparently they hadn't hired a presenter to do that part yet. That felt like an over-sight, but what did I know? Anyway, I didn't want to think about the end product too much. I wanted to be on that island. What came after, the broadcast, the interviews, returning to my life; I didn't want to think about it.

We'd be going to the island in two groups, boys and girls. That's what Sasha called us. Boys and girls. Like we were kids off on a Famous Five adventure. I didn't say that, though. Sasha didn't look like the kind of person to remember Enid Blyton.

I met my three travelling companions at Glasgow station. I was already exhausted from dragging my laden bags across the country. We'd been told to expect some building supplies on the island and tools as well as food caches. It wasn't until I'd been tipping botany books and rolls of toilet paper into my bag that I'd realised how little I could actually take with me.

7

I paused a short way from the meeting place – a taxi rank under a plastic shelter. There were three women already there, dressed similarly to me and carrying the same bulging bags of stuff. Two appeared older than me, the third was younger, glued to an iPhone. My first instinct was to turn around and run away. After my long journey these would be the first people I had to make conversation with. We were going to be sharing an island, a home, for almost a year. My anxiety levels skyrocketed, and I had to force myself to walk towards them, feeling again like it was my first day of school.

'Are you with us?' trilled the first of them to spot me. She had streaky hair clipped short with a long fringe. Her skin was wrinkled and deeply tanned, her smile glistening with pearly pink lipstick. She kissed me on each cheek. 'We were starting to think you'd never get here, weren't we, ladies?'

'Sorry. The coach got delayed. Roadworks.'

'Ah, we all came by train. I'm Gill, by the way – and you are?'

'Maddy,' I said, feeling already like I'd disappointed in some way.

I guessed Gill was in her forties, yet she seemed much younger and livelier than me despite being over a decade older. She spoke loudly, not caring that people nearby were staring. She was also cheerfully ignoring the 'No Smoking' sign in the shelter.

'This is Maxine and Zoe,' Gill said, gesturing with her cigarette and sending ash scattering over the bag

I'd just put down. 'Maxine's a retired teacher and Zoe's from India.'

'County Kerry actually,' Zoe said, raising an eyebrow.

Gill bared her teeth in a smile. 'I'll see about getting us a taxi, hmm?'

As Gill bustled off, Maxine stepped forward with a small smile. She was slightly older than Gill, maybe early fifties. She had straight grey hair and a fleece jacket that sported embroidered badges. She shook my hand and I felt the roughness of her palm, smelled a wisp of lavender. She reminded me instantly of Mum.

'Cold, isn't it?' she said, glancing up at the forbidding grey sky. 'I packed thermals, but I didn't think I'd need them before we got to the island.'

'It'll be colder by the sea,' I said. 'Still, at least there we can light a fire. Can't really do that in the middle of the station.'

Zoe snorted a laugh and shoved her phone into her pocket. 'Can you imagine, busting out the marshmallows by the loading bay?' From her bag she pulled out a jumbo pack of fluffy white marshmallows and waved them at me. 'Housewarming present,' she said, grinning. I smiled back.

She was a few years younger than me, probably early twenties, and wearing a bright silk head wrap, thick-rimmed glasses and a nose ring. I guessed she was a student or artist. She packed the sweets away and offered her hennaed hand. I shook it, already feeling overwhelmed by her effortless style.

Gill came blaring back into view, hands cupped around her mouth. 'Over here! Bring my bag!'

We traipsed over and found her still haggling with a minicab driver. Apparently our destination was not somewhere he cared to go. I couldn't blame him. On the map the village of Creel was just a dot and a name, about as far west from Glasgow as it was possible to get without a boat. Eventually, whether because of Gill's cajoling or the growing number of crumpled notes we managed to find in our luggage, the driver agreed to take us. We piled into the car, squashed between our bags. Maxine offered round some sherbet lemons and we left the station behind.

'I wonder what it's going to be like, out there,' Zoe said, after taking a few selfies in the taxi. 'Tell you one thing, I'm starting to regret bringing a bikini.'

I noticed Maxine's part surprised, part scornful look at that. A bikini on a Scottish island – not much use unless global warming really upped its game in the coming months. Still, Zoe didn't seem to be taking herself too seriously as she said it.

'What I want to know is, when do we meet the boys?' Gill said. 'Where's their boat leaving from?'

'No idea,' Maxine said. 'I imagine somewhere just up the coast from where we're going. I don't really see the point. We're all going to the same place.'

'It's fun though, isn't it? Not knowing who's going to be there,' Zoe said. 'I hope they're nice. Not too blokey or anything.'

'Blokey enough to build a house though,' Gill put

10

in. 'I'm not really into camping out for a whole year.'

'Are you sure you picked the right show?' Maxine asked, sounding mostly playful.

'Oh, I like the outdoors. I love gardening and soaking up the sun, but give me four solid walls and a floor over a nylon bag any day,' Gill said.

'I love camping. Been to Glasto four times and it's so nice to not be worried about all that domestic stuff – just mud and glitter and a pint of cider,' Zoe giggled. 'What about you, Maddy?'

I blinked, surprised to be pulled so directly into their conversation. I'd been quite happy listening and watching the world scroll by.

'Oh . . . I like camping. I used to go with my parents when I was younger. You get a lot of reading done, when there's no distractions.' We always went out of season to save money. Even if there were other kids around, Mum would forbid me from following them to the play area or pool. She wanted me close by; there was no telling what might happen if I went off alone.

The three of them chatted as we drove. The air in the back of the cab grew warm and humid as their breath fogged up the windows. The driver turned the radio up every ten minutes or so, glancing back at them in the mirror with a deeper frown each time. I rested my forehead on the chilly glass and closed my eyes.

Chapter 2

'Freezing out here,' Zoe said, pulling her oversized army surplus jacket more firmly around her. 'Where's this boat at then?'

'Not a clue,' I said. 'Maybe they're late?'

Zoe produced her iPhone. Its case was layered with charms. 'No missed calls.'

I pulled a concerned face and looked out to sea again. No sign of a boat or of anything else on the horizon. It was half an hour past the time the letter from the production company said to be there. I was already cold down to my bones. I wondered if the other four prospective islanders had been collected yet. Had they already set foot on the unmarked sand of our deserted home?

Glancing at the others I saw that Gill was still chain-smoking, drumming her foot. Maxine had a brand-new-looking thermos and was sipping something.

I put down my holdall by the iron railings at the edge of the seafront. As I leant over to get a good look at the churning sea, I noted the *fucus vesiculosus*, aka bladder wrack. A dark seaweed with large blisters on it. At least we'd not starve. Even if the idea of eating the stuff made me shudder.

As expected, Creel seemed to be a fishing village. Even to call it a village was pushing it; five weather-beaten houses leaning together around a cobbled square with a concrete ramp down to the sea. Two of the houses had 'For Sale' signs in the windows that looked homemade and had been bleached by the sun.

Despite the weathered buildings and the absence of life, I liked the place. It felt wild and semi-reclaimed by the sea. Even the concrete front was weathered and pitted from storms. It was as if these houses and this small bit of harbour had been left behind and the waves were stealing it back with hungry fingers of foam.

Tired of waiting, I wandered further from the others with the hope that walking would warm me up. At the other end of the concrete front, I let out a breath. Finally, I felt unobserved and alone, which was a welcome change after the stressful crush of my journey. I knelt to rummage in my rucksack, digging out a knitted hat and jamming it onto my head.

I was just considering layering on another jumper when a boat appeared around the edge of the craggy coastline. It was far too small to be the one we were waiting for, barely larger than a rowboat. I watched as it bobbed nearer and saw that it contained an elderly man, his face a rawish red and his overalls faded from navy to the colour of dust at the collar. He splashed out of the boat and hauled it up the ramp, then set about removing fishing creels. Inside I saw crabs scuttling like giant spiders, trying to escape.

'Morning,' I said, when he looked up and saw me there.

'Morn',' he said, the wind snatching most of the word away.

I watched him work for a moment or two more before my anxiety got the better of me. I went over to him.

'Excuse me, do you know of any boats going from here to Buidseach Isle today? Only we were expecting it to be here around now.' I indicated the others with a tip of my head.

He stood, the freshly emptied creel in one hand, then, alarmingly, shook his head.

'Not that I know,' he said. His accent, considerably thicker than that of the taxi driver, took me a moment to decipher over the wind.

'But you know of Buidseach Isle? It's near here?' I asked, wondering if I was saying it wrong.

'It's out there; no' what I'd call near,' he said, gesturing to the sea. 'Don't know anyone that'd go out there either. Risk their boat to the witch.'

I was sure I'd misheard. 'Witch?'

He sniffed. 'Buidseach means witch. Island's named for one – an' there's been stories of that island since I was a little one. Dad used to scare me with them. He said if you ever end up near it, you've gone too far out for anyone to find you should you go down on its rocks.

The witch'd reel you in and make soup from your bones.'

I'd no idea what to say to that. I didn't believe in witches, obviously, but rocks and shipwrecks were another thing entirely. My stomach turned over with new fear and the man seemed to notice, because he smiled and shook his head.

'Only stories, lass. To teach me to respect the sea.'

I tried to muster a smile back, then turned to search the horizon. No boat, not even a blur of land in the distance. The island was invisible to the mainland.

I turned back to the fisherman and found that he had gathered his bucket of crabs and was letting himself into the cottage nearest me. Clearly I'd taken up enough of his time. I jumped when I felt a tap on my shoulder. Turning I found Zoe there, a chocolate bar in one hand.

'Want some? It's dairy-free, so it's a bit shit, but I'm starving. There were no bloody vegan options at the B&B so I only had a bit of toast. I think I'd sell my nan for a chip butty right now.'

I accepted a piece of chocolate gratefully. My last meal had been at a service station. Not what I would have chosen, but needs must. Had it been up to me I'd have gone for a proper roast with all the trimmings and a creamy rice pudding with a wrinkled nutmeg skin, just like Mum used to make every Sunday.

I was about to suggest calling the contact number from the letter when a car horn shattered the peace of the harbour. A new looking 4×4 was easing its way down the hill towards us. As we turned to look, it honked again and I saw a man inside, waving excitedly.

'Looks like this could be the telly people,' Zoe said. 'Kind of blatantly flashy, isn't it?'

I nodded. Although I didn't know much about cars it was plain this one was very new. It was clean and finished with a scalding orange paintjob. It was also clear that the owner wasn't very used to it, or perhaps he was just a terrible driver. It lurched to a stop on the cobbles and out popped a young man in a suit. Zoe and I traipsed over and formed a group with the others.

'Good morning, all!' he called against the sea wind. 'Are you ready for an adventure?'

I recognised his voice from the phone interview I'd done after sending in my application. This was Adrian, Sasha's counterpart. I guessed she was the one giving the welcome speech to the men. Behind him, two guys in anoraks and woolly hats got out and started to unload bags.

We gathered around like schoolkids on a day trip, bags in tow. Adrian was underdressed for the weather in a sharp navy suit and pink shirt. His elongated black loafers were not cobble-safe and he skidded a bit as he walked to meet us.

'Boat's on its way – little technical hiccup,' he said breezily. 'Now these two,' he added, waving an arm at his two companions, one of whom had lit a cigarette, 'are your cameramen. They'll be on the island to maintain the various outdoor game cameras we've set up and to keep your body cameras in order.'

The two cameramen looked basically identical, down to their pallid skin and sparse brown beards. Both were red-eyed and slouching tiredly, I guessed from the same stressful journey we'd all just gone through. One had quickly unfolded a tripod and was setting up a camera to film our send-off.

'Eric and Ryan here will be staying on the island with you in a little command centre – but don't worry, you won't be seeing them and they'll stay right out of your way. We want this as authentic as possible. To that end, you'll each get a body camera to film each other with, and a solar power bank to keep them up and running. As you know, I do need to collect your mobile phones. Not that they'd work out there, but we can't have you distracted, playing games or making outside recordings. They'll be returned when we collect you from the island. There is, however, a communications set-up in the camera hut, for emergencies.'

He produced a large padded envelope and we unloaded our phones. I noticed that Maxine's was a decades-old handset, not even a smart phone. Zoe dropped hers in like a kid giving up their favourite toy. It was almost endearing.

'Here's the boat,' Adrian said, relief evident in his voice. I turned and saw a medium-sized open boat with a small glass cabin, chugging towards us. My heart sank a little. We'd be on deck in the cold and spray then. I'd been looking forward to getting warm for a bit.

'Just a little scene-setting before I send you off; this'll

be the opening of our first episode,' Adrian continued, gesturing to the camera guys to start recording. While they repositioned the tripod I watched the boat draw towards the concrete slip.

With everything in place, Adrian began his speech. 'The world as we know it has come to an end. Disaster reigns and the mainland is no longer the safe and prosperous place it once was.

'You are half of a team of eight brave survivors, searching for an unsullied refuge. Together you will remake society, starting again from the ruins to create utopia. You have one year to get it right, establish infrastructure, govern yourselves and build a future from flotsam, jetsam and the natural resources available to you. If you fail, humanity fails with you.'

I cast an eye around the group. Zoe looked quite emotional, the camera guys were rolling their eyes at each other and Maxine had an expression of set determination.

'Best of luck to you,' Adrian concluded, 'and I will see you all . . . in the New Year!'

Adrian slithered back to the 4×4 on the treacherous cobbles and haltingly began to turn the car around. The cameramen shared a look and one of them muttered something that made the other choke with laughter, then cough until he spat on the cobbles.

Together we boarded the boat as the sky gathered in for a storm.

Chapter 3

The sea was rough on the way out to the island.

For a while the others attempted to talk and make plans for our arrival, but gradually all four of us fell silent, watching the horizon. We were all waiting to catch a glimpse of our new home. Our refuge. I was excited, despite being drenched with icy water and scoured by the wind. The taller of the two cameramen, Eric, spent most of the journey clinging to the side and occasionally being loudly sick into the water below. The other man filmed for a while then stood, seemingly as impatient as us for the journey to end.

'There it is!' Zoe said, leaning at the prow like a kid in her gaudy mittens. 'It's real!'

The island had appeared out of the mist of the horizon, a long greyish line with a dark blur of pine forest beyond. As we got closer I could see the spars and shards of rocks around it and remembered the fisherman telling me of the wrecks. I glanced at our captain, who was steering us with narrowed eyes and lips pressed to a thin line.

The boat wove between the rocks, circling the island to its southern side, where the way was clearer. I watched as the captain threw the wheel left and right, the engine snarling and frothing like a mad dog as he fought the current. At last, we came to the shallow water that broke on the island's beach of grey sand.

Finally, we were there. I'd gotten away and left everything else behind.

One by one we collected our bags then climbed over the side of the boat and splashed into the water, wading the last few steps to land. Standing on the fissured grey rock, slick with weed and bruise-coloured mussels, we watched the boat churn the water and leave us behind without ceremony.

'Let's get on then; it's brass monkeys out here,' Ryan said, hefting his camera bag and picking his way over the rocks to the beach. We followed. Zoe was practically fizzing with excitement beside me.

'I can't believe we're really here!'

'Me neither,' I said. 'I can't wait to get a fire going, though. It's freezing.'

'Oh, that's totally step one – that and a cuppa,' she said.

Once we were on the beach, Eric and Ryan wasted no time in distributing our cameras. They were all on nylon harnesses with clips to hold them at chest height.

'Make sure you keep these on,' Ryan said. He glanced at Eric, who still looked awful from the journey and was leaning on a rock. 'They're splash-proof, so basically the only place you can't take them is right under the water. Everywhere else is fine. As long as you're OK with it going on telly.' He winked at Zoe, who rolled her eyes. 'Power packs are a doddle, just leave one in the sun when you're using the other. Should charge even on cloudy days. They're waterproof so you can use them in the rain. You break anything, we have spares.'

'Will you be watching it as we film?' Maxine asked as we all looped the straps across our chests and turned the cameras on.

'Not live, but yeah, we'll be checking that everything's coming through OK. Everything's backed up here, then when we get collected, Adrian gets to look at it and tell us we fucked up somehow,' he said, rolling his eyes. 'Now, the game cameras, like that one' – he gestured to a black box just visible on a distant tree – 'they also feed to us, but we'll use the audio from yours so it's really important you wear them. Literally the only time you'll see us is if something breaks and we need to replace it. The cameras are solar, but please try not to cut down any trees we put them in.' He zipped up the equipment case and nudged Eric. 'Right then, we're off to our generator and coffee – have fun.'

'Wait, what about the others, where are they?' I said, feeling my wet face instantly flame with embarrassment.

'That's for you guys to find out,' Ryan said, waving his fingers in a mockery of Adrian's 'mysterious guide' shtick. 'But smart money would be on them already being here. Sasha was meeting them and she called from the road to wake Adrian up.' With a snort of derision he turned away and they walked up the beach, Eric wobbling slightly. I fiddled with the unfamiliar weight of the camera and glanced around the group.

'Should we go look for them?' Zoe asked. 'I mean, if they're already out there somewhere, that's probably the right thing to do . . . Right?'

'Makes sense,' Gill said, already picking up her bag. 'Come on, ladies, let's track down the boys.'

I was reluctant to go looking for the others right away. Having grown slightly more comfortable with the other women I wanted to get to know them better before meeting anyone else. Still, I picked up my bag and followed them. We snaked our way in a short line across the beach to the edge of the woods, which straggled down one side of the sand as if trying to reach the sea.

'Is anybody out there?' Zoe shouted, grinning. 'Hello!'

Her voice bounced back from the trunks of the pines, a mess of sounds. Then came an answering whoop and a moment later a man crashed out of the woods, clutching a backpack. He turned and called back.

'They're over here! Guys! I found them!' He grinned at us like a golden retriever, a young guy around Zoe's age, a cigarette behind one ear. 'S'up guys, I'm Shaun.'

Zoe went in for a hug right away, as if they were old friends. I settled for saying my name and looking off into the trees, waiting for the rest of them to appear. They trooped into view soon enough, two guys around my age and an older man who looked to be in his mid-sixties.

'This is Duncan, Andrew and Frank,' Shaun said, waving them towards us. 'Guys, Zoe, Maddy, Gill and Maxine.'

Duncan did the rounds, shaking hands. I noticed the expensive outdoorsman sunglasses pushed up on his head. His face was pinkish and he reminded me of the posher rugby sorts from uni; pub crawl Saturday, pub lunch Sunday.

Andrew had thick brown dreadlocks coiled into a bun. They were startlingly long and would probably have reached his waist otherwise. Tattoos encircled one bicep and he had on a pair of ratty dungarees. His accent gave nothing away but, much like Zoe, he could have been from any suitably cool university town in England.

Frank on the other hand belonged in a pub, propping up the bar with a whippet at his feet and a red-top paper in front of his nose. His canvas fishing vest sported an alarming number of St. George flag patches and the frown he sent Zoe's way felt very much like disapproval. In short, he appeared to be the kind of middle-class bigot my home village was populated with. I wondered if the producers had picked him for just that reason, putting a racist on an island with a black guy and an Indian girl to create drama.

It should have been an exciting moment. It was, for

the rest of them. Handshakes all round, Zoe hugging everyone, even Frank, much to his obvious confusion. Still, I felt peripheral, like I'd stumbled on a party I wasn't actually invited to. There wasn't much else to do but paste on a smile and imitate Zoe, shaking hands and saying how glad I was that they were there.

Once the introductions were made, Duncan clapped sharply for attention. 'Well then, chaps, looks like it's time we got started, unless we want to sleep outside tonight.'

There were murmurs of agreement, but no one moved. I think we were all a bit overwhelmed. Then Gillian spotted something in the distance.

'What's that over there?' She pointed to a flash of blue at the high tide line.

We went over to investigate and found a pile of construction pallets, some broken, some whole, nylon rope and plastic sheeting. A plastic crate turned out to contain nails, a hammer, tape measure and various other tools. The blue was a plastic folder attached to a pallet with electrical tape. Duncan marched over and pulled it free, then read from the paper inside.

'"It looks like some supplies have washed up on the beach (or maybe others have been here before you?). Either way you now have materials to start building with. Keep an eye out for any supply caches previous survivors may have left behind!"' He turned the paper over. 'There's a map, with a stream and the camera hut marked on it.'

'Why'd they have to just hand stuff to us?' Andrew

said. 'Fuck sake, I thought this was meant to be "authentic".'

Zoe raised her eyebrows at me. I raised mine back, glad for the inclusion.

'I think it's just so we don't have to worry about cutting down trees or anything when it's going to be dark soon,' Maxine said. 'We can make a quick shelter with these and then start fresh tomorrow, when we have the time.'

Andrew looked slightly appeased by this. 'I still think it's stupid. And these caches or whatever – we're meant to be the last ones; it's meant to be the End. This wouldn't happen in real life.'

'That why you signed up then?' Zoe asked. 'You want to do this all for real?'

'Yeah, that's the point,' Andrew said with a shrug. 'All that stuff Sasha was saying – the oil and the pollution, that's already happening. This –' he indicated the long, barren beach '– is the future.'

I could see where Andrew was coming from – this was after all meant to be a kind of social experiment. I'd known there would be some prepper types in the bunch. For myself, I hadn't joined because I wanted a dry run of the end of the world. I'd just wanted to get away from *my* world for a bit.

'Let's get this stuff off the beach then – find a spot to set up camp,' Duncan said. I was glad someone had taken the initiative.

We carried the supplies up the beach, then went back for our bags. Beyond the sand rough grass ran right up to the treeline, and behind that was a dense forest of spruce and pine. The trees whispered in the sea wind. Beneath them was darkness.

'Might as well set up here,' Duncan said, standing on a flat spot just outside the forest. 'We should split up and have some go looking for water and wood while the rest of us get on with the building.'

I was about to volunteer to go looking for water when Zoe grabbed my arm and waved her hand in the air. 'Maddy and me can get stuff for a fire.'

'All right. Gill and . . .' He pointed, the name clearly lost already.

'Maxine.'

'Right, sorry! Maxine and Gill can go and find a water source. Take the map, see if that stream's close by.'

Zoe and I dumped our bags with everyone else's and went into the shelter of the pines. There it was still cold but at least we were out of the biting sea wind.

'Hope you don't mind me volunteering you,' Zoe said, once we'd gone a little way from the others. 'I just didn't want to get stuck with someone I didn't know. Especially not Andrew – misery guts.' She pulled a face to show she wasn't being serious, but I could tell she was, a bit.

'No worries,' I said. 'So, if you're not here for "the End", what made you sign up?'

'It's sort of my year out, now uni's done,' she said, pulling up a bunch of brown, dead ferns. 'I know that sounds mad. But it was this or visit my dad's family in Mumbai and that's just too many sexist uncles for me to be dealing with. He's the only one in his family to leave India, not to mention marrying an Irish girl so . . . they don't really get me. Plus, you know, this way I get to be on telly – people make careers out of reality shows like this. I've already got my social media all set up – @ZozoYogi, mostly about raising awareness and my yoga, stuff like that.'

'Awareness of what?'

'The environment, mostly. It's really disgusting what we're doing to the sea with all the plastic we throw away. Did you see that documentary with the turtles? Wild.'

She chatted about her upcycling projects while we picked up twigs, sticks and clumps of dry fern. It was the kind of one-sided conversation I find quite soothing – not having to contribute much more than a 'hmm' to keep it going. Zoe seemed genuinely nice and I was relieved we had fallen into such an easy acquaintance already. Even if she was doing most of the work on it.

'So, why did you sign up?' she asked, as we carried our piles of sticks and dead plants back to the campsite.

'Not sure really,' I said, which was kind of true. 'I suppose . . . I just needed a break. To get away, you know?'

She laughed. 'Funny idea of a relaxing holiday, coming here.'

I smiled back. 'Yeah, I guess so.'

As we walked I couldn't help but wish I'd been a bit

more honest. Not that I had lied, not as such. I was looking for a break. It was just that the break wasn't just from work, or stress. I didn't want a holiday. I wanted a break from myself, from my life, as it was. When I'd seen the ad for applications for *The Last Refuge* I'd not been outside for a week and a half. Not spoken to anybody since I spoke to Mum and Dad's solicitor and finalised my leave with my manager. I'd lost the only two people who really knew me and without them I didn't make sense anymore. I didn't know myself.

I couldn't really talk to Zoe about it. We barely knew each other. Besides, how would it sound? Pathetic really. A twenty-nine-year-old whose only real connection was to her parents. No old schoolfriends, because I hadn't been there to make them. No university mates, because I'd been too shy to do more than skulk at the edges of parties. Zoe, full of plans, ambitions, friends, was about as far removed from my grey un-life as it was possible to be.

By the time we returned to the campsite, the guys had made a low shelter. The sides and roof were pallets stuffed with ferns and wrapped around with plastic sheeting. Small, but serviceable.

Zoe and I dug out a hole in the sandy soil. I wasn't really sure how to build a fire properly and neither was she. We applied some common sense to get a sort of stick pyramid built in the hole. Zoe took out a plastic lighter and tried to get some of the ferns to catch.

'Bastard things are damp.'

30

I rummaged in my coat pocket and came up with some fast-food receipts from the trip north. 'Don't tell Andrew we cheated.'

She giggled, lighting the paper and getting the fern to catch. We made a couple of trips to fetch stones from the beach. With that done there was a place for everyone to put their pots for dinner.

'Look at that view,' Duncan said, standing outside the shelter with his hands on his hips. 'When you think this must be what our ancestors saw, before all the cities and towns. Amazing.'

Andrew nodded his agreement. 'Can't wait to get building properly tomorrow. Imagine calling this place home?'

When Maxine and Gillian came back they had a full plastic tank of water from the stream. Gillian was sweaty and red-cheeked; Maxine still all business. Andrew had brought an SAS book along that explained how to make a crude water filter and he set it up to strain out grit and debris. What with the long boat journey and the lateness of its arrival, it was already getting dark.

We boiled the water and finally got our much-awaited tea. The list had also said to bring a month's worth of rations as a minimum, after which we'd have to forage and fish to eat.

'Snap!' Zoe said, seeing my packet of dehydrated vegetable curry and waving her own. 'Guess we both hit the camping shop pretty hard. Want to cook together and go halves?'

Around the fire, similar bargains were being made

to get food cooked quicker. I noticed that Maxine had also gone the hiking rations route. Andrew had large packs of staples – lentils, powdered egg, oats – and Duncan had protein bars and some kind of powdered whey mixture.

'Right then, now we're all fed,' Duncan said in his booming, 'matey' voice. 'I know we've been chatting a bit but let's do proper introductions, find out where we're all coming from. So, I'm a carpenter but I'm also an IT manager, love a bit of rugger and captain my local team, and I'm here for an adventure.' He gestured to Andrew on his left. 'Your turn, Andy.'

'All right, I work at the City Farm in Bristol, mostly looking after the permaculture project we've got going on. I'm here because I love me some Ray Mears and I think this'll be a good experiment to show the public not to be complacent about our future.'

Maxine was next. 'I'm Maxine. I've been in the Guides all my life, currently Tawny Owl for my local Brownie group. I help out with the DoE award and I'm here to live up to it and show that guiding is still important.'

Zoe waved when it was her turn. 'I'm Zoe. I'm a graphic art student and I guess I'm here to learn how to do more with my upcycling and recycling. I'm hoping to get some inspiration for my artwork and generally have the gap year I never got.'

Then it was my turn. Thoughts of my inheritance, the empty flat and my old job flitted through my head. In the end I said only, 'I'm Maddy and I studied botany.

I'm a forager and I'm really excited to get working tomorrow.'

'You know plants and stuff?' asked Shaun, the guy with the cigarette behind his ear. 'Any chance of finding something for us to smoke once all this is gone?' He waved a pouch of rolling tobacco.

'Lots of things – nothing with nicotine in though, sorry.'

'Guess we'll have to hope those telly people left some in a bird nest somewhere,' he said. 'Anyway, hi all, I'm Shaun. I'm training to be a butcher and really keen to cook wild food in the great outdoors.' From the looks of him he was aiming to be the next Valentine Warner and Jamie Oliver combined – rustic and irreverent in his woolly jumper. I hoped he could do more than look the part.

Frank's introduction was even shorter than mine. He was a retired pub landlord and had come for the fishing. To me he looked ready for a nap.

'That just leaves me then,' Gillian said. 'I'm forty-two, single and looking! Up until a few months ago I was my mum's carer. Since she passed I've been running a home business selling essential oils. I do a bit of DIY and have a nice little allotment, so I'll be growing lots of lovely veg, and I'm excited to meet you all!'

With the official intros over, the talk turned to plans for the year ahead. I mostly let it wash over me. Hearing Gill talk about her loss reminded me of my own. I hoped to be as unaffected by it as she was, one day. It would take more than a few months.

The day had been exhausting and I was craving my bed and a bit of time alone. However everyone seemed content to stay up late and watch the fire die. I didn't want to seem unfriendly by being the first to turn in.

At last, as the fire fell to ashes and small embers, Zoe yawned and went to fetch her bags. The rest of us followed on and soon we were trying to fit all eight of us into the small shelter. All the bags had to be left outside under a plastic sheet. Inside I felt like a match in a box. I fell asleep listening to the muted roar of the sea and the snores of the only people I'd be seeing for the next year.

Chapter 4

'Who do you think you'll miss most?' Sasha had asked, smiling from behind the camera as a woman finished forcing my hair into crisp curls and slipped away.

'I'm not sure,' I said, mind frantically searching for an acceptable response. The studio lights were making me sweat and I worried the unfamiliar makeup might start to melt. Really, I wouldn't miss anyone, much. The only people I knew in the city were those I'd worked with and I did everything I could to avoid them outside the office. It wasn't that they were bad people, it was just exhausting trying to seem normal to them. To pretend I knew about or was interested in the TV they watched or the diets they followed. To listen to their stories of children and husbands and have only anecdotes about my small life to offer in exchange.

'Probably my friend Becca,' I said. 'We went to university together. We did the same kind of work – pharmacological botany.'

No need to mention that I hadn't spoken to her in

two years, or sent a text in four months. We'd been almost close at uni, but after we'd started working together she'd said some things. Things about Mum and how protective she was. Only she hadn't said 'protective'. She'd said 'controlling'. It hadn't helped that she'd been seeing Owen by that point. Owen who technically had the same rank as me, but spent every day passing me his work to do, taking all the credit. Owen who told me once that I was holding Becca back, that she was too nice to say anything.

After that I avoided Becca until I crumbled under the pressure and left my lab job. I hadn't wanted to bother her with the news when I lost my parents. I didn't feel like we were that kind of friends anymore.

'Do you work together now?'

'No . . . she still works in a lab; I went a different route. Botany's sort of a hobby these days, not my job.'

'And what is your job?' Sasha asked, for the benefit of the camera, as it had been on my application.

'I'm an administrator. An administrative assistant. In a HR office, at the moment. I temp around. For the experience.' Not that you needed much experience in making coffee and filing thousands of reports alphabetically. Still, temping meant I was a stranger wherever I worked and people mostly left me alone to my podcasts.

'And what thing do you think you'll miss most? Chocolate? Wine?' Sasha asked.

She'd taken the two most obvious answers, which annoyed me. Behind the blinding lights shadows moved

36

around as people went back and forth with equipment. I blinked, eyelashes stiff with mascara.

'Hot showers,' I said, eventually. 'There's nothing better than waking up with a shower.'

*

Our first full day on the island got off to a bad start. The plastic sheeting had blown off our bags in the night and rain had drenched them. This meant no fresh clothes and some of Frank's food got wet. The wood Zoe and I had gathered was also wet and refused to light.

'I think the first thing we've got to do is get a spot picked out for the shelter, so I think today a couple of us should try and scout a good location,' Duncan said.

'We don't necessarily need to scout,' Maxine said. 'We already know it needs to be near our water source, the stream – and near the forest so we don't have to drag wood so far to build.'

'But we don't want to haul all our stuff up there looking for a place to build,' Duncan countered, 'so it makes sense if some people stay behind and look for these caches we're meant to be finding.'

'We don't have to take all our stuff, but we should all go and look at the potential sites, because we've all got to be involved in the decision,' Maxine insisted. 'We should also really work out how we're going to make these decisions – a simple majority vote seems best in my opinion.'

Duncan shrugged. 'Sure, that's fine.'

'We should get on with it though,' Andrew said. 'We've got no fire and no reason to be sitting around here chatting. Let's get a shift on.'

We collected water bottles and the few things we thought we'd need and followed Maxine and Gill to the stream where they'd drawn water the day before. Following it through the woods proved a little difficult. Under the trees the ground was uneven, pitching up and down in mossy banks peppered with crags of rock and fallen trunks. Frank was soon lagging behind with a red-faced Gill. My own fitness level wasn't great, but I gritted my teeth, determined to do my best.

After a while the stream started going uphill steeply and we stopped for a rest. The trees had thinned a bit and there were some large rocks through which the stream had carved a path, creating a natural pool.

'This place isn't too bad,' Zoe piped up. 'I'm not just saying that 'cos I'm exhausted.'

'It looks fertile too,' I said, having noticed the dense grass and sprouts of fern. 'If we want to be able to grow anything near the shelter we'll need a clearing like this so the plants'll have light.'

Gillian, our gardener, nodded at this. I wondered what kinds of seeds she'd brought with her. We were all told to bring 'specialist supplies' with us; for me that meant a guide to identify edible and medicinal plants.

'There's definitely enough space to get a decent build here,' Duncan said confidently as he paced off imaginary walls. 'Lots of good straight pines too for cabin walls.'

'Is that the best option,' Maxine said, 'a cabin? That's a lot of trees to fell. Who brought proper axes with them?'

Only Duncan and Andrew raised their hands. Duncan frowned.

'We were all told to bring tools, that included an axe.'

'I have one but it's not like a "here's Johnny" axe. It's little. Probably not going to get a tree down with that – just branches for firewood,' Zoe said.

I nodded and noticed Shaun and Gillian do the same. The axe I'd brought was actually a hatchet – single-handed, with a short handle and small head. Perfect for general wood cutting but not something that stood much of a chance against one of the tall pines that creaked overhead.

Andrew didn't seem that worried. 'It'd take too long to make a cabin anyway. We need to get something up that's fast to build and durable. Otherwise, we're going to have to keep coming up from the beach every day for months before we have a proper shelter here.'

This sparked another wave of questions. Duncan and Maxine had assumed we'd be moving to our chosen site straightaway, bringing the pallets and plastic sheeting up and re-creating our current shelter. Frank, in a quiet but firm way, laid out the advantages of having an emergency shelter by the sea in which to keep his fishing supplies and get out of the rain if a storm caught him down there.

The debate went on for a while with everyone chipping in. It reminded me a lot of meetings in the office I'd worked in. All we were missing was tea and biscuits. Still, it was our first full day out of civilisation and no one was getting annoyed or sounding off. I was content to listen and weigh up the options.

'All right, we'll put it to a vote,' Duncan declared. 'Get it decided, then we'll start getting on with moving our stuff around and working out what we're putting where. Show of hands for moving our shelter up here.'

Duncan, Andrew, Gillian and Shaun raised their hands. Duncan sighed.

'That's a tie. Come on guys, we can't fall down at this first hurdle.'

'What about a compromise?' I said, after a few long moments of silence had passed. Everyone looked at me and I felt myself start to wilt under the attention. 'We . . . uh, we could stay in the shelter for the next few days, until we get enough built here to move. That way we keep the fishing hut where it is, but . . . we don't spend weeks commuting back and forth.'

Shaun nodded, slowly. 'That makes sense. I vote for that.'

Maxine put her hand up, followed by Zoe, Frank and Shaun. I raised mine as well.

Duncan shrugged. 'That's decided then.'

I felt a little thrill at having found a way to unite us and get a decision made. I couldn't remember the last time I'd even tried to volunteer an idea in a work meeting. Somewhere along the line I'd stopped trying. Just like in every other area of my life I'd sort of surrendered. Maybe this challenge, this experiment, was exactly what I needed. Maybe I'd been right to take it on.

We drew sticks to decide who would hike back down to get everyone's tools. Gill and I got the short ones. I didn't really mind.

'Everyone seems to be getting on well, don't you think?' Gill asked as we followed the stream through the trees. 'I was worried there'd be a few bad apples but, so far we're all working together.'

'So far so good,' I said. 'At least we've got a site picked out – looking forward to having a sturdier roof over my head.' After a few steps I added, awkwardly, 'I'm sorry about your mum, by the way. I just lost both my parents, it's not easy.'

'Yeah, it was a bit of a shock. I mean, she was old and had a lot of stuff wrong with her in the last few years. Still, finding her . . . Since the divorce I'd been living with her, taking care of her. My sister's got kids to be worrying about. Then one day I went up to help her after her bath and she'd had a stroke, drowned.'

'That's awful.'

'Yeah, it was pretty fucking shit, and then all the police and ambulance people going through . . . Total circus.' She took out a rollup and lit it, took a puff and cleared her throat.

'That Duncan, you can tell he's a team captain, can't you?' she said.

I nodded, realising I'd pried too far and she was probably upset, changing the subject.

'Very fit, and commanding.' Gill mused, as we picked through the supplies that had been left at camp.

That was probably the most diplomatic way to put it. So far I had no reason to dislike him, but there was something about him that made me feel like he wasn't really listening when anyone else talked. I told myself that I was probably being unfair. He was just more comfortable with people than me. More self-assured.

I should have trusted my instincts.

'I imagine we'll have that hut up in no time,' Gill puffed as we climbed the slope back to the chosen site. 'I certainly hope so anyway. That and the kitchen garden will be the most important things to get the groundwork done on.'

'Once we all pitch in, we'll get it done,' I said.

*

When we got back Duncan was standing on his own, talking away, apparently for the benefit of the camera on his chest. Meanwhile Andrew, with the help of a little notebook and a tiny pencil, had sketched up a rough plan. When Duncan was done explaining things for our audience, Andrew talked us through his sketch, pointing as if he could see the hut taking shape in the air in front of him.

'I've patterned it on an Iron Age roundhouse. It's our best bet for something we can build quickly, but large enough and sturdy enough to keep us comfortable.' He stabbed a finger at the sketch. 'We'll put thick wooden poles all around, with panels of wattle and daub in between. The roof is going to come up to a point, all thatched with pine branches.'

'What about a fireplace?' Shaun asked. 'Are we cooking outside or what?'

'We'll dig a pit in the middle of the floor for a fire,' Andrew explained. 'The smoke from it will gather above us, in the conical roof, and slowly escape through a smoke hole in the very top.'

'So what are the walls actually going to be made of?' Zoe asked.

'Basically, picture a wicker basket – only made of thick sticks. Onto that we'll put a load of mud and clay mixed with thatching like grass and moss to plug up all the holes and leave a weatherproof wall.'

I glanced at Duncan, who was sitting on a rock, axe balanced head-down between his legs. He was, after all, the carpenter.

Andrew came to the end of his pitch. 'So . . . do we need to vote or are we all happy?' We glanced around at each other. No one seemed to have any more questions.

'My worry,' began Duncan, testing the axe's weight, 'is that we're building for convenience rather than suitability. It's easy to say, "Oh well, chopping down trees is too much work", but in the end that's what's going to give us a better, warmer home.'

Zoe accepted a rollup from Shaun. 'I don't think anyone's saying that. It's just that we don't have the tools to cut down a lot of trees quickly, and I for one am looking forward to having an inside space for sleeping. So, if this hut thing of Andrew's is quick to build, and it's going to be warm, that seems like the best option.'

Shaun was nodding. I got the sense that he was going to be a swing vote in most of our decisions. So far he hadn't had a lot of ideas. Still, with Duncan, Maxine and Andrew in the group, the last thing we needed was another prospective 'leader'.

Duncan pounded the axe head on the ground absently. 'Well, if only two of us thought to bring proper axes I suppose that is the best option.'

I saw Zoe roll her eyes and I could understand her frustration. It didn't seem that fair of Duncan to say something like that. We hadn't been told to bring full-on axes with us, and we'd all had other things we needed to bring. Maxine had brought along supplies for sterilising jars, pickling and preserving food. I had my foraging book and Frank had brought his fishing equipment. Duncan's comment was allowed to slide though. I supposed as it was our first full day no one wanted to get into an argument.

Following our agreement on the hut we split into work groups. Andrew and Duncan, along with Shaun and Zoe, would be cutting down trees for the hut frame and stripping their branches with saws. The rest of us would dig holes for the poles to go into and then gather the cut branches and sticks to start work on the panels.

Duncan, who'd been irritating me a little with his bossy attitude, was at least a hard worker. By the time the sun began to slip away, we had half the trunks in the ground and two more on the grass waiting to be lifted in. Andrew was right. At that rate it would have taken months to build walls of solid logs.

We were all tired and aching, hands sticky with sap and grazed from the bark. As we walked down the hill to the beach camp we chatted in pairs and I saw only smiles.

'Isn't this great?' Zoe said, twirling under the darkening trees. 'It's like being handed the world.'

Chapter 5

Work on the hut went quickly. We were all eager to see it complete, to move in and really start our island lives. From the moment we woke up we worked on nothing else.

Slowly the roof went on. A few days from the end of our first month on the island, those of us on the ground turned to other projects. We'd taken the mud for the walls from a spot across the clearing and now turned that ragged patch into an allotment, ready for spring planting. Maxine was the first to notice the rabbits.

'There's another one!' She pointed excitedly into the forest. 'How on earth did they get here?'

'Well, it only takes two,' I pointed out.

'I suppose that's why they're considered pests,' she said. 'Very sweet pests though.'

'I wonder if anyone knows how to catch them.'

'Andrew probably. He seems like the type to know about that sort of thing . . . I used to keep them as pets,' Maxine said. 'When the girls were little. They loved them, until they got bored and moved on to wanting a dog. So, they ended up being my rabbits by default.' She laughed softly. 'I think I had more pets as a grown woman than I ever did as a child. They were forever wanting guinea pigs, hamsters – I drew the line at rats' – she shuddered – 'horrible things. They smell.'

'My mum used to say the same thing. She hated their tails.'

Maxine nodded her agreement. 'Awful little snake things. It's funny – they're both grown now, with their own families. Neither of them has pets. Maybe because now they'd actually have to take care of them.' She laughed.

I smiled but I was thinking of Mum and her aversion to all things furred or feathered. Animals carried disease and dirt, neither of which she wanted in the house. The one exception had been a goldfish, won for me by Auntie Ruth at a fairground. She'd argued that anything that lived in water had to be clean, and Mum hadn't been able to say no.

We told the others about the rabbits that evening. As it turned out, no one knew how to make a snare.

'If we could catch a few, we could keep them and breed them – like chickens in a coop,' Andrew said. 'Then we won't have to catch them all the time and we can just kill them when we need to.'

We went around and around debating how to catch rabbits. The upshot of this was that while Duncan and Andrew finished the roof, the rest of us went off to explore the island. The idea was to find evidence of warrens. Once we knew where the rabbits were, we would make a trap there and try to catch some.

I decided to go on my own. We'd all been together for days and I needed a bit of space. I was also glad to get away from everyone's cameras. It was hard to forget that we were being filmed. At least when it was just me, I wasn't actually in shot. Well, aside from on the cameras hidden in the trees, but those were easier to ignore than the bulky body cams.

I headed off into the woods and quickly lost sight and sound of everyone else. I'd thought of the island as being small when we approached by boat, but it seemed to go on and on. It was raining softly and the tall pines creaked in the wind, letting through a fine mist. Underfoot was mostly moss and fern shoots, slick and wet, greener than any grass. It was peaceful.

In the months leading up to my application, the months following the loss of my parents, I'd been angry, constantly. I snapped at co-workers and strangers alike. At home I threw and broke things. The stress of just being around other people had felt crushing. I hadn't wanted to examine why; maybe that was part of why I hadn't told Becca about the car accident when it happened. She'd called my mum controlling and I hadn't wanted to hear it, but deep down I knew she was right. I was their only child, a child they thought they'd never be able to have. Being overprotective and old-fashioned was expected for parents a decade older than everyone else's.

I missed my parents more than anything, especially Mum. She'd been more than my mother, she was my favourite teacher, my only friend for most of my childhood. She was the one I confided everything to as soon as it happened. The one I cried to and laughed with and got support from. While other people had partners, best friends and siblings, I had Mum. In the years since leaving for university though, I'd become more and more aware of just how many limits and restrictions she'd put on me as I was growing up. Keeping me out of school, wary of children my own age, shutting out 'inappropriate' influences like most TV, pop music and teen fiction. All things that had left me incredibly ill-prepared for the real world, for socialising and making friends.

They hadn't meant to hurt me, I was sure. Yet in all the grief and despair of losing my parents, there was also a kind of frustrated rage. Intentional or not, they'd shaped and pruned me into something not quite right. Now they were gone, I'd never be able to talk to them about it. I'd missed my chance. All the things I could never say to them, could never ask, just bubbled away inside me, making me angrier and angrier.

Part of wanting to leave the outside world behind was me wanting to let go of that anger. I wanted to be kinder, to myself as much as to everyone else. I wanted to push myself past my boundaries, so I could stop blaming my parents and let go of all that wasted time. So far I at least felt freer, if not yet happier.

In the spirit of that, I'd forced myself to stop

pigeonholing my fellow islanders. I decided to try to be more accepting. I'd dropped my assumptions and made an effort to get along. Even Duncan, who had irritated me at the beginning, was growing on me now. His forthright attempts at leadership pushed us forward as a group and motivated discussion.

I thought on this as I made my way up slopes and down into deep gullies. On my way I noticed the shoots of the plants my research had informed me would be on the menu in a month or so: orache, gorse and hawthorn.

At last I reached a higher point on the northern side of the island that was slightly more exposed. From there I looked down on a large swath of grassland. In the distance, nestled in another smattering of pines, was a portacabin. I wondered what our camera crew were up to. Probably enjoying electricity and a flush toilet.

After descending the steep rise I made my way west, parallel to the cabin, not wanting to get closer to the 'out of bounds' area. I'd just re-entered the treeline at the lower level when I saw it: a flash of blue in all that green.

As I got closer I saw that the blue thing was a thick piece of fabric tied in a knot around a branch of sea buckthorn. Remembering the blue folder we'd found taped to our building supplies, I was certain I'd found a cache. A quick check of the surrounding area led me to loose soil under the thorn bush and I dug with my hands.

Buried six inches underground was a large plastic storage box. Pulling it out of the hole was tricky as it was quite heavy and slick with wet mud. When I unclasped the lid I almost squealed with glee. As much as Andrew had been put out by the supplies we'd been given, I was already starting to miss some of my creature comforts, mostly milk as we'd been having our tea black.

The box was stuffed with packets and cartons, as well as some large Kilner jars full of rice, beans and other staples. The jars in particular were exciting, as we'd be able to reuse them for our own preserves once empty.

I decided to split the weight and fill my rucksack with as much as possible. The result was a box that was awkward but not impossible to carry and a backpack that was heavy but manageable. Thankfully I'd come mostly uphill from camp and so the return trip would be mostly downhill. I was looking forward to surprising everyone with my find, particularly the real coffee and biscuits I'd spotted in my haul.

What I'd not banked on was the rain. As I made my way downhill the weather got worse and soon the misty fallout from the pines became a heavy, consistent downpour. I realised with dismay that I'd started going east by accident as I fought the slippery, steep ground. I still wasn't even halfway back and was now, by my reckoning, almost on the wrong side of the island.

It was then that I made my second discovery of the day.

I came across a sort of rock cluster; two large boulders nestled against a hill, with another large, flat rock on top. The perfect shelter for a short rest. The whole thing was caked in moss and lichen, surrounded by thick ferns and brush. I hadn't realised how tiring the walk had been until I got the chance to sit down. I was in fact so tired that I didn't notice the gap between the rocks right away. Once I glanced inside, however, I realised that I was actually sitting at the mouth of a sort of cave.

There was a dynamo torch in my bag and I took it out to shine it into the gap. By lying down on my stomach in the wet greenery, I was able to slither into the hole a little way and see further in. I was fairly certain it wasn't an animal den. There was no evidence of rabbit droppings or anything like that and nothing moving inside. The place seemed a quirk of geology and erosion, formed by chance.

It was an interesting find and my mind turned immediately to what kinds of mushrooms I might find there come autumn. The possibility of even farming some species in there was quite exciting, as until then I'd been resigned to the capricious and elusive nature of wild fungus.

Once the rain cleared a bit I hefted the box on my shoulder and slid my way back to camp. Everyone else was already back and gathered inside the hut. In my absence Andrew had finished the roof, not before time given the weather.

The floor was still unfinished dirt with no fire pit,

but with everyone packed inside it was warmer than outside. I shrugged out of my wet coat and took a seat on the dry ground. The box immediately caused a stir of excitement. So much so that I forgot to mention my second discovery; the cave.

'Just in time for our housewarming party,' Zoe said, brandishing a bottle of whisky. 'Irish coffees and cookies for dinner!'

'More handouts,' Andrew sniffed, looking into the box. 'This is a fucking joke.'

'Will you lighten up, please?' Zoe said, half serious. 'Look – you get tobacco! Can't find that washed up on the beach.'

The pouches of rolling papers and tobacco seemed to mollify Andrew somewhat. He might not have any interest in sugar and processed food, but he did go through his skinny rollups like he was trying to beat a personal record.

'I've been thinking,' Duncan said, after we'd shared round the packet of biscuits as a mid-afternoon pick-me-up. 'I know we all have our own rations and we've been sort of sharing between ourselves informally – but now we've got our first group supplies, maybe we ought to think about putting all our stuff together into one larder.'

'Could be a good shout,' Shaun said. There were other mutterings of agreement.

High on our first processed sugar in a week, we all agreed to create a shared food store in the new hut. Andrew started making plans with Duncan for some shelves across the back wall, pegged into the upright posts.

After he'd finished his biscuit Frank cleared his throat and quietly revealed to me that he'd found a large rabbit warren. He'd already told the others. Apparently to the east of us was a hillside riddled with burrows. This meant that we'd have to fence our garden before we planted anything. But we were also now in with a shot at trapping some rabbits for our 'rabbit coop'.

With work almost finished on the hut Andrew was excitedly talking to anyone who'd listen about other building projects. He wanted to get the kitchen lean-to done right away. Then a shelter for our long-drop latrine and another for us to strip down and wash in.

That night we stayed so long at the hilltop camp that the sky was darkening from blue to black as we reached the beach. Maxine and Gill made our first 'group meal' over the fire, a kind of pilaf seasoned with curry powder from the cache box. Afterwards I volunteered with Shaun to wash up.

We sat around the fire and I thumbed through my foraging guide, turning down corners of things I'd found. Zoe was using her hand drill on a thin slice of log, Andrew had a book and Shaun was lying down, looking alternately at the stars and Zoe. It was the first time in a long time that I'd enjoyed the company of other people without feeling anxious or irritated.

That night we went to bed knowing that it would be our last night on the beach. Tomorrow we'd finish our hut and move in. Our first milestone, a testament to our skills and combined effort.

Looking back, it almost makes me sick. To think how naïve I was to consider the building of the hut, together, as a sign of things to come.

Chapter 6

I haven't yet had a good night's sleep. In the police station and hospital, it was to be expected, but in a quiet, comfortable bed I'm still jerking awake every few hours. Scrabbling upright, feeling my heart pounding away, slowly easing back to normal as I blink away the nightmare. I'm in bed. I'm home. I'm safe.

I get up and put the light on. The central heating has clicked over and the carpet is warm under my feet. Downstairs, in the kitchen, I fill a glass with milk and drink it down, slowly. I can do that now; flip a switch for daylight, walk around barefoot and cosy, lock a door against the world. I wonder when it will begin to feel normal again. When it will feel like my life and not a short reprieve from cold, hunger and danger.

I notice the answer machine blinking in the hall. Thirty-seven messages. The first time it had rung I'd dropped a cup of tea and had a small panic attack. Now it's on silent but the calls are still coming in. I sit on the stairs and push play.

'*Miss Holinstead, this is Emma Gilroy from the Guardian . . .*'

'*. . . The News on Sunday . . .*'

'*. . . BBC News . . .*'

'*We're really interested in your story . . .*'

'*. . . your side of things . . .*'

'*. . . what happened to you . . .*'

'*. . . just awful . . .*'

'*We're looking for an exclusive . . .*'

'*. . . a great opportunity for you . . .*'

'*. . . very generous offer . . .*'

On and on. So many messages. So many people clamouring for the truth of what happened to us. To me. I look around me at the silent house, the carpet soft with dust, the clocks winding down, losing time. On the wall opposite me is Mum and Dad's wedding picture. I get up, take it down and add it to the pile of things I've already boxed up in the hall. I'm ready.

One last test of strength, one last battle to win, and I'll be free.

I'm done running. Tomorrow, I face the world.

Chapter 7

We had our first real argument about five weeks into our stay on the island.

In many ways I was surprised it hadn't happened sooner. After all, we were toting cameras everywhere we went, aware that we were being watched. It added an extra sense of discomfort that had me on edge most of the time. The others must have felt it too. Besides that, we were all virtual strangers living in extremely close quarters. We didn't have any outlets for our frustrations; no friends or family to vent to, no internet to distract us. There was only one hut and although we could go out and walk for a bit, we had to share the same space a lot of the time.

It was obvious that cliques were forming. Andrew and Duncan had bonded while building our hut and they brought Shaun into that. They were always together, chopping wood or sitting around the fire messing about. Maxine, Zoe and I were all friendly and tended to sit together for meals or work together at chores. Though Maxine did sometimes complain to me a bit about Zoe's 'freewheeling' attitude towards washing up and keeping her part of the hut tidy, I mostly ignored it and steered the conversation elsewhere.

Gillian moved between our two groups, spending more and more time with the guys. Frank sometimes hung out with the guys, but mostly he went off on his own for long periods, returning with a few crabs or some mussels at the end of the day.

The problems began when Zoe and I went beach-combing. There were no set jobs or 'working hours' so we'd all been self-managing. In the evenings people volunteered to get water or wood but for the most part we just talked over our plans for the day at breakfast and then did our own thing. On that day the guys were starting work on a rabbit enclosure, Maxine and Gill were fencing the garden and Frank was making some creels for catching crabs. Zoe and I had taken to walking the beaches, specifically around the tidal pools on the east side of the island.

Since we'd arrived we'd found a number of things that had been left for us by the production team. These things seemed basically new: buckets, a plastic laundry basket, rope. They had been positioned around the beaches as fake flotsam, above the tide line so as not to be washed away. Mixed in with that, though, was stuff that was actually washing up on the island. These things were smaller, more damaged and tangled in seaweed. So far we'd found torn fishing nets, planks with the varnish chewed off by the sea, a short metal pole (currently holding our pots over the hut fire) and bits and pieces of plastic rubbish.

However, since we'd started going to the beach every couple of days to see what there was to find, Duncan had started to comment on it quite pointedly. It was just little jabs, 'How's the tan looking today, girls?', 'Need one of us to knock you up a beach umbrella?', stupid stuff like that.

On the day of the argument we were going down to the beach on the first clear morning we'd had in a week of rain. The sky was wide open, so blue it was like August had come early. My hopes were high for the day and Zoe seemed equally uplifted. I was hoping for a good haul from the storm-roughened seas.

After an hour or so we had a good pile of things on the pale sand. I was very happy with an orange fishing buoy in particular; it would be a great addition to Frank's fishing pots. Zoe had found a number of pieces of blue nylon rope and a chunk of wood riddled with nails, which we were hoping to extract at camp. I'd also bagged a lot of kelp and laver seaweed, which I was excited to turn into laverbread.

'While we're here do you want to go for a swim?' Zoe said, eyeing the calm sea.

'Are you kidding? It's freezing on the beach. I'm not after losing a toe to frostbite today.'

'But it's not as cold as it's been,' Zoe wheedled. 'Come on, I haven't washed more than my face in over a week, I need a good dunking.' She dug a large towel out of her backpack. 'Look, I came prepared.'

She had a point about the wash. It had been so cold and we'd had so little privacy around the guys that a full wash had been pretty impossible. I'd kept my face and hands clean but I was worried I was developing fairly vicious BO. Icy salt water wasn't exactly the bath I had in mind but it was better than nothing.

Since arriving I'd had to get used to stripping off around the other girls. No one had made fun of me so far. It was still kind of embarrassing but the idea of being clean was too tempting. I got down to my under-wear, keeping my eyes on the sand and hoping Zoe wasn't looking at me.

We splashed into the cold waves, shrieking and shivering. I instantly lost feeling in my feet. I only made it up to my waist and then forced myself to duck down until my shoulders were submerged. I was doing a quick scrub with my hands when Zoe sent a wave of freezing water over my head. I emerged, spluttering and wiping my face, cold needles stabbing through my greasy hair.

Zoe was laughing, not meanly, but like we were having fun together. I whipped up a large piece of bladder wrack and threw it at her, making her scream. I felt a stab of fear that she'd get pissed off, but she was grinning as she shrieked.

'That's so gross!' she shuddered, eyeing the drifting, bladder-covered weed with disgust.

'That's going in your dinner tonight.'

She mimed being sick. I snorted.

We exited the water and pelted back to our pile of clothes. We shared the towel, and I was overjoyed to cram my damp body back into my smelly clothes and pull my woolly hat over my wet hair. We gathered up all our finds, including the bladder wrack, and headed back to camp.

When the weather was clear we'd been cooking outside. It was easier than working in the cramped hut. I took a seat by the fire and went through my bags of foraged seaweed. I was occupied for a while washing and chopping by the fire. Then I checked my guidebook for the recipe I needed. It was then that Duncan came over, Andrew and Shaun trailing behind with mugs of coffee.

'Can we have a word?' Duncan said.

'Sure, can I just finish this first?' I asked, gesturing to the seaweed with the book.

'It's actually about that.'

They sat down on the logs we'd moved around the fire. Duncan was between the other two, across from me, his knees wide and hands between them, fiddling with his outdoorsman sunglasses.

'Look, we just wanted to have a chat about what you and Zoe were doing today.'

'Oh . . . well, she took most of what we brought back over there if you're looking for rope or something.' I pointed to the lean-to outside the hut. What had been intended as a kitchen had turned into a sort of toolshed instead.

'We're just a bit concerned that you guys going down to the beach all the time might not be the best use of your time when there's so much work to do around here.'

I blinked, not sure I was understanding him. He was making it sound like the two of us had been down there making sandcastles every day. I decided to just assume he had somehow not noticed what we were actually doing.

'We've been going down there to bring back all the stuff that ended up on the beach. Like the planks for the lean-to and all the stuff for Frank's creels.'

Duncan waved a hand. 'But it doesn't take hours to get that stuff and Shaun saw you guys messing around in the sea.'

I could feel myself getting angry, mostly at the thought of being spied on while I was basically naked. Still, I forced myself to explain as tactfully as I could. I used my polite 'work' voice, hoping it would hide my growing irritation.

'We walk around half the island looking for this stuff. It isn't just all sitting there in one place. We were taking a fifteen-minute break to have a wash, in private.' I glanced at Shaun pointedly.

Shaun turned a blotchy red colour and looked at the ground. Andrew snorted and nudged him. They were like a pair of grubby schoolboys. Duncan's ears went pink, but his face was set and he wasn't wavering.

'It's just a bit of a piss-take if we're up here working and you guys are down there messing about. I'd love time off for a swim or whatever, but we have stuff we need to do.'

'Like I said, we weren't messing around – we went into the sea to get clean. No one is stopping you doing the same,' I said, trying to be diplomatic. 'If you want to go tomorrow, that's fine too.'

Duncan held up his hands. 'We can chat about it when you've calmed down.'

I dropped my professional voice. 'I am calm. I'm just disagreeing with you.'

I held his gaze evenly and only looked away when Zoe spoke up behind me.

'Hey, guys, what's going on?'

'Nothing,' Shaun said, 'just havin' a chat about what we've been doing all day.'

'Oh, OK. Have you guys seen the stuff we brought back? There's nails! How cool is that? I've just been yanking them out.'

Andrew started talking about the possible uses for the nails and Duncan slipped away. I felt stiff and tense all over from the confrontation and not in the mood to make conversation with either of the guys at the fire. I made quick work of the rest of my chopping, distracting myself.

The laverbread patties seemed to go down well. Frank had managed to bring in some fish too, though they were small, barely a mouthful each. Still, it made a change. Since we'd all thrown our rations in together, meal quality had varied a lot. Sometimes we had a dehydrated meal bulked out with plain rice, other times someone, usually Maxine or Shaun, put a bit more effort in.

Once the meal was almost done and we were sitting around the fire, Duncan cleared his throat. My stomach flipped over. I had no desire to get into another argument. Especially not a public one.

'Guys, I think it's time we worked out a firmer rota for getting things done. At the moment everyone's just doing their own thing and that's been all right for some of us but . . . I just think structure would be the best way to make sure everyone's pulling their weight.'

Zoe asked the obvious question. 'Who's not pulling their weight then?'

Maxine caught my eye with a raised eyebrow. It was becoming clear to me that she was not Zoe's biggest fan. Something about the way she looked at her reminded me of how Mum used to treat her little sister, my Aunt Ruth. That same kind of disapproving pinch to the mouth.

Duncan shrugged. 'I don't want to call anyone out – it's just becoming clear that some of us are doing more work than others. That's just how it's happened. I get it because some of us have skills that are more useful right now, but we should all be working as hard as we can.'

I didn't want to cause an argument. Duncan wasn't naming names, he wasn't accusing anyone. If I took offence it was going to be on me. A public blowout wasn't going to solve anything. I pressed my lips together and pushed the last of my laverbread around my plate.

'So, what kind of rota?' Zoe asked.

'We've got things we need to build that should take precedence over the more frivolous stuff. I think we should all be part of the building crew in the morning. In the afternoon everyone can get on with their own projects, like the allotment and the fishing.'

The mention of fishing got my back up. Aside from shellfish, Frank hadn't brought in much else. Either he wasn't catching anything around the island, or, more likely, he was falling asleep next to his rod of an afternoon. Unfortunately none of us knew the first thing about fishing, so it wasn't as if we could just replace him.

'What about the general work – the cooking and getting water?' Maxine asked.

Duncan shrugged. 'We can keep that as it is, just take turns. But no one should be sitting on their arse reading if there's work to be done.'

I couldn't tell if I was just being sensitive or if he was actually having a dig. I had been reading after all. If checking a reference book while doing work could be called reading. I glanced at Zoe, who I knew also had a book on bushcraft that she routinely carried around with her. She didn't seem to be taking Duncan's words personally. I decided not to either. That didn't mean I was going to sit there being a doormat.

'I think we ought to have a rota for the "housework" as well,' I said. 'At the moment it tends to be me, Maxine and Shaun who do the cooking most nights. When it's not us it feels like there's a reliance on the pre-packaged meals that we should really be saving for emergencies. There's wild food available, plus our staples. There's a lot of scrap wood around from the building so I don't see that gathering wood is a daily task. Not until we have the wood store.'

Maxine nodded. 'I'd like to point out that the washing-up should also be a rotating chore. It seems to be me that gets left with it – unless Maddy or someone else takes care of it when they cook. I don't mind doing it sometimes, but I didn't come here to spend a year washing up.'

Duncan spread his hands nonchalantly. 'Hey, I don't mind taking a turn at the cooking – I'm not just very good at it, but if you're OK with eating my crap food . . .' He shrugged. 'And with the washing-up, we can rota that, absolutely. You just had to say.'

I ripped a blank endpaper from my foraging book and, using a marker from Andrew, we drew up a rota. Two work parties would spend alternate days on building, one led by Andrew and one by Duncan. The domestic work would be given to a different pair every day who would be responsible for three meals and all the admin around them. The dehydrated camping meals and protein bars were to be kept for emergency use.

Following the meeting it seemed that everything was settled. No hard feelings, all back to normal. Maxine made some 'tea' with the bags from that morning and we sat around the fire for some recreation time.

Zoe was trying to work out how to make a basket

from sticks and Andrew was helping to split them. With nothing else to do I ended up whittling a wooden spoon that Zoe had started work on, then abandoned.

After a while Maxine came over to sit with me and have a chat. In the month we'd been on the island I hadn't noticed any change in her neat appearance. She was still as put together as she'd been when we arrived. Everything about her was quiet, purposeful and direct. I appreciated that immensely.

'Bit of a tough talk that,' she said under her breath.

I shrugged. 'Seems to have all worked out in the end.'

She hummed doubtfully. 'Everyone's definitely said the right things, but I'm going to wait for the follow-through.'

She had a point. I'd seen enough of it at work. Everyone shows up to the meeting, everyone agrees, or, at least, doesn't dissent. Then everyone just does what they planned on anyway and six months later we have another meeting about why nothing's changed.

'I wanted to ask about fruit actually,' Maxine said. 'I want to start on making vinegar and that means making alcohol first. When is there most likely to be fruit to pick?'

'I think there might be some hanging around still actually. Sea buckthorn fruits around September but I read there might be fruit left into the New Year. I'll keep an eye open while I'm out tomorrow.' I yawned widely and instantly felt guilty. 'Sorry! I'm just super tired.'

'Time for an early night, I think,' Maxine said,

sounding mildly amused. 'Lots of work to do tomorrow.'

'Isn't there just.'

I was the first to head into the cosy darkness of the hut. Our beds were laid out like the spokes of a wheel around the fire pit. On the back wall were the shelves of rations and below them the plastic box with more of our food inside. When the pines had been stripped of branches to make the poles of our hut Andrew had left the stumps of some in place. These made natural pegs for us to keep our clothes hung on. Already I had become used to the smoky smell that clung to everything, undercut by that of drying pine sap.

Snug inside my sleeping bag I looked up at the criss-cross of branches overhead, listening to them creak and settle in the breeze. It was only as I turned over to go to sleep that I thought of my book. I'd dropped it on top of my sleeping bag earlier, yet hadn't seen it as I'd got into bed.

I sat up and looked around, finally spotting a slice of white paper in the gloom. The book was under a small heap of clothing I intended to wash. When I pulled it out I saw that the cover was bent and dirty. Had someone kicked it under my laundry to hide this? Or just to make the book harder to find when I needed it?

With the book in my hands I sat frozen. From outside came the muffled sounds of chatting and laughter. Face-to-face disagreements were one thing, but this, damaging my things behind my back felt . . . pointed.

It felt underhanded and devious and I wasn't sure how to deal with that. If it was an accident, why had they hidden it? If it was deliberate, what had I done? I had my suspicions as to who had done it. I also knew how Duncan would react if confronted. It was only a bent book, not worth making a fuss over. Just an accident. He hadn't seen, hadn't meant it. I would be the one causing trouble, making accusations.

I finally tucked the book into my backpack. The best thing to do was to ignore it, I decided. I would not give him the satisfaction of a public shouting match. It was one childish thing and I wasn't even sure it had been deliberate. We were building a community; there were more important things to worry about.

Still, as I dozed and listened to my fellow campers entering the hut and going to bed, I felt suspicion gnaw at me. Since arriving there had been trust. We had shared our rations, we had stored our supplies in the open and side by side. Now I was worried about my belongings and found myself thinking of hiding places within the small hut we all called home.

I did not sleep well that night. Though, if I had known then what would follow, the escalation that was to come, I might not have slept at all.

Chapter 8

'How do you think your friends or your family would describe you?' Sasha had asked, not looking at me. Someone had brought her an iced coffee and she was smiling at them, probably as keen for this to be over as I was. I supposed she didn't have to seem enthusiastic; they were going to re-record her parts with an actual presenter. I only got the one chance.

To be honest I had no idea how Becca would describe me. Probably in the same bland terms you would an appliance you wanted to give away: reliable, hardworking, just slightly old-fashioned. Not exactly the thrill-seeker these people were looking for.

I knew how Mum would have termed me; sensitive, a wallflower, reserved. Her catchphrase during my childhood had been 'you're a good girl'; simultaneously praise and an admonishment. Good girls did not argue or 'strop'. Good girls didn't beg their parents for nail polish or 'tawdry' teen magazines. Mum had moulded me in her image – pinafores, plaits and none of those 'vulgar Barbie dolls'.

I thought suddenly of Auntie Ruth, Mum's little sister who visited sporadically through my childhood, sometimes staying for weeks at a time. Back then I'd not realised this was because she'd lost her job, her flat, her boyfriend or all three at once. Or because she'd gone travelling again and returned, full of amazing stories but flat broke, again. I'd assumed that staying with us was a treat for her. A kind of holiday, or that she'd missed us while she was abroad. Looking back, she must have hated it, having to rely on Mum's pursed-mouth charity.

I had a clear memory of Auntie Ruth taking me down to the stream behind the local church. She had bright red hair with sunglasses on top, nails to match. A long swishy peasant skirt with bells on the hem. I thought she looked like someone from a storybook, all colours and patterns. We went looking for fairies in the weeds and wildflowers. She showed me how to suck nectar out of white nettle buds. Once, she gave me a 'magic stone' – one of those little tumble stones they sell in gift shops for a pound a scoop. It was blue and partly clear. I liked to hold it up to the sun and look through it.

'You're filling her head with nonsense,' I heard Mum say to her, after I showed off my 'fairy gem' and went to wash my hands, stopping just on the other side of the door. I did this a lot, listening. I wasn't sure for what exactly, maybe just to see what they said about me when I wasn't there.

'She's being creative, it's good for her. Her mind needs opening up, some imagination.'

'Rubbish. And what would you know about it?'

A long, frosty silence. I remembered feeling like I should move away, not listen anymore. But I stayed.

'She's enjoying herself with a little make-believe. There's no harm in that, is there? Let her be a kid. She's got the heart of a dreamer and the head of an old maid. Why don't you let her out to play with all the other kids that're home for the holidays? Summer's when they should run wild.'

Mum sniffed. 'They're too rough. She's only little. Just watch what you say around her. She's very sensitive.'

Where was that stone now? I wondered. Probably somewhere in my old room. Surrounded by the prim china dolls Mum had given me over the years. Unless she'd thrown it away. She did that a lot, making decisions about what I needed and what was just 'collecting dust'. When Auntie Ruth died, far away in a foreign hospital, Mum didn't tell me for months. Claimed it didn't occur to her that I 'needed to know'. It would only upset me while I was meant to be studying. After all, I was so very sensitive.

I smiled at Sasha and the camera, the smell of hairspray reminding me of hennaed hair and giggling as Ruth painted my toenails.

'I think anyone that knows me would say I was a dreamer . . . ready to run wild.'

*

75

From then on, Zoe, Shaun and I worked under Andrew in one group and the others worked with Duncan. Fortunately, we got to organise ourselves. I did not relish the thought of working under Duncan. There was an edge to our interactions now that had not been there before.

Most of our group work involved stripping branches from felled trees and carrying logs back to camp. Andrew and Duncan took care of the finer details like chiselling holes and joints. Every morning the clearing rang with the sound of hammer on steel and the scrape of saws on wood. Together we finished the shelter for our latrine, a shower 'cubicle' and a log store.

In the afternoons we were 'allowed' to pursue our own projects. For me this meant foraging. I spent a very sticky few days milking sea buckthorn berries into a series of empty jars. The berries were too fragile and thin-skinned to actually pick. Maxine was pleased with the results though.

We still hadn't caught any rabbits for our enclosure. This was set on a large, half-buried rock. Anything else and the rabbits would tunnel to freedom. Since the work party on building seemed to be winding down, we had a meeting to work out what to do about the rabbits.

'I'm not going out hunting for rabbits,' Zoe said, right off the bat. 'I'll help feed them, I'll build whatever we need – but I'm not OK with hunting them down.'

'Andrew's veggie and he's not fussed,' Duncan pointed out.

Zoe didn't look at either of them, but shrugged. 'What Andrew's OK with is his business.'

'I am here,' Andrew said. 'Look, just because I feel differently about eating meat while we're here doesn't make me a fake vegetarian, OK? I'm against the meat industry, not hunting my own.'

'Let's split the work detail,' Shaun said quickly. 'Two out of the four can go hunting. And maybe we have one person go when Zoe's meant to go.'

'I'm fine on my own,' I said.

'That's settled then,' Shaun said, giving me a grateful smile. He was clearly trying to get on Zoe's good side. It was kind of sweet.

Our trap was simple: an empty bucket balanced on a scrap of wood. Frank had punched a hole in the edge of the bucket's lid and made a hinge of fishing line. The idea was that the lid could be propped up on a stick and when a rabbit entered the bucket after the bait, it tipped, dropping the lid in place. The whole contraption had to be propped up with sticks so it wouldn't fall over when, and if, we caught a rabbit.

For over a week we stalked Frank's warren. We caught nothing. So we had another meeting. They were fast becoming our speciality.

As we sat around the fire after dinner, Duncan cleared his throat. I looked up from my foraging guide. If given the choice I preferred not to be around Duncan unless we were in a group, the same with Andrew and Shaun. I hadn't forgotten about Shaun spying on me and Zoe, even though she seemed to be quite keen on him. I wasn't holding anything against them per se, but I wasn't as open with them anymore.

'I think we need to discuss the rabbit situation,' Duncan said. 'It feels like we're not getting anywhere, and we've wasted a lot of time on it already.'

'I think it's pretty important to have a source of meat for the winter,' Shaun said. 'And I'm not just sayin' that because it's sort of my job to do the butchering. I'm also getting bloody sick of rabbit *food*.'

There were murmurings from around the fire. The hardest part of the experience so far had been the food. Although the wild greens and shellfish were quite plentiful, they were also not as filling or calorific as we needed them to be given our hard work. Frank seldom caught anything big enough to be worth gutting. If he caught anything at all. Even Zoe, already used to a vegetarian diet and quite healthy, was losing weight rapidly.

'I would full-on murder someone for some halloumi,' she muttered to Shaun.

'Or a Big Mac,' he snorted.

'Uh . . . fries,' Zoe sighed wistfully.

I noticed Maxine glaring at them in a sort of head-mistress way. It was the same glare she had at mealtimes when food was most often discussed. We all missed things and it felt like we talked about nothing else sometimes. Maxine seemed to take it personally, as if wistful longing and imagination were a slight against her cooking. I supposed she'd rather not think about what she was missing, and found it annoying when other people harped on.

'Maybe we need a new way to catch them?' Andrew said.

'Like what?' Duncan asked.

'Like a snare or something. Maybe I can work it out.'

'We don't have any wire though,' Zoe pointed out. 'Don't you need wire to make something like that? Besides which, it seems super cruel to like, leave them tied up for ages.'

'Maybe we can try trapping somewhere else, further from the warren?' I said. 'I mean they probably have all the food they need around there, but if we move further away we might get some stragglers that aren't part of the main group.'

'The weak sickly ones?' Duncan said, unimpressed. 'Oh, delicious.'

'We only need them to breed. Then we'll have lots of rabbits to choose from.'

He sighed and sat back. 'I don't think it's worth wasting more time on. The work parties should go back to building.'

'But we've built everything we need for right now,' I said. 'We're just making furniture, which is sort of more your thing – as the carpenter.' I was aware I should just give it up, but I wasn't ready to let Duncan just have his way.

'So, you want us to all go out hunting rabbits? That seems like a massive waste of time.'

I was fighting to stay calm. 'No. I'm saying some of us should keep trying. We already have the hutch so it seems a waste to just give up without trying a new tactic. Maybe the rest of the work party should be helping with something else, like the allotment.'

Duncan looked over at Gillian. 'I'm sure she would say if she needed any help on the allotment. She's got it all in hand, right, Gill?'

'Right,' Gill said, looking up from her hair-thin rollup. 'It's going along quite nicely. Fence is in, seeds planted, nothing to do now but watch it grow.'

'See?' Duncan said.

No one was taking my side, so I shrugged and let the matter drop. It was too hard to push uphill against the tide of indifference. Everyone was tired from a day of work and an unsatisfying dinner – they didn't want to get involved. If Gill said the allotment was fine, it was fine. There was no point trying to argue about weeding, monitoring for pests or any of the rest of it.

'Right, so, tomorrow we're back on building parties,' Duncan said. 'Sound good?'

There were mutterings of assent around the fire. Duncan looked across the ruddy, crackling flames and smiled at me. 'You can take the traps out in the afternoon, when you're done with work.'

I turned in early, as was becoming habit. Partly this was because I was quite tired. Foraging meant I was hiking all over the island on a daily basis. Every log and twig overturned, every hill crested and stream crossed, it all cost energy. Energy that was not being replaced by the food we were eating. Food that was going down steadily as the days went on.

Another reason to turn in early was to check on my things. Since the incident with my book I was keeping my possessions close. While there was nowhere to hide anything, I had taken to leaving my stuff in a plastic carrier hung up underneath my thin raincoat. So far nothing else had been damaged. Maybe that was because the book had been an accident. I felt mildly ridiculous for my suspicion. Clearly, I wasn't used to living with other people.

*

Next morning we all broke into our work parties as usual. We spent a good few hours cutting more trees and stripping branches. I didn't dispute that furniture would be nice. Still, having all eight of us work on it instead of Duncan, whose only job was woodwork, seemed unfair. Was unfair.

Lunch was leftovers from dinner: soup of vegetable stock cube, wild greens, mussels, razor clams and seaweed. After a thorough re-heating on the fire the shellfish was like rubber. I was craving soft white bread and butter so strongly that I was nearly hallucinating it. I could feel the butter melting in my mouth.

I left the camp with grim determination to come back with a rabbit.

No one volunteered to come with me, which suited me just fine. What annoyed me was that while we were all off working on our personal jobs, Duncan, Andrew and Shaun would bring the scrap wood to the log store and call that an afternoon's work. When I'd left the camp they were sitting at the fire with Gill, smoking.

I pushed thoughts of the fair and unfair from my mind. I was going to catch a rabbit. It didn't matter what they were doing. I hiked away to the eastern side of the woods, where the rabbit holes honeycombed the hills. Further on there were fewer holes and less vegetation, the rainwater having been sucked up by the perpetually parched pines. I laid out the trap, tapped in some stakes, and retreated.

Hiding a way off in the trees, behind a crumbling hillock, I kept my eyes on the bucket. There was nothing to break up the time except the stirring of the branches and the thoughts of meat that kept filling my mind. I sat as still as possible, hardly daring to breathe, willing myself invisible.

Finally, after so long I wondered if moss was going to sprout on my jacket, a rabbit appeared. I watched as it hopped slowly from its hole and looked about, sensing for danger. Finding none, it started to graze.

I watched for a long time as it took maddening moves both towards and away from the trap. My teeth dug into my lip and my hands cramped into anxious claws, waiting for it to go into the trap. In my mind a litany had begun – *pleasepleasepleaseplease*, as if begging some unseen god of rabbits. I was so consumed with the need to catch it, that I almost didn't see it hop into the bucket.

It was as if I'd conjured it. One moment I was staring at the rabbit, willing it to enter the trap, the next the lid fell down and the bucket sat, filled. I sprang up so fast I felt dizzy. In seconds I had the trap in my arms and was looking down, through the half-opened lid, into the black, liquid eyes of the rabbit. I snapped the lid down as if it might slip through the crack. I could feel its weight shifting, the panicked scuffle of paws.

I must have seemed mad when I burst into camp, waving the bucket over my head and shouting. It was Zoe who first realised what I'd done. She jumped up from her half-finished kiln, hands clotted with mud, and came running to see. Shaun followed suit and soon I was surrounded, showing them my prize. The joy of it was incredible. Even Zoe, who had no stake in the rabbits, was practically glowing at this success and cooing over the 'cute little bunny'. Our first failure had been averted. We had won.

I let the rabbit out in the enclosure and it bolted into the little wooden shelter as soon as it was down. Maxine, ever practical, had set aside an empty pilchard tin for a water bowl and it was already full from the rain. Zoe ran off with Shaun to get some grass and leaves for it. They were like a pair of kids who'd been given their first pet.

'Now I just need to do it again, and again,' I said to Andrew, who was leaning over the hutch.

'Give me two secs and I'll come with you. If you get another, I'll bring it back in a box – get that trap turned around faster.'

'Good thinking.'

With renewed excitement we hurried back to the

place I'd caught our first rabbit. This time the waiting was charged with anticipation. Now we knew it was possible, it was no longer a question of if, it was a question of when.

A second rabbit tripped into our trap an hour or so later and Andrew leapt on it. With the captive in an empty box he ran for camp, while I reset the trap and went back to watching. When he returned, I had another rabbit waiting for him.

By the time it grew too dark to carry on we had caught five rabbits. At camp, Maxine sexed our catches and discovered we had three does and two bucks. They had also proven quite hard to handle. Maxine had a history with pet rabbits, but these bit and kicked with their clawed feet when picked up. Duncan, who had tried to record a diary segment about our first rabbits, had a nasty bite on one hand. I can't say that didn't amuse me.

'How long until we get to eat them?' Duncan asked, looking down on the hutch and the small shelter in which the rabbits were cowering.

'After the does have a litter – which takes about a month, once they're actually pregnant,' Maxine said. 'And we have to wait for those rabbits to mature slightly. I think six babies is about average.'

Duncan groaned. 'A month? We'll be skin and bones by then.'

'We can catch more, now we know where the best spot is,' I pointed out.

'Then we could eat one of these today,' Duncan said, 'and get more tomorrow.'

I looked to Maxine, who had the only experience with rabbits out of all of us. She shrugged.

'We don't really need two males – one and the does would be fine for now.'

'Aren't the females going to be easier to catch though?' Duncan said. 'We can replace one of them easier.'

Maxine raised an eyebrow. 'You caught them. What do you think, Maddy?'

'I mean, they belong to all of us, right?' Duncan said. 'Why not vote?'

I didn't have any strong feelings about killing one of the rabbits and said as much. After all, I was missing meat as much as the next person.

'I do think it should be one of the bucks though. Three litters from three does is better than having an extra buck getting territorial,' I pointed out.

Duncan muttered something to Shaun, who snickered. I kept my face blank. It was a good day, a successful one, and I wasn't going to be the one to ruin that.

We voted in the end and the decision was almost unanimous. Zoe abstained and also left the fireside while we discussed how best to kill the rabbit. In the end we agreed that breaking its neck would be fastest. Andrew caught one of the bucks and quickly dispatched it. Shaun, finally getting a chance to show off his butchering skills, skinned and gutted the body.

There is precious little meat on a wild rabbit when divided between seven people. Especially on a rabbit excluded from the best grazing, the better territory.

They don't have the security, the luxury of getting plump. Still, to me it was definitely cause for celebration. We made a soup, extracted Zoe's portion, then cooked the rabbit in the stock. The meat slid off the bones, making the soup richer and more flavourful than anything we'd eaten in weeks.

A holiday mood filled the camp and, for the second time, we broke out the booze. Maxine made some effort to convince us it would be best used in preserving – but was overruled. Some comforts were to be treasured. I felt like my body finally had enough energy to replenish itself. There were more smiles around the fire than I'd seen since the early days. When I caught Duncan's eye he raised his mug, and I raised mine.

I suppose we were all feeling more human after a good meal. It was very much a case of rabbit soup being good for the soul. After dinner Zoe broke out her marshmallows to celebrate. I guessed she felt a bit left out of the rabbit feast, having just the same old soup. She took sticks from the kindling pile and we stuck the large mallows on them like teens in an American film.

'Now we just need a campfire story,' Zoe said, wafting her marshmallow in the direction of the fire. 'Who knows a good one?'

'I know one about two girls that go skinny dipping,' Shaun offered.

'Pass,' Zoe said drily. He grinned.

'Come on, someone has to know a scary story,' Zoe said, looking around the group.

'I have one,' I said, almost without thinking.

'If it's about a man with a hook for a hand, I know it,' Shaun said.

'It's about a witch,' I said, 'one that lives on this island.'

There were various sarcastic 'Oooos' around the fire. Mostly from Shaun and Andrew. I ignored them.

'Let's hear it, Maddy,' Zoe said, settling against Shaun's side.

I cleared my throat. 'While we were waiting for the boat to come and pick us up, I asked a fisherman about Buidseach and he said that the island is called that because a witch lives here. A witch that sinks ships and traps people here.'

'Is that it?' Andrew said. 'Not very long, was it?'

I clenched my teeth together. It was true that I hadn't found out much else from the man on the dock. I thought about Auntie Ruth and her stories of fairies and gnomes at the bottom of the garden. What would she say?

'Well, years ago, when he was a young man, he and a friend decided to spend the night on the island. See if they could find the witch. They knew if she existed, she had to live somewhere.'

'What happened?' Zoe asked, eyes round above the molten marshmallow she was trying to bite into.

'They took a small boat and managed to land between the rocks, like we did. All that day they went about the island having fun, scaring each other. They didn't find any trace of a house, but they hadn't really thought they would. It was just a game. But the woods, which had been fine during the day, were very different at night. The two of them got split up and even though the fisherman called out, he couldn't hear an answer from his friend.'

No one was laughing now. I glanced around and even Duncan seemed to be caught in the spell of the story. I was making it up as I went, yet I felt I could see those two young men in my mind, running scared through the woods. Afraid of the witch.

'After a while, the fisherman realised he was very lost and had no idea how to get back to their camp. But then he saw a fire through the trees and thought he must have ended up there by accident. Only, it wasn't their fire. When he got closer, he saw a house. A house they hadn't come across before. It was very old and made of branches. On the outside were bones and skulls, taken from the sea where the boats had been wrecked. A cauldron sat outside and from it came a smell unlike anything he'd ever smelled cooking before. And over that cauldron stood the witch, all dressed in black, her face hidden by a hood. As he stood there, frozen, she turned to him and said, "Won't you sit down and share a bite with me?"

'Well, that was all it took. He ran. He didn't stop running until the sun came up and he could find his way back to the beach. But he did not find his friend there. And though he waited until the sun was high, no one came out of the woods.' I stopped and plucked a marshmallow from the bag, threading it onto a stick.

'That's not the end,' Zoe said in disbelief. 'What happened to the other guy? Did the witch get him?'

'No one knows,' I said. 'When he came back with a search party there was no sign of a house, or a fire, or of the witch. Only an empty bowl and a spoon, left on a stump where someone might have sat for a meal from the witch's cauldron.'

Zoe cuddled up to Shaun and he squeezed her tightly under his arm. 'That was really creepy,' she said.

Shaun laughed. 'He probably got off with whatever weirdo was living there and they went off to have weird kids together.'

Andrew laughed, and then started telling a story he remembered from a book, about a staircase that went down without ever ending. While he spoke I sat and thought about the story I'd just made up on the spot. It was rather a good one. I'd surprised myself and was glad the others had liked it. Maybe I'd been worried about nothing; I was starting to fit in after all.

What a fool I was.

Chapter 9

With a wet spring at our backs, the weather began to improve. The wind had lost its teeth and the formerly grey and brown landscape appeared suddenly green and vibrant. It was a much-needed boost to morale.

Unfortunately the start of summer brought its own unique problems. The first and most crushing was the loss of our shellfish. May marked the beginning of the off season for mussels. The warmer temperatures meant all shellfish were off the menu until September. With them went our most plentiful source of protein. We were left with only Frank's occasional catches of tiny fish. The second problem was of our making. We had depended a lot on the staples from the cache and our own supplies. These supplies were now almost gone.

One evening, after a dinner of soup containing half a cup of rice, some wild greens and a tablespoon of fish, the subject was raised. Andrew put aside his tin cup and cleared his throat.

'We need to talk about the apricots.'

A general tenseness spread around the fire. The theft of the apricots had been at the forefront of gossip for the last few days. Zoe and I had talked of nothing else during a whole morning of digging clay. Glancing at Andrew I saw how stringy and lean he looked now. We had all lost a lot of weight. Seeing each other every day it went unnoticed, but sometimes I caught a glance at someone and was shocked at the raw-boned appearance of them.

'We all know that there's been some nicking,' Andrew continued. 'We've all had our snacks and stuff out from the food stores. But this is getting stupid. Dried fruit is a pretty essential part of our diet. It also makes this shit' – he gestured at the pot on the fire – 'the watery fucking porridge and the endless fucking soup, marginally more interesting.'

Duncan nodded. 'The odd protein bar is one thing, but this is our food supply. We can't just keep dipping in when we feel like it.'

'We are basically out of everything now,' Maxine put in. 'There's a bit of rice, some flour and other bits, but if that's going to last another month, until July when we start getting stuff from the allotment, we need to be more careful with it.'

'I think we need to put someone in charge of the food,' Duncan said.

'How's that going to work?' Zoe asked.

'We've got a couple of luggage padlocks from our bags – I say we punch a few holes in the box and lock the food up. One person has one key, one person has the other.'

'Like a nuclear weapon,' Shaun laughed.

'Is that going to keep anyone out though?' Maxine said.

'Well, if they really want to they could smash the crate, but at least this stops the casual picking. If someone wants to steal, we'll all know about it,' Andrew reasoned.

'So who gets the keys?' I asked.

'Andrew's sensible, he should get one,' Duncan said immediately.

I glanced at Maxine and she was already looking at me. We were both thinking the same thing; Andrew and Duncan had a tendency to not be around when it was their turn to cook. Either they'd go out early to 'chop wood' – aka smoke in the forest – and we'd all end up getting our own breakfast. Or they'd hike off somewhere to 'look for supplies' and not come back until late, usually wet from swimming. Usually it was Maxine and I who made dinner on those nights as I had foraged food and Maxine was the better cook.

'Do you not think we ought to give the keys to the cooks?' I said.

'We all cook,' Duncan said with a frown. 'I don't get what you mean.'

'We're all rota'ed to cook,' I said slowly, taking the time to pick my words with caution, 'but sometimes people aren't around when it's time to cook, so other people fill in. So . . . it doesn't really make sense to give the only keys to the food to people who might not be around when we need to access it.'

'Do you want to name some names, Maddy?' Duncan asked.

'I'm not *accusing* anyone, I just—'

'You're just saying that you'd rather me and the rest of the guys were here making soup instead of chopping wood, so that you can do . . . what exactly?'

'I never said it was an issue. If you don't want to cook, fine, whatever – but if you're not going to, let's have it out in the open and not have you guys off on the other side of the woods with the keys to the food store,' I snapped.

'Don't get upset,' Andrew said.

'I'm not upset. I just wish you guys were doing what we all agreed to in the first place with the rota.'

'We can't cook if we don't have any wood.'

I gave up. 'Can we just decide on the key thing, please?'

'We should draw for it,' Maxine said. 'That way it's fair.'

She plucked up some bits of dry grass while the rest of us watched. I was seething. The cooking rota was an irritation, but it had been getting to me of late. Duncan and Andrew's reaction was as expected. It was everyone else I was annoyed at. I knew Maxine and Zoe were as sick of it as I was, but they didn't want to get involved in an argument. They were too tired and hungry to do more than complain in private.

We drew sticks. Andrew and Gillian got the keys. I went to bed.

*

The next morning, at breakfast, I decided to try and put it behind me. It was exhausting trying to be the person attempting to get everyone to do their jobs. I decided I needed to do something positive. Of course if I'd known then how horribly wrong it would all go, I'd have kept my foolish mouth shut.

Shaun and Zoe were on rota to cook and had made our usual thin porridge with dry fruit and nut butter. Our teabags had been used and re-used so many times that the brew was more a memory of Tetley than anything else.

'I was thinking,' I said, as we ate our small portions of porridge. 'We're getting into the prime season for forage now and with food stocks so low, it might be worth having one of the work parties go out and look for food.'

As it stood the work parties had been all but abandoned. Currently the only work party activity was carrying logs from where the guys were felling trees further back in the woods. This only lasted an hour or so, after which we all just went our separate ways.

Frank, usually silent as a stump when in camp, nodded. 'No shellfish to gather, might as well have a go at the seaweed.'

'Does anyone else already know anything about plant identification?' I asked.

Maxine raised her hand. 'We did a bit with the guides. Mostly about berries though.'

Surprisingly Shaun was the other person to raise their hand. 'Done a bit when I went on a game prep course. They showed us what greens went with what.'

'I'll go with Shaun,' Zoe said. 'I need to let my clay settle anyway.'

'Is that a good idea?' Maxine asked.

Zoe glared at her. 'What do you mean?'

'That perhaps if both of you keep to your separate tasks you might have more success,' Maxine said, her cheeks turning a bit pink.

'I'm sure we'll manage,' Zoe said coldly.

Maxine only shrugged. Point made. Inwardly I sighed. The two of them were my only friends within the group and I desperately did not want to get involved.

'Anyone else?' I asked. 'I have a book that can help with some tips, and I'll go over everything when we're done so we don't accidently get poisoned,' I laughed.

On the edge of my vision I saw Duncan shake his head and walk away.

'All right then,' I said with forced brightness. 'Shaun and Zoe, you take the book – go check the grassy bit on the other side of the woods. Maxine and I can take the dunes and Frank, you probably already know where the most seaweed gathers.'

Zoe went to do a quick check on her clay. She'd

commandeered two buckets and had mixed the dirt with water to start filtering out the heavier clay particles. Maxine and I donned our backpacks and headed for the dunes.

'I don't know what she thinks she's going to make with all that muck,' Maxine said once we were a decent distance from camp.

'I think the idea is to make extra bowls and things to store what we gather,' I said, keeping a neutral position. I was surprised that Maxine would be so negative about Zoe's project. OK, so pottery wasn't the most pressing thing, but at least it didn't take up any resources other than dirt and water, both of which we had plenty of.

Maxine huffed. 'Not what you'd call essential work though, is it? More of an art project. And I needed one of those buckets for something that's actually useful.' I was shocked at the amount of spite in her tone. Usually Maxine was disapproving of Zoe, not outright hostile. I guessed their little standoff had annoyed her.

'I tried to get her to help me with the rabbit skin – I'm building some frames for stretching them for curing, so they don't go to waste. But she wasn't interested.'

'She's veggie,' I pointed out.

'Exactly why she should want to use every part of the animals we kill, even if she isn't eating them,' Maxine snapped. 'Squeamishness is not a characteristic we can afford to have.'

I hummed, non-committal. I saw her point, but I also saw Zoe's. Besides which, if pottery was a non-essential I couldn't see how preserving rabbit hides was something we had to worry about.

'She's just wasting time,' Maxine continued, voice rising as we moved further from camp. 'And the way she's carrying on with that boy. This is meant to be a serious experiment, not some rubbish about who's sleeping with who. Have you seen she's still wearing makeup? Makeup, in the woods, I ask you!'

'Maxine,' I said, sharper than I intended. She turned to face me and there was colour in two high points on her cheeks. She was furious. 'I really don't think you're being fair. We're allowed to have fun. She's allowed to have fun. And if she and Shaun want to get together, if she wants to wear glitter and make pots – I don't see how that hurts you, or the rest of us for that matter.'

Maxine's lips pressed into a thin line, almost invisible. She'd never looked as much like my mum as she did then. I could almost hear her patented huff, that 'well then' that seemed like a reflex whenever I contradicted her, stood up for a book or song or skirt that was deemed 'inappropriate'. When it became clear Maxine wasn't going to say anything I started walking again, only to stop when she suddenly found her tongue.

'She's not your friend, you know. She calls you boring. When you're off on your walks.'

I turned back, trying not to let the deep hurt she'd just inflicted show on my face.

Maxine swallowed, had the grace to look uncomfortable. 'She told Shaun she thinks you're probably autistic.'

I wasn't, nor did I think it was such a terrible thing to be called. It hurt though, that Zoe had discussed me behind my back, called me names to Shaun. Maxine didn't seem to be lying. The worst part was that I could imagine those words coming out of Zoe's mouth.

'I thought you'd want to know,' Maxine said primly, walking past me and on down towards the beach. I kept my face blank and followed.

We made it to the dunes and I set to picking what we could find along the shore and in the more protected areas. It was the beginning of the season for rock samphire and there was a bit of it around. Mostly I just wanted to avoid Maxine, who was gathering further away and not speaking to me.

I wasn't sure Shaun and Zoe would find anything. Thinking of them off alone sent a pang of hurt through me. Perhaps even now they were talking about me. Theorising about my weird ways. I shook my head and told myself not to be stupid. That they wouldn't be as interested in me as they were in time alone together.

We sat down for our midday meal beside our spoils for the morning. It seemed as though Maxine was adopting a technique my mother used after an argument; she spoke stiffly and without looking at me, as if I'd done her a great wrong. While we ate half a protein bar each she looked out at the sea. There was

99

nothing between us and the horizon, only the grey-green water and the tips of rocks. No boats, no land, not even a plane scudding trails in the sky.

'I hope my girls are doing OK,' Maxine said at last. From this I understood that the argument was over and that if I mentioned it I would be even further in the wrong than I already was.

'What is it they do?' I said, begrudgingly taking the olive branch.

'Lydia runs a bed-and-breakfast in Devon and Felicity owns a riding stable in the New Forest. We used to talk on the phone every week. I completely missed Mother's Day, back in March. We would have gone to the pub for Sunday lunch.' She sniffed and produced a handkerchief from one of her pockets.

'They'll be happy to see you, when you get back,' I said. 'You'll have so many things to catch up on and talk about.'

She nodded, dabbing her eyes. 'I know. It's just . . . hard, missing them – and Douglas of course, my husband. He's probably drowning in washing by now. Never did learn how to use the machine. But we're all missing someone, aren't we? You must be looking forward to seeing everyone at home?'

I shrugged, not willing to bare my soul to her, to anyone, now that I knew it could be used against me later. 'Like you said, we're all missing someone.'

*

As predicted, Zoe and Shaun hadn't found much. The sum total of their gathering was some nettles and what Zoe claimed was wild parsnip, but was undoubtedly poison hemlock, which I discarded. Zoe also had her shirt on inside-out. I didn't fancy talking to her, not with the hurt still fresh in my chest. I noticed Gill nudge Maxine and the two of them regarded Zoe's clothing situation with raised eyebrows. More gossip for the mill.

Frank hadn't returned to camp, so I went off and looked for mushrooms. There weren't that many to be found. Still, a handful was better than nothing. At least it would add texture to our watery soup.

When I got back to camp Frank still wasn't there. Everyone was gathered around the outdoor fire and trying to work out what to do. It was getting late in the day. In another hour it would start getting dark.

'We should go and look for him by the tidal pools,' Maxine said, as I put my bag down and joined the discussion.

'He could have gone anywhere on the island from there. We should split into pairs and go check all the beaches,' Shaun said, earning him a shoulder squeeze from Zoe. I'd never thought of Shaun as being keen on the stoic fisherman, but he was clearly worried.

'Someone should stay here in case he comes back,' I said.

'Like who?' Duncan said.

'Any of us. We all did that first-aid course, didn't we?'

'I'll stay,' Gill said immediately.

'All right, Gill stays here, to wait and get dinner started, and the rest of us can go look,' Shaun said, already standing up and putting his backpack on. 'We've already wasted enough time.'

We quickly organised ourselves and found our torches. Maxine insisted we all take sterile packs of bandages from the first-aid kit in case Frank was injured. Shaun and Zoe headed down to the tidal pools on the east side of the island. Duncan and Andrew went south-west to check the fishing hut and the beach we'd arrived on. Maxine and I would go north to the craggy rocks and small pebble beaches. If Frank wasn't found we were all to walk counterclockwise around to the next point of searching, thereby covering the entire coastline.

No one wanted to decide what we'd do if we still hadn't found him.

Maxine and I hiked north up the steep, pine-covered hill. At the island's highest point, I looked down into the gathering gloom. At this time of day the pines looked especially sinister, the wind rocking their branches like a second sea. In the distance I could just make out the shape of the portacabin where the cameramen were. That too was in darkness.

'Maybe we should tell them – just in case. It might take hours to get emergency help out here,' I said.

'Makes sense – one of us should keep looking though.'

'I can,' I said. 'I'll carry on around the shore.'

We split up and I picked my way down to the island's

edge. There were many cliffs on the northern side, but eventually I found a way down to the water. Clinging to the barnacle-covered rocks I looked along the shore, called Frank's name and felt the growing wind snatch my words away. The temperature plummeted and soon it began to rain, hard.

It was now well and truly dark and the beam from my torch picked out a mess of footprints in the sand. I'd reached the fishing hut and the others had already searched there. I decided to head back to see if Frank had been found.

Slipping and sliding my way uphill I noticed that the stream was already flowing fast. The rain was really coming in and we had not been ready for it. I could barely feel my hands in the freezing downpour, God only knew what condition Frank would be in if he was out in the open.

When I finally arrived in the clearing it was to see one of the camera guys leaving. He passed me by in a drenched waterproof, his face set in an angry frown.

'Is Frank here?' I asked. 'Is he all right? What's happening?'

'They found him. Next time you guys drag me out of bed in the middle of the night, in the middle of a fucking storm, it had better be an emergency.' He stomped off into the trees, swearing as he stumbled in the dark.

I shifted the rocks that held the door curtain down and went into the hut. Frank was lying on his bedroll, surrounded by the others, minus Andrew and Duncan.

'What happened?' I asked, going straight to Frank's side. 'Are you all right?'

'I'm fine,' Frank croaked. 'Just fell.'

'He fell on the rocks at the tidal pools,' Zoe put in. 'His ankle's all swollen and he got cut up on the barnacles. We bandaged it.'

'Did you wash his leg before you put the dressing on?' Gill demanded.

'Yes.' Zoe gave her a look. 'I'm not an idiot. I used some Dettol as well.'

'He needs a cold compress on the ankle,' Gill said.

'I'll find something,' I said. There was a spare flannel in my bag. Maxine came over while I was wetting it from the water carrier.

'He wasn't very impressed – the cameraman.'

'No, he didn't seem it. But it could have been more serious.'

Maxine nodded. 'Though to be fair if I was asleep in a warm cabin I wouldn't want to go out in that rain either. It took a lot of convincing to get him to come down to camp to see if Frank was back – he didn't want to call in the cavalry without cause. Good thing he didn't or we'd be surrounded by annoyed producers and paramedics right now.'

I handed the flannel to Gill and she wrapped it around Frank's ankle. Zoe went to grab some clothes to wad up and create an ankle rest.

Frank sighed and closed his eyes. 'Stop fussing.'

'You had us really worried, mate,' Shaun said.

'No use worrying . . . but I'm glad you came along. No chance of a nip or something for the pain?'

Shaun went to check but returned empty-handed, unable to find the remaining whisky. The curtain rustled and Duncan came in, followed by Andrew. Both were drenched to the skin and rain dripped from their jackets and all over the compacted dirt floor.

'Thank fuck, was hoping one of you lot found him,' Andrew said. 'Jesus, Frank, you gave us a scare and a half.'

'No bother. I just had a bit of a slip on the rocks. Couldn't walk on my ankle. I knew one of you lot would come looking after a while. Took you long enough though.'

I glanced up and found Duncan glaring at me. He quickly looked away, but guilt had already lanced through me. I knew logically that Frank could have fallen while fishing or been injured any number of ways. The accident was not my fault for involving him in foraging – I knew that. But that didn't stop me from feeling terrible.

'So, now the excitement's over, what's cooking?' Andrew asked Gill.

'I haven't had time to get started on anything,' Gill said, flushing. 'I was getting ready in case we needed to administer serious first aid.'

There was no evidence of this. There was, however, an open novel on her bed. She noticed me look at it and blushed further.

'Who's on rota for dinner today?' Duncan asked.

'Frank and Shaun,' Gill said.

'I'll help,' I said immediately.

We built the fire up in the hearth. What with Zoe and Shaun not finding anything useful and Frank obviously having not been able to gather, we had only what Maxine and I had brought. The result was a soup similar to what we ate every night. Mostly it was water, stock cubes, wild greens and mushrooms, with a little pepper and some lentils. As usual it cried out for crisp bacon, bread and butter. None of us were satisfied with our meal.

The rain continued to sigh and rattle against the panels of the hut. Some seeped through at the edges of the floor. The smoke hole let in a barrage of rain which hissed into the fire.

We sat, huddled around the hearth, nursing cups of hot water with a suggestion of coffee in them. Zoe and Shaun had his sleeping bag draped around them. Maxine was wearing a fleece over her pyjamas. I had a blanket around me like a shawl.

Duncan cleared his throat. 'I think we can all agree that this is pretty miserable.'

There were murmurs of agreement and I joined in.

'Until now we've been quite lucky, we've not been trapped indoors like this. But when the weather starts to get bad – when we have to live out the winter here – things could get uncomfortable pretty quickly.'

'We've been talking,' Andrew put in, 'about building a cabin – like we talked about when we arrived. A log cabin, to give us more space. Now we've got a good shelter to be going on with we can afford to build something that might take a bit longer.'

'So we need to get the work party on it,' Duncan said. 'It seems like the most worthwhile thing we can be doing with our time.'

He didn't say 'rather than foraging', but it was there all the same. I'd had part of the work party on my side for a single day and we hadn't produced results. Worse, there had been an injury. I felt too awful about Frank to raise any objections.

'That settles that then,' said Duncan.

It was the beginning of the end then. I sort of felt it at the time but, had no idea what that prickle of unease might mean. I'd lost a battle without even realising it, and a tiny bit more control was his for the taking.

Chapter 10

I sense my interviewer's unease in the quick, constant movement of her hands. They flutter like nervous birds as she picks her acrylic nails and twists her rings. A hair and makeup person approaches from behind her and I divert them with a glare. I've seen off every attempt to mask the lines around my mouth and eyes, the scars on my face and hands.

My shorn hair is growing in and has been freshly washed. My clothes are ones provided by the wardrobe team; none of my old things fit anymore and I haven't had time to buy anything other than leggings and hoodies. The thick Fair Isle jumper and dungarees are ridiculously picturesque, as if I've spent a year raising goats and smiling brightly at sunsets. They are warm though and painfully thin as I am, I need the insulation.

Camera people start calling out and someone dashes past us. The lights grow slightly brighter and the interviewer receives her cue.

'Good evening, I'm Rosie Donnelly and tonight I'm

here with Madeline Holinstead, one of the Buidseach Island survivors. Maddy – now that the trial is over, we are all dying to hear your story. What can you tell us about what happened on Buidseach Isle and your miraculous rescue?'

Rosie smiles like a lightbulb, bright and empty. I do not return her expression but meet her gaze with my own, feeling my heart beat steadily in my chest, like the pounding of the waves.

'I'm going to tell you everything that happened on that island, but I'd like to say something before I start.'

'Of course,' Rosie says smoothly, moving a little closer, as though we are friends and she is waiting for a whispered secret. 'We're here for your story.'

'So, let me be clear: my story has no miracles, and no rescue. I survived. I escaped. And despite the best efforts of everyone else involved, I'm here to tell you about what we did on that island.' I sit back and think for a moment that I see a familiar dark shape just beyond the halo of studio lights. I take a breath that smells of hairspray and pine needles.

'I'm going to tell you what no one else can stomach . . . the truth.'

Chapter 11

Following the disaster of work-party foraging, all efforts were directed towards building our cabin. In the mornings we worked to cut down and strip trees. All of us as one big work party, minus Frank.

The afternoons, however, were a different story. Andrew and Duncan, our primary builders, saw their work as being done. They mostly hung out around the fire chatting, or as the weather got warmer and we slid into June, they went diving off the rocks near the beach, staying there until late. Gill invariably joined them, though I suspected she was mostly an audience. Sometimes Shaun went with them. On one occasion they came back obviously drunk. The missing whisky was no longer a mystery; but no one else seemed to notice, or at least, they didn't say anything.

The island had stopped feeling like a new and bewildering place. It was starting to feel, if not like home, then at least like a familiar holiday destination. We were no longer out in the open and scrambling for shelter. Our hut was warm and our routine established. Waking up to campfire meals and a cold shower was starting to feel normal.

The argument over foraging had not been forgotten. I imagined that somewhere a producer was happy about that; after all, it made for good television. It made things awkward for me though. For her part, Maxine never got really nasty about Zoe to me again. I suspected she was taking that kind of thing to Gill. The two of them were getting quite chummy, despite Gill's laziness. After what Maxine had said about Zoe I found it hard to really trust her again. I wasn't sure she noticed that I wasn't really reciprocating in our conversations. I began to see that she was talking to my camera, rather than me.

Our rabbits were doing well – several escape attempts notwithstanding. There had been some efforts at trapping more wild rabbits for the pot. None had been particularly successful. Mostly it was Shaun who went, as I was busy foraging.

The food situation wasn't getting easier and although we weren't starving, our staples were running low. Frank wasn't bringing in any fish while he was injured, and nothing in the allotment was ripe yet. To date, Gill had supplied only a handful of green tomatoes. So when Andrew found another cache down by the beach it was like Christmas day. The sight of pasta and rice had smiles going all around. Then the bombshell.

'If this stuff is going to last we need to really step up our game on the rationing,' Andrew said, snapping the lid closed. 'We've been talking and we think we ought to cut back to two meals a day – no dinners.'

'Should we not discuss things like this all together?' I asked.

'That's what we're doing now,' Andrew said.

'But after you guys have already made up your minds.'

'Do you not think it's a good idea?' Andrew asked.

'It seems like a good idea, but—'

'Then why are you arguing about it?' he said, raising his voice slightly.

'What about our energy levels?' Zoe said, cutting off whatever else Andrew was about to say. 'Won't we get hungry and tired and not be able to get on with stuff?'

'That's why we're cutting out dinner – we don't need calories to sleep on. We'll eat while we work and then when we rest we'll be saving food.'

'What about foraging?' I asked. 'At the moment I have to do that in the afternoon – and we eat what I find for dinner. We're losing nutrients if we don't eat greens and things until the next day.'

'Fucking Christ,' Duncan muttered, audibly.

'If you have something to say—'

'Well, do you have to bitch about everything?' Duncan demanded.

'For God's sake, what is your issue with me?' I said, stung.

'I don't have an "issue" with you. It's the fucking bitching I can't stand.'

'I'm not bitching, I'm pointing out that we could be

shooting ourselves in the foot if we don't make use of foraged ingredients while they're fresh.'

'So you want to bunk off the work party, is that what you're saying?'

There was a long moment of very tense silence.

'I wouldn't be the only one,' I said, finally. 'When was the last time Gill was in the work party?'

'Gill is taking care of Frank, who you got injured with your nagging about foraging!'

'And yet somehow Gill isn't caring for Frank when it's time to fuck off down the beach for the afternoon with the rest of you!'

Gill squawked in outrage and Duncan jumped to his feet. For a fraction of a second I thought he was going to hit me. His face was red and blotchy, his eyes dark slivers beneath his creased brow. His hands were clenched into fists. Shaun leapt up as well and held his arms out.

'Look, it's gettin' a bit heated so maybe we should all calm down . . .'

Zoe was standing beside Shaun now, echoing the need for a moment's calm. Somehow Duncan had been persuaded back onto his seat but was shaking his head and muttering angrily to Andrew. Gill, on his other side, fixed me with a glare as hurt as it was mutinous.

'Let's just all leave it and we can talk more tomorrow morning,' Shaun said.

'Fine,' Andrew said.

I nodded. In truth I was as angry as Duncan seemed

to be. It wasn't fair that Gill didn't have to join the work party. But mostly I was annoyed at Maxine and Zoe. Both of them had done their share of complaining about the others, in private. Yet around the fire they remained silent and let me get all the stick for putting my head above the parapet.

The next morning I got up and as usual we congregated around the outdoor fire. Andrew and Shaun were rota'ed on for cooking. Maxine, the earliest riser of us all, had lit the fire and was boiling water for tea. Everything else was in the hands of Shaun, already wiping sleep from his eyes at the fireside, and Andrew, who was still asleep. Shaun was keen to make a start, but we needed Andrew's key to the rations. Gill sat on the opposite side of the fire to me and wouldn't look at me or talk to me directly.

At last, after we'd drunk cups of watery tea that tasted of woodsmoke, Andrew appeared. He and Duncan were already dressed and awake. I got the sense that they'd been talking in the hut for a while.

'Morning, guys,' Andrew said, taking a seat on a bench. 'Listen, before we get down to breakfast I think we ought to revisit what we were talking about yesterday. Obviously there's a need for rationing – are we all agreed on that?'

I nodded. Everyone else did as well. I ignored Duncan, who was ignoring me just as studiously.

'Right, so, are we all agreed that cutting out one meal a day is the best thing, or, are we saying we'll reduce all meals by a third to make the supplies last?' Andrew looked around the group. 'Votes for ditching dinner, raise your hands.'

Only Maxine voted for smaller meals all round. I threw my vote behind the majority. One fight in twenty-four hours was enough for me. I had also decided not to mention foraging again. Andrew had other ideas.

'With the foraging,' he began, and I felt all eyes turn to me. 'What if you go before work party in the mornings and then we'll have the stuff for breakfast and lunch? And in the afternoon you can help someone else out with their work.'

It was clear I had a choice to make. Either I could stir shit up all over again and cause another fight, or I could accept the olive branch being thrown at me. Not that it felt like much of one.

'Sure,' I said. 'No problem.'

With everything decided we were finally allowed to have breakfast. Andrew unlocked the rations with Gill. Shaun made watery porridge with nut butter and some raisins. Afterwards we trooped off to the worksite to get on with building the cabin. I noticed that for the first time in over a week Gill was with us.

I wasted no time in getting to work, hacking the branches off of felled pines with my hand axe. After a while Zoe came over to join me. Her dark hair was held back by one of her seemingly endless supply of colourful silk scarves.

'You OK?'

I shrugged, annoyed by her overly sympathetic tone. 'I'm fine.'

'Duncan got a bit aggro, didn't he?' Zoe said quietly.

'Yeah . . . I kind of wish someone else had said something,' I said.

'Not really to do with me though, is it? I mean, what do I know about all the food side of things? He stresses me out anyway. Can't be doing with it.'

'But you'll talk to me about it,' I said, a little more forcefully than I'd meant to.

Zoe looked a bit taken aback. 'Did I do something to upset you?'

I took a breath. If I wanted to talk the talk, I should walk the walk. I couldn't tell her to voice her feelings if I hid my own.

'Maxine told me what you said about me, to Shaun.'

Zoe's eyes sharpened. 'I don't know what you mean.'

It was very clear that she was lying. That hurt me more than her words had.

'It's not a big deal, it just upset me a bit, that you guys were talking about me behind my back.'

'Like Maxine talks to you about me, you mean?' Zoe said. 'She's just a bitter old cow. You shouldn't listen to her.'

I shrugged, not wanting to get in another argument by calling her a liar. I think she knew I didn't believe her, because she dropped it as well.

We carried on with our work. Occasionally Zoe would make a crack about Duncan or Andrew, both of whom were working on the cabin proper. I didn't

117

reciprocate. I wasn't in the joking mood. As the morning dragged on Zoe finally nudged me and nodded her head to the other side of the clearing.

'Have you seen what Gill's doing?'

I glanced over and fought not to roll my eyes. Gill was with Andrew and Duncan by the cabin site. As I watched she handed a chisel to Andrew, then went back to leaning against the log pile, chatting. There were plenty of trees to strip and plenty of logs to move, but Gill was passing tools three feet. Clearly a great use of her time.

'Sort of takes the piss, doesn't it?' Zoe muttered.

I hummed in agreement, but went back to my work. Gill was an adult. We were all adults. I had raised the issue and been shot down. I'd attempted to mollify Maxine and she'd turned to Gill. I had tried to confront Zoe and she'd lied to my face. I had tried. The only person I had control over was myself. I wasn't going to be the one constantly coming down on people for their shitty behaviour. Not if no one was going to stand with me.

At around noon we went back to camp. My grumbling stomach was eagerly awaiting a decent lunch. Shaun took charge of things once again, making instant-potato cakes with the rest of yesterday's mushrooms fried and dumped on top. With that put away I filled my metal flask with straw-coloured 'coffee' and went on my way, bag in hand.

My quarry for the day was *amanita rubescens*, the blusher. Without any meat or fish on the menu, mushrooms were the closest thing we had to a main course. I was looking forward to July, when more varieties would start popping up: ink caps, parasols and the large puffballs. I prowled the woods for a few hours, pondering over a cluster of what turned out to be *amanita pantherina*, the deadly panther cap, a ringer for the blusher. Mushrooms were tricky that way, pretending to be something they weren't.

As I picked I tried to come up with interesting things to say for the camera around my chest, but everything I came up with sounded pompous or boring. I wasn't a gifted speaker, even about things I was passionate about.

I was picking my way through the jagged rocks to the far west when I heard voices. Slowly, I knelt between two spars of rock, still clutching a clump of pepper dulse. What stopped me was not just the voices, but the smell of smoke. And meat.

'Is that almost done?' Andrew asked.

'Nearly there, couple more minutes,' Shaun said. 'You sure no one knows we've been turning our cameras off?'

'They'd have sent those camera blokes down if they were on to us,' Duncan said. 'Not sure I even care. No one came down to have a go when we had that whisky, and the cameras were on for that. Gill's the one paranoid people'll talk shit about her when this goes out on TV.'

'I just don't want us to look bad,' Gill said.

'Well, you were talking a lot of mad shit,' Andrew put in. 'But it was just a laugh.'

'We're not doing anything wrong,' Duncan said. 'And no one's going to know anyway. Stop worrying.'

I heard shuffling, the scrape of enamelled tin plates. Something was poured, tea or coffee? Then Duncan sighed.

'That smells so good, Shaun.'

'Cheers. Got a nice fat one for once.' He cleared his throat and I could imagine him doing that neck-scratch, shifty-eyed thing he did when he was nervous. 'I feel a bit bad, not telling Zoe, like.'

'She's veggie though, right?' Duncan said.

'She's a poser. Said she was vegan until she fancied some fish,' Andrew said.

'I know but . . . it feels a bit bad, keeping secrets.'

'Well, if we didn't keep it secret, we'd have to put this bunny in the hutch with the others. Or we'd have to share it between all eight of us and that's what, a couple of bites? If that?'

'I know but—'

'I can hear Mad Maddy now, "That rabbit belongs to the collective",' said Andrew, in a shrill parody of my voice. I heard Gill laugh and Shaun snorted.

'Besides, we're the ones doing all the heavy lifting with the cabin,' Duncan pointed out. 'And blokes are meant to have more calories a day anyway. Ipso facto, we're just doing what's natural.'

'It's ready,' Shaun said.

I crept away in the general scuffle of plates and the ripping of meat.

My mind was turning over what I'd heard as I picked

my way along the beach in the direction of home. I was annoyed, of course. Mostly by the sheer unfairness of convincing the rest of us that dinner was unnecessary while they were eating rabbit. I was also astonished that I hadn't seen it sooner. Shaun's 'bad luck' with the trap was such a thin lie.

I had a choice. I could tell the rest of the camp, or I could keep it to myself.

If I told everyone there would be an argument. Feelings would be hurt, grudges held and I would be even more disliked than I already was. And it was clear that Duncan and Andrew did dislike me. They were mocking me, pitting themselves against me over any issue. That much had become obvious over the past few weeks.

My other option was to say nothing. I had it on my camera after all. It would come out eventually. I could keep my head down and wait for everyone at home to see them stealing food from us on TV. OK, so it meant putting up with it for now. But why did it always have to be me that called him out? Why was everyone happy to let me be the bad guy? If I kept it to myself I at least wouldn't have to deal with the arguments or the blowback.

I wasn't ready to make a decision and go back to camp, so I started beachcombing my way along the shore. Not much to be had, just more washed-up rubbish.

By the time I hiked back to camp I was ravenous. I must have covered miles on my foraging walk. I was annoyed all over again when I saw Duncan, Andrew and Gill all happily chatting by the fire.

As I walked past Duncan said something to Gill and she yipped with laughter, half-heartedly smothering it with her hand. I ignored them and went inside to the food store. There wasn't much in the way of space, so I hung my foraging bag on a protruding stump of branch. With some spruce in hand I went to the fire to make some tea.

I sensed eyes on me as I was steeping the green needles and struggled to remain casual. I intended to take my tea and retire to my bedroll to mull over my decision on the rabbit. My stomach was grumbling and though it wouldn't provide much in terms of calories, the tea would at least fill me up.

'What've you got there?' Andrew asked.

'Tea,' I said, not looking up.

'You not sharing?' he said, and I sensed his smirk, shared with the others. What was it they'd said on the beach? Ah yes – the spruce 'belonged to the collective'. I had no idea where that had come from.

I waved a hand towards the towering trees around us. 'Take all you want.'

Shaun came over to join them then, hand in hand with Zoe.

'What's up?' he said cheerfully.

'Maddy's just helping herself to a snack,' Gill said.

Shaun's smile shrank a little and he looked uneasy, glancing at my mug of greens and water. 'Doesn't look like much of a snack. Y'all right, Maddy?'

'Fine,' I said, levelly. 'Catch anything over the woods today?'

A blush crept along his cheekbones. 'Nah . . . It's a bit quiet over there.'

I nodded thoughtfully. 'Well . . . I thought I might take the trap over there tomorrow afternoon – see if my beginner's luck holds up.'

Shaun swallowed. 'Right, sure. Uh . . . won't you be . . .' He glanced at Andrew as if for help, but Andrew was looking at me, a steady, assessing gaze.

'Oh, I'm foraging in the morning now, my afternoons are wide open for rabbit trapping,' I said sweetly. 'Can't have your butchering skills going to waste.'

'Yeah.' Shaun stuttered a laugh. 'Yeah, sweet, well . . . Hope you catch something.'

'Hopefully. I do like doing my bit "for the collective",' I echoed, then raised my cup. 'Anyway, long day and an early start tomorrow. I'll see you guys at breakfast.'

I went to the hut and sat down on my bedroll, balancing the cup on my bed as I opened Andrew's SAS guidebook. It was appropriate reading material. So far I'd tried to come at problems head-on, have discussions out in the open. But clearly that wasn't what we were doing anymore. Now was not the time of community, it was the time of politics and out-manoeuvring one's opponent. Guerrilla warfare. And I'd just won my first skirmish. The trap and the rabbits were mine now. No more secret feasts.

Chapter 12

'What was it that made you realise, this is it? The gloves are off – I'm in real trouble here?' Rosie asks.

It makes me smile. She sounds like she's asking me about a business deal gone sour. Some kind of technical hiccup. She might as well ask when I threw up my hands, said, 'Oh bother' and really had to 'rethink things'.

She can't possibly understand that it wasn't just one thing. I can't pinpoint the beginning of that subtle shift, the slide towards full-out war between us.

I know where it ended though. It ended with them coming for me in the night.

I still find myself back there in my nightmares. In the thick, black dark it can only be without electricity, without streetlamps and glowing windows. The fire still etched on my eyelids as I run. Their fire.

Days of rain and snow melt had made the ground a slurry of mud, the moss sloughing off it like burnt skin. I slid and slipped, my heart in my throat. That kind of dream running where you try and try but can't get anywhere.

There are voices behind me.

'Maaaaaddy! Where aaaaaare yooooou?'

'Maddy! Get back here!'

I run headlong through the trees. If I stop, if they find me, they will rip me apart. I've no doubt that they will kill me right there in the woods, with their bare hands.

Then my foot hits air, instead of mud. In the dream, this sends my stomach plummeting. Heart racing. It seems like I fall for ever.

Then I smack onto the ground, hard. Winded and seized with pain.

I hear footsteps, right on top of me.

That is when I wake up, usually. Jerking awake in my bed. Only that night it had all been real. There was no waking up from it. I lived in that nightmare. My life hanging by a thread.

Chapter 13

I tried my best. I woke before dawn each day, then picked mushrooms, woodland greens and seaweed until the sun was fully up. I chopped wood with the others and then, in the afternoons, I trapped rabbits, working until the sun went down.

I'd thought I'd scored a win when I'd stopped their secret barbeques. Yet it was only a week later that I noticed food missing from the locked storage box. It should not have surprised me. After all, Andrew and Gill were the ones with the keys to the stash. I had convinced myself that our food, the communal stock pile, would be off-limits. That was stupid of me.

Again, I deliberated over telling the others. The problem was that my only proof was my word, versus the testimony of Andrew, Gill and Duncan, perhaps Shaun too, who would all swear they hadn't been near the box. They'd also probably turned their cameras off, so I'd end up looking paranoid to anyone watching the show. I was outnumbered.

A few weeks into the new arrangement I got back to the fire with my foraging to find no one there. Looking over to the cabin I saw them all hard at work already. Duncan was looking at me, the sun winking off his dark glasses.

I put my bag down and checked the pot, which was empty. They had eaten the remnants of yesterday's lunch. For a moment I thought about going over and starting work on the cabin, but I was already shaky from the long hike on an empty stomach. I went about making myself some spruce tea and threaded mushrooms on a stick to cook over the embers. The food box was locked, so I made do. I took my time eating but inside I was seething.

Once I was finished I went over and started work with the others. Still there was this sense of a divide. They had risen together, eaten together and started work as one. I had arrived later, eaten alone; I felt their disapproval. I told myself it was just my imagination.

I noticed that Gill was not in her usual place chatting and holding a saw. Apparently even showing up for work detail was now beneath her. Perhaps she had one of her new 'backaches'. These had seemingly come from nowhere. She never did enough work to strain her back. But it was a good excuse; everyone lapped it up.

Gill returned just in time for lunch, hair wet from a swim. Had she been in the sea for the hours we'd been working? We didn't have the calories to spare for swimming. She caught me looking and looked away quickly, almost guiltily, as if she knew what she'd done was unfair. Perhaps she had a conscience after all.

That afternoon I made myself scarce. The silence around me felt tense and pointed, as if I'd done something wrong. I wasn't sure what it was I was meant to be guilty of. Yet I did feel guilty, just through the coolness I was being treated with. I went to the allotment and sat down amidst the tall ferns and clumps of chickweed. There, shielded from view, I felt more relaxed. Aside from brief meals, this was the first time I'd sat down in hours.

For something to do I started pulling weeds, sorting them into piles of useless and edible. No weeding had been done for some time, that much was clear. The sprouts of our vegetables were almost hidden under grass, tangled weeds and ferns.

I noticed that there were gaps in the rows of young plants and small pebbles of rabbit shit. The fence was clearly not proving effective at keeping the buggers out. As we ate them, they were eating our crops.

I briefly entertained the idea of raising this at a group meeting. We needed to build a better fence and take care of the garden. Surely Maxine would agree with that, no matter her annoyance with me or her new closeness with Gill. But as I tugged weeds out of the soil my resolve weakened. It was obvious to anyone who cared to look that the allotment needed work. Yet no one else was talking about it or putting some time in on it. Even I'd not noticed until I needed a space to be by myself. I was just as guilty of shirking my responsibilities as they were. Calling attention to this would only start more arguments and that morning's events had already shaken me enough.

I stayed in the allotment for most of the afternoon. The sun warmed my neck and aching shoulders as I sat on the ground and picked weeds. Occasionally I stopped, stretched and sat for a while to listen to the birds and the insects around me. For a while I stretched out on a patch of bare dirt and soaked up the sun, feeling it enter my bones like liquid fire. I think I even dozed a little.

For the next few days I kept the same routine. I woke, foraged, worked on the cabin and then retreated to the garden to weed in peace. I wasn't working hard at it; I didn't have the energy. But I reasoned that a little daily effort was better than nothing. It also kept me away from the others.

Clearly, I wasn't the only one with a new routine. Over the following four days only once did I arrive at camp to find everyone around the fire, ready for breakfast. That was on the day I was on rota to prepare it. On the other three days they had already eaten when I returned. This really got to me. Zoe and Maxine had to be aware of what was going on, yet they were allowing it to continue.

On the fifth day of this happening I went to ask for the keys. It felt very much like begging, as if I was handing over some form of power. I told myself it was only my pride. I went over to where Andrew and Duncan were chiselling a log. Gill was sitting nearby, her back against the rear wall of the cabin, out of sight of the others.

'Can I get the food box keys, please?' I asked.

Andrew glanced at Duncan. 'Sure . . . Gill, can you go with Maddy?'

'She doesn't need to come with me, I just need the keys.'

Again that shared look.

'I think it's better if someone goes with you. For accountability's sake.'

'Accountability for . . .?'

'The supplies,' Duncan said, like it was obvious. 'We can't just give anyone free access when we're already rationing. You understand that.'

'Anyone other than Andrew and Gill, you mean.'

'Well, they can't open the box individually, can they – that's the whole point of having two keys.'

'No, but they can open it together, can't they?' I met Duncan's eyes and held them. I wasn't going to seek a fight by chasing everyone to do their jobs, but I also wasn't going to stand there and be lied to. It was obvious they had been dipping into the stash. Pretending that I was the one who might steal was a power move, even I could see that. I couldn't accuse them, because they were the majority. I was just one person; what they said, what they pretended to believe, was true by consensus.

'Look, we've already wasted enough time on this. The rest of us are trying to work,' Andrew said. He went and got Gill's key from her and handed the pair over. 'Just get on with it. We know what's in there.'

I took the keys, ignored the warning in his tone and went back to the hut. With the box open I measured out a third of a cup of oats (the ration we used per person to make porridge). I put this in my billycan along with some dried fruit and a bit of powdered milk, then topped it off with water. Then I paused.

At the bottom of the food box were the rest of the dehydrated meals. The things we'd all brought with us and added to the stockpile voluntarily. Looking at them, I was sure there were fewer than when I'd last looked. I could have sworn we had several treacle sponge packs, but now there was only one. The rest I couldn't be sure about. Sitting there, knowing I had to get back as soon as possible, I made a snap decision.

I picked out the few meals that I had contributed. It was easy to tell mine because they all had the price stickers on the back from my local outdoor supplier. Looking at the friendly yellow logo I felt a spasm of unreality. I had driven to the shop and browsed the shelves. I could remember clearly how I'd picked out each packet, tapping my foot to the instore Christmas music. I remembered the carrier bag on the car seat next to me while I sipped a scalding cup of hot chocolate with marshmallows, watching the windows steam up.

Blinking snapped me back to reality, to the growl of my flattened belly and the dirty, broken nails on my calloused hands. I flattened any trace of guilt. This food was mine and I had paid for it, however much of a foreign concept that seemed in my current reality. I refused to be denied access to my own food while Andrew, Gill and the rest ate it out from under me. There was no fairness in that. I picked up the packages, hid them in my backpack, under the folded foraging bags, and then locked the box.

I made quick work of my porridge and joined the others, but all the time I was thinking of where to hide the food I'd reclaimed. There was no privacy in the hut and I couldn't risk keeping them in my backpack. I'd have to put them somewhere out of the way. Somewhere safe.

It wasn't until we had eaten our meagre lunch of greens with a handful of rehydrated chickpeas that I remembered the cave. I'd not thought of it much since discovering it. In fact, I'd only been back once to look for mushrooms sometime in March. Having found none I'd not bothered to check again. It was the best place I could think of.

After lunch I waited a while, then casually donned my rucksack and left camp with my foraging bag in hand. On my way I noticed that Maxine was washing the plates we'd just used, but that everyone else seemed to be sunbathing in the clearing. For once I was pleased to see them not doing anything. It meant no one would happen on me while I was out.

Finding my way back to the cave was a little tricky. Everything had grown so much since then that it was disorientating. Previous markers like fallen trunks and oddly shaped rocks had been swallowed by the rising tide of greenery. The opening of the little crevice was chock full of ferns and tall grass, so I had to fight through it to get inside. The air in there was cool and damp, the floor packed earth and dry leaves. A prickle went over my neck as I remembered my own stupid horror story – the witch's house. How easy it was to picture her in here, waiting for the unwary.

After rooting around on the floor for a bit I found a stick and used it to gouge out a decent sized hole. Once I'd put the foil packets of food inside I covered them over with dirt and leaves. When I left the cave I packed the entrance with ferns and greenery again to keep it from view. Otherwise I could foresee it being used by Zoe and Shaun for a bit of privacy.

I snatched up some chickweed and nettles on my way back to camp, to sell the idea that I'd really gone foraging. I needn't have bothered because there was no one there when I returned aside from Frank. I left him dozing in the sun and followed the sounds of shrieking and whooping down to the stream. All of them were splashing around in the water, aside from Gill who was lying on a large rock. For a moment, looking at them being so happy, I felt a stab of guilt. I quickly squashed it. I wasn't stealing from them. That food wasn't for myself. As soon as stocks were depleted I would bring it back so that we could all enjoy it, not just the select few.

Part of me wanted to join them, but I was too self-conscious. How could I have fun when it felt like Duncan, Gill and the others were recording my every moment for later mockery? I had no idea who I could trust, if any of them. Instead I opted to spend some time in the wild greenery of the allotment. I was too tired for much actual work, but it felt like a rest day. Everyone else was enjoying the sunshine, so I stretched out and basked.

Chapter 14

'How do you typically handle conflict, or arguments?' Sasha had asked. 'With all the stresses you'll be under, it's only natural that there will be times when the group has to handle disagreements.'

'I'm quite a calm person,' I said, 'I don't really like all the shouting and screaming that goes on, like . . .' I faltered.

'Like on reality TV?' Sasha said, with a small laugh. 'You can say it. After all, this isn't really "reality TV" – it's a social experiment. A new reality.'

I nodded, internally cringing. I wasn't sure if Sasha really believed that or if she was just parroting the brief. Conflicts definitely sounded very much in the realm of reality TV.

'How did you handle your last falling out?' Sasha said, as clearly I'd been silent too long.

I thought of my last visit home. Nausea crawled into my stomach. This was not the place for that. Still, I couldn't stop the memory surfacing. Couldn't unhear Mum's voice.

We'd been cutting out scones together, listening to Radio Four. I'd just left my job in the lab, unable to cope with doing Owen's work on top of my own. It had just sort of happened. One day I was struggling, the next I was being disciplined for falling behind. Then I was giving my notice. I was angry with myself for not standing up to him, but how could I go over his head and tell anyone what was going on? I couldn't even tell Becca; she was his girlfriend, and we'd only been growing apart. Owen was friends with everyone, a team player. I was nobody.

I'd just started my first temp role and was bored out of my mind. Every day I wished I'd stood up for myself a little bit more, told someone what Owen was doing. But I hadn't, and it was too late.

'We worry about you, Maddy – all alone in that big town. Are you taking care of yourself?' Mum asked, pouring milk into a bowl.

'Yes, Mum,' I'd said dutifully.

'I don't see why you have to spend hundreds of pounds a month on that flat of yours when we have a room here for you. It was good enough while you were saving for your master's.'

'I work in the city, Mum.'

'Well, there are jobs here, since you're not working in pharmaceuticals anymore. You can work anywhere. And here you wouldn't be on your own. We hardly ever see you anymore.'

I'd pushed the cutter down hard without meaning to, sliding it over the veneer counter with a squeal of metal on plastic. There was a short silence.

'We just worry,' Mum said again, softly. 'You're not a city person. You're a homebody. You need people around you.'

I'd looked away, not wanting her to see the shine of tears welling up in my eyes. I'd thought it myself, of course, a hundred times. What was the point of struggling to hold onto my horrible flat in a city where I didn't know anybody? Where I was miserable? Wouldn't it be better to be at home, with people who loved me, whom I loved? After all they were the only ones who really knew me, had been there my whole life. They understood me better than anyone.

Only, I could see the danger there. If I went home, back to my old room with its camberwick bedspread and rows of dusty Enid Blyton books, I would never leave. I would stay there for ever; making scones with Mum, walking the dogs with Dad. I would never change. They wouldn't let me. There wouldn't be room for me to change. In the city, I was miserable, but at home I would be numb, slipping back into old routines. Being a good girl. I didn't want that to happen. I had to be pushed, to open up, to grow. And Mum had never pushed me. She liked me just where I was: in her kitchen, listening to Radio Four.

'I'm fine,' I said at last, when I could trust myself to speak without bursting into tears.

'Madeline—'

'I'm fine. And I'm not moving home, so can you drop it, please?' I said, standing up for myself at last. Far too late.

Mum sighed and I recognised the sound as a signal that she was not going to drop it, but for now she would be content with wounded silence. It would be up to me to apologise, or to pretend no disagreement had taken place. Mum did not apologise.

Somehow we'd got through the rest of the visit without incident. Partly this was because I made up a work emergency and left a few days early. Back to my musty flat for the rest of the time I'd booked off. I didn't see or speak to anyone until I went back to work at my temp role.

That was the last time I went home to see my parents. Being there, enfolded in the familiar warmth of their home, was too tempting. To stand any chance of changing my life, making it work, I had to stay in the city and try to live like any other person my age. I couldn't risk being persuaded to give that up.

So I made excuses: work commitments, social engagements and holidays, none of which existed. We spoke on the phone but that was it. I would not allow myself to be convinced or cajoled into making the trip to my home village, not until I was stronger. There would be plenty of time, when I was ready.

Only there wasn't, and I found that out far too late.

An icy road, a sharp bend. Just like that, I was on my own. And all my reasons, all my ideas about what I needed and why, felt suddenly very hollow. I had traded time with the two people I loved most for a job I hated and people who barely knew me. I had given up the chance to confront them, to fix myself. I could never get that back.

'I think it's best to handle things up front,' I said, hands clenched into fists in the folds of my skirt. 'Burying them, ignoring them . . . It just builds up, until somebody snaps.'

*

The summer brought out midges and horseflies that bit and stung. We all dreaded leaving the fireside, where the smoke drove them away. Duncan declared that the cabin would be finished in autumn, in time for winter. As of August, it just sat there, humming with insects and with walls barely at waist height.

The next big blow-up had nothing to do with me, at least, not directly. Maxine's disapproval of Zoe hadn't been dampened by my outburst; instead I seemed to have made it worse by driving her towards Gill, who relished gossip.

Maxine's barely hidden disapproval started to bubble over. First it was 'forgetting' to put aside vegetarian food for Zoe. Then it was Zoe's birth control being misplaced whenever Maxine took it on herself to tidy the hut. She nagged and criticised Zoe whenever she got the chance. Gill joined in and the two of them formed a spiteful coven of two.

With Shaun gone during the day, chopping wood or

just pissing about in the woods with the guys, Zoe turned to me for sympathy. I felt guilty for being glad of Maxine's jibes. At least it gave me someone to talk to, even if I didn't want to be in the middle of their row.

'She treats me like a naughty teenager,' Zoe complained as we wedged clay together, throwing it down on a flat rock. 'If she had her way, me and Shaun would be in separate huts.'

'I think she's just a bit . . . old-fashioned,' I said, trying to be diplomatic. 'You probably remind her of her daughters.'

'I feel sorry for them then, landed with a tight-arse like that as their mum. Can you imagine? Bet they never got to do anything.'

I hummed, non-committal. Zoe's annoyance cut too close to my own thoughts about Mum, the ones that had kept me away from home.

'I just want her to get off my back. It's none of her business who I sleep with,' Zoe huffed. 'And just because I don't do meat-and-two-veg doesn't mean I don't know how to cook. I'm an adult.'

Zoe was laying a lid on some leaves to air dry when Maxine came by. I watched her eyes narrow as she took in the mud that was all over us both and the pile of plain pots.

'I hope you're going to rinse your clothes before they go in the laundry.'

'Yes, Miss,' Zoe said acidly. 'Right away, Miss.'

Maxine's lips thinned to invisibility. 'There's no need

to act like a brat. I was just reminding you that this –'
she waved a hand '– creates a lot of mess and waste,
which other people have to deal with.'

'I'm not wasting anything – I am using natural
resources to make something we need.'

'Because we desperately need pots we can't cook in
and plates that harbour germs,' Maxine said, shaking
her head. 'Meanwhile you're using our firewood, all
the buckets, a perfectly good towel—'

'Guys, maybe we should—' I started but was interrupted when Zoe leapt up and jabbed a clay-covered
finger at Maxine.

'Oh my God, shut up!' Zoe snapped. 'No one cares.
Stop trying to control everything I do! I bet your daughters are made up that you're not at home bossing them
around. Probably couldn't wait to be shot of you.'

Maxine reacted like she'd been slapped. Her face
went white aside from a few patches of mottled red on
her cheeks. Her eyes hardened and she shot an accusing
glare at me before storming off. I winced watching her
go; clearly she thought I was on Zoe's side. Really, I
just wanted them both to be friendly again, to each
other and to me.

It was obvious to me that Maxine's behaviour came
from missing her family. Sometimes I caught her
looking wet-eyed as she held the picture of them she
used as a bookmark. I knew what it was like to miss
someone that much; to not know who you were without
your family. She was lashing out to distract herself.

Zoe simmered down once Maxine was out of sight

and we didn't discuss her further. There were plenty of pots left to make and get dried out before firing. By nightfall the two still weren't speaking, but were at least around the same fire. Least said, soonest mended. I hoped.

Despite Maxine's comments, Zoe managed to produce some very rustic ceramic crocks. We used them to keep foraged berries and nuts in as they dried or waited to become preserves.

Each day I went out in the pre-dawn and then again straight after breakfast. It became the norm that I would make my own food when I returned from the woods. It was annoying being left out, but anything that reduced my exposure to Duncan was its own silver lining. After the argument about the keys, I made my meals from forage alone. I busied myself bringing food into camp. There was a lot of it to harvest and preserve before winter; mushrooms to pickle, berries to turn into jam and seaweeds to dry and crumble into jars. We were in a time of plenty.

Plenty would seem a foreign concept within a few short months. I looked back on that time a lot and bitterly regretted every leaf, root and berry left ungathered. Every scrap wasted. It was a task too great for any one person. Had anyone thought to help me bring it all in, had they not deprived me of food, of fuel to do my work, we might have had more. Had enough. Things might have been different. Lives could have been saved.

I found Maxine by the fire one afternoon, monitoring

two of our largest pots as they steamed and spat over the glowing wood. Since the blow-up with Zoe I'd been treating them both with caution. Maxine in particular still carried an air of hurt feelings and mild disapproval wherever she went.

'Got more of those ceps,' I said, by way of greeting. 'How are we for vinegar? Do you need more berries?'

'Could be doing better,' Maxine said, nodding towards an empty squash bottle half full of murky liquid.

'I could get some more juice for you. Or you could come out with me if you like – have a break from camp?'

'I'll see if there's time; I've got a lot to do at the moment.' She glanced up, her face red and sweaty from the fire. 'I picked some of the tomatoes from the allotment earlier. It's not looking great over there.'

'Yeah, it's not produced as much as it could have,' I said diplomatically, thinking of Gill and her 'bad back'. I wasn't looking to spark another disagreement.

'That's an understatement, don't you think? The rabbits have been at everything – what isn't choked by the weeds. We'll be lucky to get a third of what we could have grown. It's disgraceful.'

'I know . . . It's a let-down. I was looking forward to a bit of a feast at the end of the growing season,' I said, trying to keep things light. 'Still, not much we can do now.'

Maxine sniffed and turned her back on me to check on her pots. 'Then you should have worked harder on it, shouldn't you?'

I was taken aback. 'Well, I did my best. I was on my own after all – Gill was meant to be working on the allotment. That was her job.'

Maxine rounded on me. 'But you took responsibility for it when she hurt her back. You can't just say it's not your problem when we were relying on you.'

I stood there a moment and just blinked. While Maxine hadn't been friendly to me for a while, she had at least been coolly polite. She hadn't directed her annoyance at me before, only at Zoe.

'I was working in the garden – I didn't "take responsibility" for it. I was just doing what I could. I never said that I would take it on all by myself – no one ever bothered to help with it.'

'Did you think to ask?' Maxine demanded, face no longer flushed with steam, but with anger. 'You can't just go off doing your own thing all the time – we're a community. We have a responsibility to each other.'

'Where is this coming from?' I said, astounded. 'You've had months to talk about this, why are you getting at me now when there's nothing to be done on the allotment?'

'Because it doesn't make any difference! You never listen, you just argue and complain about everything, to anyone who will listen. You're old enough to know better.'

I was shaking, completely blindsided. How could I be 'complaining to everyone who would listen' when I hardly spoke to anyone and was out of camp most of the time? I wasn't bitching and backbiting like Gill and the others were behind my back. Maybe I'd got into arguments, but always for good reason. Or so I thought. I'd avoided as many as I could by keeping to myself and not dragging up the food theft incidents.

Looking her in the eye, I suddenly realised what was going on. Really, it should have occurred to me sooner. Maxine had been taking her misery out on Zoe, but Zoe was standing up for herself now. She'd proven that with what she'd said by the kiln. Besides which, Zoe was with Shaun and he was friends with Andrew and Duncan. Maybe something had been said, or maybe Maxine had realised it on her own. Either way, Zoe was protected. I was not.

Words choked me. I had so much I wanted to say in my own defence, but Maxine was just glaring at me, her eyes flat and full of anger. My skin turned hot and cold with shame and fury at the unfairness of it all.

'Maxine . . . I—'

'Will you just go away!' Maxine shouted.

I took a step backwards, shocked by this sudden outburst. It was then I noticed that she was crying. I was still standing there speechless when Gill came running over and put her arms around Maxine, bad back momentarily forgotten. In the distance I saw Duncan, Andrew and the others in the shadow of the pines, axes leaning against the tree trunks.

'What is it, what's going on, eh?' Gill asked softly, rubbing Maxine's back.

Maxine choked on a sob, clinging to her, suddenly looking so old and hopeless that I felt myself tearing up as well. She reminded me so much of Mum, I wondered if this is what she'd looked like every time I'd made excuses not to come home.

'I want to go home. I . . . miss . . . my . . .' she sobbed into Gill's shoulder and Gill glared at me.

'Maybe you ought to give her some space,' she said sharply.

I swallowed, something in my chest hitching. I didn't want to leave, I wanted to stay and talk to Maxine, try to fix things and make it all right. But there was a sort of line between us, with her and Gill on one side, me on the other. I couldn't cross it.

Gill led Maxine away, shushing the whole while. I was left by the fire, alone. I felt eyes on me and knew that the others were still watching from the treeline. Glancing up I saw Zoe hurrying after Gill and Maxine. Maybe they'd make up after all.

I did the only thing I could think of: picked up my foraging bag and left the camp. As much as I hated to admit it, Gill was right, I had to give Maxine some space.

Picking my way north, up the steep hills and gullies, I stopped only to squeeze clutches of sea buckthorn berries into one of the empty plastic bottles in my gathering bag. A peace offering. It was how I'd always made things right with Mum. A cup of tea, asking about her book, little gestures to bridge the gap. Perhaps I could convince Maxine I wasn't her enemy. I didn't want her to pick on Zoe, but if it was a choice between being stuck between them and being completely ostracised, I would choose the former.

146

Being outside and busy had always been able to lift my spirits, but I found I was struggling. Maxine's words had hit me hard. She held me responsible for the failure of our allotment, blamed me for neglecting it. The unfairness of that, the hurt of it, followed me through the trees. It was there, waiting for me whenever my mind wandered from the task at hand. The worst part was that the further I went, the longer I thought, I started to agree with her. The allotment might not have been my job, but I had been working on it. I should have worked harder. If I'd left off foraging for a while, yes, we would have gone without, but we'd also have a better harvest now. I could have done more, I knew that. I should have done more.

Still, a tiny part of me railed against the unfairness. Obviously Maxine was stressed and missing her family, her husband and daughters. That was the real reason behind her outburst. She needed to get that stress out and had chosen me as a target. That didn't make it hurt less. Was there anything I could have done differently? Even as I thought it I knew that bringing in less forage at the time wouldn't have gone down well. I had been forced into working on the cabin, bringing in daily food and cooking it too – but that hadn't been enough. I knew that if I'd raised the idea of the work party shifting to the allotment, I would have been shouted down. If I had tried to pass the duty of foraging on or cut back on it, I would have been accused of shirking, of depriving them. But hindsight could be capricious. In a few months' time would anyone remember the food I'd provided, or would they instead lament the food they *could* be eating, had the allotment flourished?

Alternating between guilt and anger, I reached the crest of the hills and looked down on the meadow below. The grasses were long and green, sizzling with insects. Birds flew low over the waving tide of green, snatching up flies. In the distance the cabin of our two camera techs was almost hidden in the newly lush undergrowth, the door slightly ajar to let in the warm breeze.

I sat down on the hard earth and raised my face to the sun. This was what I was here for: freedom, and space to heal. I didn't want to be angry all the time, trying to force people to listen to me, to value my input. The lonely life had driven me out here to find some kind of respite from it. But so far, most of my moments of peace had come away from camp – away from the others. I'd had some good moments with Zoe, with Maxine, but . . . things were getting tougher. If today was any indication those relationships were fragile at best, transactional at worst. It was clear from the way things were getting with Duncan and Andrew's clique that we were all only as good as our contributions. And my contribution wasn't exactly feeling valuable at that moment.

I took a deep breath, then wrinkled my nose. There was something fetid on the sharp sea-salt-and-pine air. Rot. Rotting meat. I sniffed again, but the air was clean once more. The wind must have changed direction, most likely. I thought of Frank and his abandoned fishing gear. Hopefully he'd get back out there soon, replace the forbidden mussels with mackerel. Though so far in our time on the island he'd caught barely any fish. All of them tiny. Either he was slacking off or there were no fish around to catch. I could imagine all the boats out there scooping them up in big nets. Not much left for us, with our single rod and lazy fisherman.

I'd wandered far and darkness was starting to gather under the trees. Still, I didn't want to go back to camp. I thought of my flat with a longing I'd never felt for it before. To have somewhere that was mine, where I could shut the door and shut out the world at the same time, that was a luxury I missed more than coffee and butter put together.

I made my way back and found everyone else already gathered around the outdoor fire. The flames were high, more logs than usual spitting and sparking over the glowing embers. It looked more like a celebration bonfire than a campfire pit, but no one looked in the mood for celebrations.

Maxine was sitting between Zoe and Gill, a hankie screwed up in her hand. As I sat down I tried to catch her eye, but she was looking at the base of the fire, where the embers winked out their last light.

'Maddy, we've been having a chat,' Shaun said, after glancing at Duncan. 'Just, you know . . . about what happened today?'

'Right,' I said. 'Look, I . . . I was thinking about it and, maybe I just needed some time to see how it must have looked – to you, Maxine. And I wanted to apologise for not being clear about the allotment thing. Obviously there was a lot of room for misunderstanding and I should have asked for help with it before, if I wasn't, you know, going to be spending all my time on it. So, I'm sorry and, I hope that going forward we can all try and make the best out of the plants we have yet to harvest, like the late crops and the squashes.'

Frank coughed in the ensuing silence. Shaun exchanged another, pleading look with Duncan, then Andrew. Zoe swallowed and took Shaun's hand, squeezing it.

'The thing is,' Zoe said, 'we get you're sorry about it and, that's fine – thank you for saying so. But . . . we've been talking about basically everything that's gone down since we got here and we think that it might be best if, for the rest of the experiment . . . if you maybe moved out of the camp.'

I blinked, unable to process this, coming from her of all people. 'What?'

'Just for the community,' Zoe said quickly. 'The whole point of being here is to pretend like this is the last of everything, you know? We're meant to be a community, working together and . . . it feels like you'd be happier doing more your own thing, not collaborating.'

'We think it'll cut down on the arguments,' Andrew put in. 'You know, if you don't agree with ninety per cent of what this community is doing, maybe you shouldn't be in it.'

I looked from one person to the next, at the faces

around the fire. Maxine and Zoe wouldn't meet my eye. Clearly this was the price of their truce. Gill was looking at Duncan expectantly and Frank looked like he was asleep under his broad-brimmed fishing hat. I couldn't think of a thing to say. Being confronted like this had utterly thrown me. I'd been expecting an argument, recriminations, but I'd thought an apology might smooth things over. It was just one silly argument. Finally, I opened my mouth.

'Are you . . . serious?' I asked. 'Over one misunderstanding . . . you're just . . . throwing me out? Where am I meant to go?'

'We thought the fishing hut would be most logical,' Andrew said.

'There's a latrine down there and it's pretty solid so . . . you should be all right,' Shaun said. 'And we'd obviously let you take your stuff.'

'*Let* me!' I exploded, the unreality of it all boiling away to leave only pure fury behind. 'Well, that's awfully big of you, Shaun. Thank you so much for letting me take *my* stuff.'

'This is what we're talking about,' Maxine said, making me flush hot and cold with humiliation. 'I don't want to deal with this kind of thing for the next four months. It's ruining this experience – for everyone.'

'And you constantly getting at Zoe was what, community-mindedness?' I said, instantly regretting my words when Maxine folded her arms and glared at me.

'We already voted,' Duncan said, speaking for the first time since I'd sat down. 'It was unanimous.'

151

I glanced at Zoe, but she was looking anywhere but at me. All the fight in me died. Even she'd gone against me on this, after everything Maxine had said and done. All right, if I wanted to stay they couldn't force me out. The hut had no real door so it wasn't like they could lock it in my face. But . . . how could I stay when every single one of them wanted me gone? Coming back into camp that evening had been hard enough just knowing that Maxine was angry with me. How could I come back to that day after day, knowing it was all of them?

Andrew correctly took my silence as assent. 'You can go pack up your stuff – we found most of it and put it on your bed.'

'But . . . it's night?' Zoe said quietly. 'Couldn't we wait until morning?'

That tiny sliver of concern did what their anger and betrayal had not. Tears sprang to my eyes.

'I'll go tonight,' I said, not recognising my own voice. 'I'll get my stuff.'

I took two steps, then faltered and turned around. 'Maxine, I brought back buckthorn juice for you. It's in that bag.'

No one said anything as I went to the hut.

Andrew was right, it looked like all my belongings, even my tools from the storage lean-to, had been heaped on my bed. I started packing it in a jumble. I just wanted to get away.

It was only as I was stuffing my few toiletries into my coat pockets, that I realised I hadn't seen my books.

I'd brought three with me; foraging guide, plant-based medicine and *The Physician*, a seven-hundred-page historical novel so dense it had lasted me two months. I went to the little almost-shelf where the rest of the camp's battered paperbacks were, usually. It was empty.

I headed outside and found Andrew waiting by the door.

'All done?'

'No, actually – I can't find my books?'

'Oh . . . well, we can drop those down to you if we find them.'

From his tone it was clear he would be doing no such thing. With all the other books suddenly gone it was fairly obvious mine had been hidden.

'I can't leave until I have them,' I said.

'What's the problem?' Duncan asked, appearing at Andrew's side.

'She wants her books,' Andrew replied, making it sound like I was a five-year-old demanding my special blankie.

'If you've lost them, they'll probably turn up. Though they really are a community resource, so . . .'

I fought the urge to slap him. 'They're mine. I brought them here as part of my allowance of supplies. Also, have you split my rations up from everyone else's so I can take them with me?'

More shuffling and glances between the two of them. 'Again, that's food for the community, for people working on the cabin and the—'

'Fuck. The fucking. Cabin,' I said, clearly and loudly.

'You haven't done any work on it for weeks and you're still eating with the rest of us. I foraged that food, I found a cache, I was the only person working on the sodding allotment – I'm taking my share. And if you even think of stopping me –' I tapped the black plastic shell of the camera I'd been wearing so long that I'd ceased to notice it '– you're going to be on national TV, stealing a woman's food.'

I couldn't see Duncan that well; he was backlit by the raging fire. Only his eyes caught the light, gleaming like broken glass. For the second time I thought he might hit me, camera or no camera. Thankfully, my threat seemed to work.

'Get her some fucking rations,' Duncan muttered to Andrew. 'Just get this bitch out of here.' Duncan poked me, hard, in the chest. 'Don't even think of coming back for more. We don't give handouts to lazy cunts.'

'Better tell Gill then,' I said, thankful he couldn't see the trembling of my hands in the dark.

I turned and went to the food store, waiting for Andrew to get the keys. Inside I was pure adrenalin, fear and fury sloshing around like oil and water. I felt sick. I wanted to hit something, to cry, to dig my nails into my own skin. I wanted to be anywhere else than on Buidseach Isle. I wanted my mum.

Andrew came in, unlocked the box and waved my hands away when I reached for it. He took out bags and boxes and jars, creating a small pile on the ground. In the dark I couldn't see any of the labels. I doubted he could either. Andrew snapped the lid of the box shut, letting me know he was done. There was very little in my pile, but I took it anyway.

'My books?' I said.

Andrew didn't say anything, just shoved the box aside and pulled my books from underneath, practically throwing them at my chest. I grabbed them and scooped the food into my arms as well, dumping the lot into my holdall.

I left the hut and walked past the fire. With my anger burning a hole in my gut I reached the edge of the clearing and turned on my heel.

'Maybe now Duncan and Andrew can share their secret feasts with all of you, not just Gill and Shaun!' I called. It was petty and stupid, but I couldn't leave without outing them to the others. I couldn't walk away while they pretended to have the high ground. I would rather be angry than feel the gaping hole of despair in my chest.

No one said anything as I went. Even Zoe let me go without a word.

Chapter 15

'How do you think you'll get on with the other islanders?' Sasha had asked. 'We've chosen from quite a broad pool of people; lots of different personalities and backgrounds. How do you see yourself fitting in?'

'I fit in very easily, it's one of the things I got used to when I started temping,' I'd said, relieved that for once I didn't have to lie. I did work hard at fitting in when I started somewhere new. I didn't enjoy it, constantly felt awkward and exposed, but I could do it just the same. It was just a case of dressing like everyone else, listening to them, mirroring their rivalries and concerns. Whether I could keep it up for a year was another question entirely.

'You must meet lots of new people all the time then. Any kind of personality that you don't mesh well with?' Sasha asked. 'People that just set your teeth on edge?'

People in general set my teeth on edge, strangers in particular. It was always a relief to shut the door of my flat, slough off my work clothes and be myself again away from prying eyes.

'Bullies, I suppose,' I said. 'Sometimes I've worked places where there are just . . . bullies. You grow up thinking that's just playground stuff, but some people never grow out of it. They like throwing their weight around, having control over people. Especially in offices. You know, the CEO's secretary who can get you in trouble for eating at your desk, when she does it every day. The HR manager who can get away with being a complete pig. That kind of thing.'

Sasha nodded. I wondered if she'd ever been bullied. I couldn't picture it. You could tell with most people. Either they'd been bullied, or they'd been the one preying on someone else. There was a third kind, those that liked to watch, to laugh. Most people fell into that category in my experience. They liked to watch, as long as the bad things were happening to someone else. Wasn't that why I was there? Wasn't that what reality TV was all about? Throwing a group of bullies and victims together for the viewing public to bet on, like horses in a race.

'How do you deal with people like that? Generally?'

That was a tricky one. Generally, I'd always followed my mum's advice. Ignore them, and they'll go away. Eventually they'd come to the end of their game, move on. Then I'd become the unreasonable one. 'Why don't you talk to Kirsty, she's so nice' – never mind that she made my first year in halls a nightmare, stealing my food, banging on my door in the night and running away with her friends, laughing. Condoms on my door handle, hiding my post, reading my letters from Mum aloud in the kitchen. No, once the game was over it was like none of that ever happened. I was just an antisocial freak.

Auntie Ruth's advice had been very different. 'You've got to fight back, Mads. The only way you can get that cow to leave you alone is to get back at her, better and smarter than she got at you.'

I'd never had the guts to retaliate. Too afraid of what might happen to me if I did. Kirsty and the others were loud, vicious. I'd seen her get in a fight once in the student union. I wasn't looking to have my hair pulled out at the roots. But I thought about all the things I could do, from the big to the small. All the ways I could get revenge. If I was ever brave enough.

'Forgive, but don't forget,' I said, one of Auntie Ruth's other aphorisms. 'I always try to remember that. Because if someone can hurt you once, they can do it again.'

*

Getting down to the fishing hut in the dark wasn't easy. I nearly turned my ankle a few times on the exposed roots of pines. The bags I was carrying were heavy; I'd not had to carry it all up to the camp in one go and had forgotten how unwieldy they were. I was also weak from hunger.

When I arrived at the fishing hut I shone my torch

inside. It had been largely abandoned since Frank had his accident and the seasonal embargo on mussels had kicked in. Inside there was a lot of sand blown in through the tattered plastic curtain that made the door. It smelled of damp and there was rainwater trapped in the plastic, turning yellowish-brown. I was too exhausted to care.

I crawled in and dragged my bag in after me. There was no cloud cover and the heat of the day's sunshine had evaporated. I didn't even bother to take my coat off, just toed off my boots from a prone position and shuffled onto my bedroll. I was too weary to dwell for long, and quickly fell asleep.

The following morning I had to face my new reality. I'd been numb with shock, exhaustion and cold when I left the camp, but in the blistering light of morning there was no hiding from the challenge I had to face. Everything we'd built in the eight months we'd been a community was now essentially off-limits to me. The food stocks, the water filter, the shelter and allotment crops, all out of reach. I was back where we'd been on arrival.

Panic rose in me like bile. There was so much I needed to do that I didn't know where to begin. How was I going to manage? I was going to be alone for the next four months. Unwanted, shunned, hated, without even the most casual contact with a neutral outsider. On top of all of that, how would I look now, when all this went on television? A stubborn bitch no one could stand to be around? A weirdo who couldn't get on with anyone and who created disaster wherever she went?

For a moment, sitting there in the musty shelter, I considered giving up. I had in my head an image of me walking up to the portacabin and asking for the emergency radio. The producers would have to send someone to get me if I wanted off the island. There was no prize at the end of this, nothing worth soldiering on for. They couldn't keep me there a prisoner against my will. I could be on the mainland by nightfall. Perhaps they'd put me up in a hotel. I could take a long, hot shower, lie on a real mattress, watch television, crank the thermostat up and order in a pizza to eat all alone. Even the thought of that brought tears to my eyes. It was humiliating. Worse, though, was the idea of returning to my previous life, to the inheritance I couldn't stand to think of, to the loss that threatened to break me.

I felt for the straps to my camera and undid them. Turning the little black box around I looked at my tiny reflection in its dead-eyed lens. I wasn't alone, not really. Everything I did, everything any of us did, was being recorded. One day people would see what I'd gone through. I refused to give Duncan or the others the satisfaction of being rid of me. I wanted every moment of their mean-spiritedness, their bullying, to be on show, for anyone to see. If I left now they could forget me. If I left, I would be the one losing out on the island and its beauty.

'I'm not giving up,' I said, aloud to the camera, to jolt myself away from thoughts of hotels and hot food.

'I'm not letting them win. I refuse to be forced off this island.'

Those three phrases formed a mantra for the rest of my day.

I got up, reattached my camera and forced myself to find twigs and dry seaweed for a fire. With that done I went down to the rocks and picked an obscene number of mussels. September loomed and there were only a few weeks left of the mussel-ban. I would take my chances. I gathered enough for two people, two greedy people. I had a full day's work ahead of me and I would not be much good on an empty stomach.

I steamed my mussels in a small amount of water, added ghee from a tin Andrew had definitely not meant to give to me, and ate the mussels using a shell half as a spoon. It wasn't pizza in a warm hotel, but it was almost as blissful.

With a blank page from my novel and a pen I wrote myself a list of everything I needed to get done. If I had a moment to think of the others, of the way things had been last night, I knew I'd freeze up and sink into despair. I needed focus, goals and, above all, something for dinner.

*

I spent that first day alone foraging, for food and supplies. I swept out the fishing hut with a pine branch and turned a plastic bottle and a handkerchief into a primitive water filter.

My main worry was the food. Mushrooms would be plentiful right through until the end of November, but everything else would be unpleasant to eat or just absent altogether within a month or so. I had to preserve as much as possible. I had no jars and no vinegar, no sugar or salt, so pickling or brining was out of the question. Drying and smoking would have to do.

I would not go crawling for assistance that would not be forthcoming from my fellow islanders. I would not beg the production team to send pasta over by boat. I would not leave now that I had started to discover myself again.

For the next few days I kept busy, talking as I did so to the people who would one day watch my endeavours. It helped me to feel less alone. It was ridiculous; I'd spent so much time longing for a bit of peace from all of them and now I had it and it was driving me crazy. Even when I'd thought myself lonely before I'd still spoken to people; at work, in shops, waiting for the bus. On the island all that incidental contact was stripped away. I spoke to the camera because, otherwise, I wouldn't have spoken at all.

There were plenty of mussels about and I was eating well for the first time in months. The strength I got from that was incredible. I'd forgotten what it was to not feel tired and annoyed all the time. I quickly put together a small wattle and daub structure out of the sea wind, large enough to surround a fire pit. Inside this approximation of a smoke shack I hung clumps of seaweed and mushrooms to dry.

I stored the dry food in washed-out tins, lidded with squares of torn-up T-shirt tied on with string. Dried berries and nuts I hung from the ceiling in pouches made of the lining of my holdall. None of it was ideal, but it was better than nothing.

Hunting for food took most of my time and led me all over the island. It was a hard task to find places I'd not previously harvested. I crawled around, overturning leaves and dead plants looking for precious mushrooms, often going out at dawn and not returning until late afternoon.

It was on one such day, almost a week into my isolation, that I noticed something amiss in my hut. It was the beginning of the season for *sparassis crispa* – cauliflower fungus. I'd had quite a successful day of it. On returning I went to find my mushroom brush, as cauliflower fungus has many, many holes for mud to get into, when I noticed a cep on my bed. The small mushroom was almost hidden under the fold of my sleeping bag. I picked it up and looked into my billycan, which was hanging on an exposed nail. It was where I kept the food I planned on eating for my meals, and it should have been full. It wasn't.

When I'd left that morning it had contained a large handful of ceps, a few lobes of chicken-of-the-woods and the remainder of a small puffball I'd found the day before. Now only half of the chicken-of-the-woods and the puffball remained. The rest was gone. Still holding the lone cep, it took me a moment to realise what had happened. When I did, I felt my stomach clench in anger.

While I'd been out, searching and foraging for myself, after filling their larder for them, the others had been treating my hut like a supermarket. For a moment I was so blinded by rage that the thought of checking my smoke hut didn't occur to me. As soon as it did I ran outside and untied the little door to peer in. It didn't look like anything had been taken. Had they stolen stuff from there before? I couldn't be sure.

I documented the theft for the camera, which assuaged some of my anger. They could say whatever they wanted about me. In the end they were the ones who were stealing. They were the ones who had thrown me out. Everyone who watched our footage would see that.

The next day, before I set off, I made sure to remember what was in the can for dinner: cauliflower fungus, seabeet and kelp. I climbed up into the hills and went hunting as usual, trying to put it out of my mind. By the time I returned to camp I'd almost forgotten about my suspicions.

It was clear immediately that someone had been in my hut again. There was nothing missing from the can, but my foraging book was out from under my bed. I flicked through it and noticed with great irritation that a page had been ripped out. I'd not needed to refer to it for a while and so couldn't say if the page had been missing before I'd been ousted from the camp. But the fact remained that the book *had* been moved. Someone had been in my shelter.

My first thought was to go confront them, to demand the return of the page and some sort of compensation for the stolen mushrooms. My second thought was that this was probably what they were waiting for. It would have been easy to hide their intrusion if they'd wanted to. Clearly, they hadn't been bothered that I would notice. They wanted me to. This was an act of petty aggression, something working in an office had taught me all about. In that environment taking someone's stapler was an act of war and missing someone from a tea round a clear signal of contempt. They had probably turned their cameras off and if I started making accusations I'd only make myself look crazy and paranoid. If I went roaring up to camp to shout and stamp my feet, they would win. I would have succeeded only in making myself more of a pariah.

That didn't mean I was going to take it lying down, of course.

That night I made a decision that was to prove essential to my survival. Though I didn't know it at the time as I packed up all my tins and packets of food. It was dark by the time I picked my way out to the cave. Inside all was as I'd left it. No one seemed to have stumbled across my hiding place. Yet.

Once inside I came across a problem. I'd buried my packet food but the tins with their loose coverings and the permeable bags of dried food required hiding in a dry, airy space. Shining my torch around the roof of the little cave showed me only long, tangled roots and spider webs. If I hung anything there it would be seen by anyone coming in. Not to mention water might drip down those roots and rot my supplies.

The torch picked up the jagged line of the crack in the back wall. I went over and peered through. Back there I could see no roots; it looked mostly like stone and hard, dry clay that far under the hill. The two sides of the crack were not opposite one another; one was about ten inches back from the other. Maybe more. Experimentally I removed my bulky coat and camera, slid my shoulders into the space and wriggled. For a moment I was worried I was stuck and that worry jolted through my heart like a shard of ice. But I managed to push my way through and found myself in the full darkness of the cave interior.

It was indeed mostly stone and clay. No roots had found their way through and even fewer dry leaves had blown through the crack. The air was dry, stale, but suitable for my needs. I wriggled my way partially back through the crack and pulled my belongings in after me.

I lined up my tins on a ledge where two rocks met, so any damp from the dirt floor wouldn't rust them. I wedged my foraging book beside them and put the cloth pouches on top. It was a semi-decent solution and would at least keep my food from being stolen. Sitting there, I thought for a moment of moving all my things into the cave, but logic stopped me. If I disappeared from the beach the others would notice and would go looking for my new camp. Then the stealing would begin all over again. Besides, the beach hut was close to the shore and suited me fine for foraging and beachcombing. The one drawback to it was not being able to have a fire indoors. Come winter that would be impossible to live without.

Building a new shelter seemed my only option. Yet more work to undertake alone. I sighed and eased my way out of the cave. Tomorrow I would make a start on my own hut.

*

Three weeks after being ousted from the community, life was almost back to normal. At least, as normal as life could be on an island populated by only ten people, two of whom I never saw and the rest of whom hated me. I'd seen the other islanders around and they mostly ignored me. A few times Zoe had come down to the beach to take a quick dunk in the ocean; she nodded hello, but that was about it.

I'd made myself a little hut on the edge of the beach, where it turned to earth. It was of tipi style, three reasonably thick branches sunk into the dirt and lashed together at the top with scraps of rope. Onto this frame I'd nailed crossbars of pallet from the demolished fishing hut and heaped on pine boughs, held in place with the plastic sheeting. The result was snug, smoky, but warm. I could also now cook inside when it rained, as it did often now that September had washed away the last of the warm weather and was edging into October.

My stock of food was still not enough to feel confident about, but with some rationing, it would keep me going until January. I kept a bit on hand in the tipi as a decoy and made sure to pick lots of woody, bitter vegetation as bait. Food still went missing, but at least it wasn't food I wanted.

I was out among the tidal pools, looking for clams, whelks or anything else edible hiding in the wind-furrowed water, when I felt eyes on me. Looking up I saw Zoe standing on the beach, her dark hair whipping in the wind. She waved, then beckoned me back. Curious, I picked up my bucket (a child's yellow castle one I'd found, handleless, on the beach) and made my way towards her.

Zoe had given up her summer uniform of sarongs, skirts and tank-tops for more cold-resistant leggings and wellies. I noticed that she was wearing Shaun's bulky fisherman jumper under her purple anorak.

'Hi,' she said, as I came within earshot. 'Find much?'

'Not especially,' I said. 'How about you?'

'Oh, I'm not looking . . . not today.' Zoe looked out at the sea, which roared and foamed behind me. 'Can I talk to you about something?'

'All right,' I said, sensing that I was not going to like where this was going. 'Can we walk and talk? It's bloody cold out here.'

'Um . . .' Zoe glanced around. 'Sure, but not to the beach hut.'

'Worried about being seen with the island pariah?' I said, only half joking.

Zoe lowered her eyes and didn't laugh. I realised that was exactly what she was worried about.

'What is it you wanted to talk about?' I asked, swallowing the hurt I felt.

'Well . . . You're a herbal doctor or something, right?'

'Or something.'

'I need some medicine.'

'Gill's got the first-aid kit.'

'Gill can't help with this,' Zoe said, looking pained.

'If it's serious you need to go to the camera guys and use the emergency radio,' I said, feeling a stab of alarm. 'What's wrong?'

For the first time I noticed that Zoe wasn't wearing her camera. I had got out of the habit of wearing mine all the time, mostly I left it in the tipi if I was gathering. I had a half-formed idea that maybe it might get footage of the food thieves even if they had left their cameras off, then when the show went out, people would know.

Zoe met my eyes for the first time. 'I'm pregnant.'

'Oh . . . wow . . . congratu—'

'I don't want to be. I can't be, not right now,' Zoe said, all in a rush. 'I have plans, for my career, for my life. I don't want to be a mum. I've never wanted to be and . . . I'm on the pill, but I don't know if I missed one when that cow was hiding them, or if it's not worked right but now . . . now I'm pregnant.'

'So . . . you want an abortion?' I said slowly.

'No! It's not even a . . . thing, yet. I just need for you to give me something that'll make me get my period, because it's over three weeks late now and I can't leave the island, leave the whole show behind just

170

because I need a pill. And if I wait until it's over it'll be too late to actually have an abortion.'

I was already shaking my head before she stopped speaking. Possible side-effects of herbs like tansy, pennyroyal and white dittany flashed before me: seizures, organ failure or coma. I'd studied them as part of a dissertation. The last recourse of truly desperate people where abortion remained illegal. The case studies of women using homemade poisons to expel unviable pregnancies the law required them to see through to the bitter end. A choice no one should have to make. Zoe had no idea what she was asking. If she did, she wouldn't have come to me.

'Zoe, there are plants with the right chemicals to do what you want but . . . it would be far too dangerous for me to even try to administer them to you. I don't have the right training, we're quite far from any real medical help if things go wrong and . . . Have you discussed this with Shaun? Does he even know?'

Zoe looked away. 'It's my decision.'

'Yes, but have you spoken to him about it? He'd probably be worried about you if he knew what you wanted to do.'

Zoe's brows drew down and she glared at me. 'So you're not going to help me because he might want me to be pregnant.'

I'd had enough. 'I'm not going to help you because I know the risks here, and I have no desire whatsoever to poison you by accident, several hours from the nearest hospital. If you need medical care you should get on the radio and get someone to take you to the mainland where you can get it. I'm not discussing this further.'

I took a step round her and started to make my way back along the beach. Zoe caught up with me after a few steps.

'I stood up for you, you know!' she hissed. 'I thought we were friends – that I could rely on you, but you're worse than Maxine. You think you're right about everything and that we're just a bunch of fuckwits. But she's right – we're better off without you.'

I turned around so fast she bumped into my chest. Our noses were almost touching.

'If you've got such a handle on things I suggest you stop stealing my fucking food,' I said in a low voice. 'Now get yourself out of my face and go gossip – it's what you're good at.'

I turned and stalked away, my heart beating heavily in my chest. I was shaking with anger. Over the past few weeks I'd been anxious, but calmly working towards my own goals. Just one run-in with Zoe and I was back to where I'd been the night I was kicked out: furious and on the edge of tears.

'Fuck off then!' Zoe shouted at my back. 'Who needs you?'

I refused to turn around and instead made my way off into the woods. I was half convinced she'd follow me to my hut and trap me in there until I gave in. I didn't have the energy for it.

Once I'd calmed down a bit I started to worry. I

remembered the old horror story Mum had told me of the girl who attempted her own abortion. It was something that had circulated at school during my brief attendance and which she'd fleshed out and retold, drilling the warning into me. I'd had nightmares about it. It was one of the reasons I'd chosen to study those herbs in the first place.

If Zoe was in fact pregnant, her dietary needs would not be met by the rations they were on at camp. Even just in terms of calories she'd be undersupplied. Then again, perhaps that restrictive diet and its ensuing dramatic weight loss were to blame for her late period. We only had a few months left; my hope was that if she was pregnant she'd see sense and leave the island to get medical care. If she wasn't, well, then there was no problem.

I was also worried for myself. Neither of us had been wearing our cameras, so the content of our conversation was between us two alone. If Zoe did try to brew up some concoction and did herself some harm, she might still implicate me. It would be easy for her to say I'd given it to her, as the island's botany 'expert'. Of course, she'd have to find plants at random; my foraging book was well hidden. Although it didn't tell you how to induce an abortion, it did advise on herbs to be avoided in pregnancy. Not really a leap to work out what to use. It was then that I remembered Gill had a book of her own, from some company that made essential oils. Most of it was pseudoscience – I'd flipped through it out of boredom – but they did warn against using some of the remedies during pregnancy. I hoped that Zoe wouldn't take that information and use it to work out what plants to ingest. Hopefully Gill would have more sense than to let her borrow it.

After a few hours of foraging I returned to my tipi and found that the cold ashes of my fire had been kicked over my bed. It was annoying but a petty act easily put right. It still hurt. I carried the sleeping bag outside and shook it into the sea wind. Then I put things to rights and put my camera on. From now on, I wasn't going anywhere without it.

Chapter 16

'You were, at several points during the time following the split from the others, accused of acting against the group, weren't you?' Rosie asks, head tipping to one side, mouth a sympathetic pout, as if to convey empathy to a scolded puppy.

'Accused of trying to attack them, yes,' I say.

'I can't imagine what that was like for you.'

'No, I don't think you can,' I agree, watching as the pout purses up in slight annoyance. I wonder, for the first time, what Rosie would have been like on the island. I can picture it quite easily, shuffling her in with the rest of them. She looks most at home beside Gill, gossiping with that same insincere look of concern. Perhaps she would have joined in the finger-pointing as well. Echoing the hisses of 'poisoner' just like the others.

'Why do you think it was that they became convinced you were responsible? As opposed to anyone else, or simply bad luck?' Rosie asks.

'Because it's very easy to think the worst of someone you already hate. People assume that people they dislike are secretly revelling in their failures, and it's not a huge leap to start thinking that they are causing you to fail. That used to be something you'd be killed for; just looking at someone before they fell ill or lost something valuable. Ill wishing. The others hated me, and they assumed I hated them, enough to go after them.'

'But you didn't hate them?'

'I did, sometimes,' I allow. 'Mostly I found myself asking if they really meant to hurt me or if it was just unintentional. I fell into the opposite trap, you see. They thought I was out to get them, when I wasn't. I thought they wouldn't deliberately harm me, when they obviously could.'

'So you think that's the only reason they suspected you, the fact that they disliked you, and it was easy for them to believe the worst?'

'No. Not entirely. It was also easy for them to believe, because I knew how to do what they were accusing me of.' I sit back and watch as Rosie tries to cover her surprise with a knowledgeable nod. 'I knew how to survive, to cure, so I also knew how to kill.'

Chapter 17

My worry about Zoe did not go away as easily as a scattering of ash. In fact it worsened as the days went on. Finally, when I could take it no longer, I decided to check on her, from a distance.

I went for my morning forage and deposited the haul in my tipi. Some interesting specimens that would require careful preparation later. I took some winter chanterelles and jelly ear fungus with me as a sort of excuse. If I was caught I planned on saying I was there to trade them for packaged food. I took a circuitous route up to the northern hills and from there found a good spot to peek down on the camp.

Nothing seemed so very different, not that I'd expected it to be. The only obvious change was a smoke hut, much like mine, which had been put up by the unfinished cabin.

Frank, Shaun and Andrew were sitting by the fire, drinking something out of mugs. I thought at first that it was spruce tea but then noticed the plastic bottle on the ground, half full of brownish liquid. Homebrew.

After a while Zoe came out and went to the shower shelter with a billycan of steaming water. She looked fine, waving to Shaun as she passed. Satisfied, I crept back into the woods and went hunting for more mushrooms.

It was late afternoon when I got back to my tipi. The sun was on its way down and gloom was settling in, making space for nightfall. I busied myself firstly in cleaning a puffball I'd found. Once I had my cooking fire going, I went to fetch what I'd put aside for dinner. Only what I'd gathered wasn't there; all of it was gone.

The theft was so brazen that for a second all I could do was stand there. To take some and hope I wouldn't notice was bad enough, but to make off with everything was a blatant 'fuck you'. Anger clouded my mind for a moment, but quickly gave way to panic.

The mushrooms were *amanita muscaria* – fly agaric. I'd left them out because I'd not thought anyone would take bright red mushrooms with white scales, so similar to storybook toadstools. They looked inedible and many books called them so. If not chopped and boiled to remove the ibotemic acid, they could induce vomiting, hallucinations, seizures and other horrible side effects. Even death.

My heart was racing. If the others had taken the mushrooms they wouldn't know how to prepare them properly. I grabbed my torch and ran for the camp without a second thought.

As I ran I tried to think. How many mushrooms had I gathered? Deaths from *amanita muscaria* were rare, but the effects could be nasty and Zoe was potentially pregnant. I couldn't remember exactly how long it would take the combination of toxins in the fungus to work – maybe an hour. If they'd taken them while I was at the camp and eaten them for lunch they'd be fully in the grips by now and possibly unable to get to the emergency phone for help. I knew symptoms could last for at least eight hours and if the person was already drunk, weakened by hunger and without access to clean water . . .

I burst into camp and was hit by the smell almost at once. Shit and vomit. Sounds of retching came from both the latrine and the shower shelter. From somewhere close by came the sound of something semi-liquid splashing into a bucket.

Around the fire I could see huddled shapes of people and I went to them first. It was Frank and Shaun. Frank appeared to be asleep, but Shaun was staring into the embers of the fire, pale and unmoving.

'Are you all right?' I asked, but neither of them answered. Shaun just blinked slowly. I realised he was high. Fly agaric had a reputation for being a 'magic mushroom'. Even reindeer tripped on the stuff. I was about to try and take Frank's pulse when I was shoved from behind. I stumbled, flinging myself away from the fire, regained my balance and turned around.

Zoe stood behind me, breathlessly furious and wide-eyed, her face streaked with tears and glitter.

'You!' she shouted, pushing me again. 'What have you done? What the fuck is wrong with you?'

'Zoe, I haven't—'

'You did this! You knew Duncan'd take those mushrooms, you knew!'

She started to sob. 'What've you done to them?'

I grabbed Zoe by the arms and she struggled, starting to cry harder.

'Zoe, I need you to listen to me. Those mushrooms are edible. I picked them for me. I don't care if you don't believe me, there isn't time right now. I'm here to help, but you need to tell me who ate what and when. Can you do that?'

Zoe sniffed thickly, but nodded. 'OK . . . OK . . . the mushrooms. Duncan brought them back here and I said – I told him! – they didn't look good to eat. But he said they must be if you had them. So he cooked them up and I said not to be stupid but he ate them and I went off because he was being an arsehole. Shaun came after me and when we came back a while later everyone still seemed fine. Duncan offered Shaun some of the stew he'd put the mushrooms in. It had rabbit in so, I couldn't have any but Shaun ate a bit. Then about an hour later everyone started feeling sick, except Shaun. He just . . . he's been acting really weird. Is he going to be OK?'

'I think so,' I said. 'He looks like he's tripping, so I guess he must have had a small dose of the actual mushroom. But you said Duncan was eating them before that, was that with Andrew and Gill?'

180

She nodded. 'I don't know who ate the most of it, but Gill was the first one to throw up. She went off over there and we heard her. Duncan thought she was drunk at first.'

'What about Frank and Maxine?'

Zoe snorted. 'Frank's been asleep the whole time. He drank a lot of Maxine's wine and he wasn't awake for the stew. She had some though, with Gill and the others.'

'Right . . . I need to see how they're doing. In the meantime can you find me Gill's first-aid kit and make up some of those re-hydration powders? If the others are being sick a lot they'll need them. Then can you just stay with Shaun and make sure he doesn't hurt himself?'

Zoe nodded. I let her go and went in search of the four missing members of the community. I had to make sure they weren't in danger. I found Maxine first, holed up in the latrine. After some coaxing she opened the door a crack and I saw her pale face and sweat-soaked hair. The smell of sick made my eyes water. I told her about the mushrooms and promised to come back in a bit with something to drink. She only nodded weakly and eased the door shut.

Gill was in the unfinished cabin, one of the buckets close by. She was leaning against the wall with her eyes shut. There was a bottle of water next to her. She'd clearly been sick a lot but had at least tried to stay hydrated. She didn't look as bad as Maxine. Since Gill had been sick before any of the others, I suspected she'd thrown up most of the toxins before they'd had a chance to work fully. Luckily for her.

I found Andrew behind the hut, wrapped in his sleeping bag and dozing next to a bucket of shit. He didn't look in any serious danger and he had a steady pulse. I decided to let him sleep until it was absolutely necessary to move him.

Zoe had prepared a few water bottles of orange-flavour re-hydration crystals. I snatched some up while she checked on Shaun, and went to see about Duncan.

I tapped on the door of the shower shelter, a wattle and daub panel on rope hinges. Inside I heard a groan. The smell of vomit and excrement was very strong. If he'd been the first to eat the mushrooms and had eaten the bulk of them, he was likely the most affected. I felt a guilty surge of satisfaction that it was Duncan who was faring the worst.

'Duncan?' I said softly. 'It's me, Maddy. Are you awake? Can you open the door?'

'Fuck you,' came the rasping reply.

I felt like in the current situation he was justified. At least he wasn't unconscious. 'Can you tell me if there's any blood coming up, or . . . um . . . out?

There was a short silence then a quiet, sullen response. 'No.'

'OK. I've got some water here with something in it to re-hydrate you and balance out your system a bit. Can you open the door a bit?'

The door opened a crack and a waft of pungent air set my eyes watering. I held a bottle out and fingers snatched it away. I didn't look at the smudges on the hand too closely.

'I'm going to sort you out a change of clothes and something to clean up with,' I said. 'Call out if you have any pain or if the symptoms get worse.'

There was no reply but I knew he'd heard me. I went in search of hot water, soap and rags of any type. Since arriving we'd been using leaves and moss as improvised toilet paper. This was usually kept in a plastic bag hanging off a nail by the latrine. I found the bag empty, and set about collecting more moss and large leaves in the dark.

'Zoe, can you dig out some cloths to wash with?' I asked as I returned to the fire with my full bag and started to add wood to the flames.

I built up a good fire and rounded up all the billycans I could. I boiled up water and sliced a bar of soap from the hut into smaller pieces. Zoe came back with a hand towel and we cut that up too.

While Zoe coaxed Frank awake and gentled him and Shaun to bed in the hut, I took care of the others. I started with Maxine, handing her a hot soapy cloth, then clean clothes. When she was out of the latrine I gave her a water bottle and sent her to the fire to sit. Gill was able to get to the fireside under her own steam once I woke her up.

Andrew came around when I tapped his shoulder. His eyes were unfocused and he had trouble walking, but I held him up while he wiped himself down. Once he too was lying down by the fire I went to Duncan.

This time he had to open the door to me fully. His jumper and sparse beard were both caked in vomit. He was naked from the waist down, his khaki shorts and underwear trampled into the effluent on the shower floor. He was visibly trembling. He wouldn't look at me and didn't say a word as I passed him a clean cloth and some jogging bottoms. When I offered a hand to help him to the fire he refused it.

Soon all four of them were around the fire, curled up in sleeping bags and full of water. I was already exhausted by this time. After a full day of foraging the last thing I'd needed was a run up the hill to camp. I'd also not had anything to eat since breakfast. Though after smelling the lot of them I didn't think I'd be able to stomach anything.

In the pit of my stomach was a hard little knot of guilt. All this was because of my mushrooms. All right, they'd stolen them, but had I expected anything different? Hadn't there been a moment when I put them aside that I thought, 'Wouldn't it be great if . . .'? It made me feel sick to admit it even to myself but yes, I'd thought there was a small chance they might take the mushrooms, assuming they were safe. I'd had the idea, deep down, that maybe they'd be taught a lesson if they were stupid enough to eat them. I hadn't actually thought they would. Apparently I'd given them too much credit. Still, even the possibility should have stopped me leaving the mushrooms out. It was irresponsible. Any one of them might have been seriously affected.

My penance would be cleaning up the mess I'd caused with my carelessness. I went to work, forcing myself to remain awake and in motion.

'Do you need a hand?' Zoe said, yawning widely as she spoke.

'Get yourself some sleep; I'll wake you up if anything changes,' I said. The image of her stricken, tear-stained face still very much at the forefront of my mind. She'd been through enough.

'All right . . . if you're sure . . . and thanks, Maddy. For everything.'

I shrugged, uncomfortable. This was sort of my fault after all. Duncan might have been underhanded, but I had been irresponsible. I should have known better.

Once Zoe went off to bed I rinsed out buckets of shit with boiling soapy water and sluiced down the latrine and shower stall as best I could. I gathered up all the discarded clothing I could find and went a fair distance from camp, lit a small fire and boiled up the dirty clothes in the one metal bucket. Lastly I refilled the filter so that there'd be plenty of clean water to drink when everyone woke up.

By the time I was done exorcising my guilt a pale dawn had found its way through the trees. The camp was revealed as a confusion of footprints, buckets and puddles of spilled water. Everything at least smelled cleaner, aside from me. I did a last check of the sleeping patients. They all looked all right, with colour in their faces. By my rudimentary calculations they were past the worst of it.

I woke Zoe to tell her I was going to the beach for a wash and to come and get me if anyone deteriorated, or to go for the emergency phone if it was serious. She grabbed my arm as I went to leave.

'Will you come back? Please? I don't want to be here on my own.'

Guilt flared again. I couldn't leave her to deal with my mess. I hadn't planned on returning; this wasn't my home anymore. It was humiliating really, how quickly I caved to the slightest hint of Zoe's need to have me there. To the idea that I was wanted. I'd been on my own for too long if that was all it took to change my mind.

I nodded. 'I'll grab a few things and come right back.'

I hurried down to the beach, stripped and took a hasty dip in the freezing sea. Dripping and shivering I ran to the hut, towelled off and put on a clean pair of leggings, T-shirt and oversized jumper. With my hat pulled on over my wet hair I packed a change of clothes, my camera charger and my sleeping bag into my rucksack and headed back up the hill.

For the next few days I was back in the communal hut, but I could never mistake things for being as they were. For a start everyone was still weakened from their tussle with *amanita muscaria*. Most of them showed symptoms like getting over a bad flu: exhaustion, aches and grogginess. Frank and Shaun were mostly back to normal the day after the event itself, aside from Frank's hangover. The four of us shared the necessary work, chopping wood, fetching, filtering and boiling water, preparing meals, feeding the rabbits and digging a new latrine. Still, I felt like an outsider and more often than not I found myself working alone.

Despite Zoe's initial gratitude for my presence, she started to avoid me as soon as Shaun was awake and sensible. I wasn't surprised, but it did still hurt. I'd foolishly let myself hope that she'd forgiven me for not helping her that day on the beach. Clearly, she had not. The crisis had forced her to depend on me but now that it was over, we were back where we had been before.

I steered clear of ministering to the others directly. I had no desire to spend more time with them than was absolutely necessary. Instead I busied myself with the water and the wood. I foraged what I could and cooked solo, unwilling to ask for rations and knowing they would probably not be forthcoming. At night when I bedded down in my old spot in the hut, the air felt strained. I knew I wasn't wanted. After all, every one of them had voted to kick me out. They weren't looking for me to come back.

After two days of this I knew I had to leave. Their hostility helped to ease any residual feelings of responsibility I had over the incident. I'd more than paid for my moment of carelessness. I packed my things and left just after breakfast. I'd been planning on saying goodbye to Zoe at least, but she was nowhere to be found. Shaun and Frank had also disappeared from camp. I told myself that they weren't avoiding me and that I didn't care if they were.

It was almost a relief to return to my little tipi. The silence there was natural, calm, not pointed and weighty with disapproval. I stowed my things inside and went to look at the smokehouse. Without me there to tend the fire it had gone out and the mushrooms I'd been drying had gone soft and dark. I buried the spoiled food in the woods with regret. I'd lost three days of foraging for food that I sorely needed.

I had a small calendar in my things and carefully crossed off the last three days. The remaining weeks stretched on as unfeeling black numbers. Although we had arrived in February, we would be rescued on the first of January – missing out the coldest month of the year. Before we'd set off I'd felt as if it was cheating to only live for eleven months on the island. After all, they were calling it a year, weren't they? But now I could hardly wait for Christmas to pass and the boat to return for us. Already the wind coming off of the sea was like a knife through my clothes. I couldn't imagine what it would be like in a few weeks' time, when the snow started to fall.

Chapter 18

'I think my biggest mistake was giving them too much credit,' I say, pulling at a loose thread on the sleeve of the jumper. It grows longer and I imagine that somewhere a wardrobe assistant is wincing. As if a loose thread is important.

That's the strangest part of being back; not the crowds, noise, hot showers and soft beds. It's the thousand and one mundane concerns everyone seems so preoccupied with. Parking tickets, missing wheelie bins, long queues, bank holiday sales and loose threads. None of them seem to realise how little it all means. How much of it is window-dressing. Play-acting at being a superior species, somehow apart from the rest of the animal kingdom. I've seen what hides behind all that.

We are all animals when cornered.

'I thought they didn't realise what they were doing, or that they were just selfish, lazy. I tried to back away, not get involved. I thought, after they kicked me out, *if I just got on with what I had to do it would be OK. But they wouldn't let that happen. Hating me was the only thing they had holding them together. Without me I think they would have turned on each other much sooner. Not that it made any difference . . . No matter what we did, we were doomed as soon as that boat dropped us there.*

'*The things that started happening to us, after Christmas . . . I thought it was all just random tragedy; accidents, mistakes. If I'd known then that there was some reason to it, some intent, I don't know if I could have held on like I did.*'

'*You might have given up hope?*'

I almost smile. '*I'd lost hope by then. No, I might have given up holding on to my delusion that somehow we were all still civilised people at heart. I might have tried to get them before they came for me.*'

Chapter 19

Snow shrinks the world down. When I'd lived with my parents in their little village, it had kept us inside for days at a time. The roads outside slick as glass and unsalted, our cars useless in the driveway. There were always accidents, every winter.

On the island it was much the same, only now instead of being stuck in a three-bedroom house with wifi, TV, cupboards full of food, and central heating, I was confined to a small tipi with a fire, no toilet and a single novel. It was the first time I'd been jealous of hibernating creatures.

Inside the smoky darkness of my tipi I kept myself wrapped up in my sleeping bag. Reading was possible in the dim light and I was grateful I'd brought *The Physician* with me. I eagerly drank up the descriptions of scorching deserts and hot, dusty towns, imagining the same sun baking my face.

I left the tipi for only two things: to use the latrine and to bring in wood, which was stored in the now defunct smokehouse. Each time I braved the outside world the ferocity of the wind surprised me. It wasn't just the strength of the sea wind but the hard, sandy pellets of snow it threw at me. After a few minutes outside I felt scoured down to the bone.

Wary of running out of wood I reluctantly went out every few days to dig through the snow for fallen branches and sticks to store in the smokehouse. It was while I was out shovelling half-frozen snow that I found the camera. The end of the spade bounced off the tough plastic and I pulled it up out of the snow. It was a game camera, one of the ones we'd been shown on arrival. Glancing up I saw a broken branch, probably snapped by the weight of the snowfall. The camera must have fallen.

I held on to it, wondering what to do. Clearly the camera guys hadn't found the fallen camera. It had probably been buried in the snow for a while. I assumed they wouldn't want to be trekking all over the island in the freezing cold, checking on them. I hung the smashed camera on a low branch to make it easier for them to find when the weather got better.

Every day I crossed another square off of my pocket calendar. It was the only thing I looked forward to, aside from hot meals. When I wasn't reading, sleeping or making daring trips to the latrine, I daydreamed about what I would do when I was back on the mainland, back to reality. It was a game that could go on for hours and though it never bored me, it did often leave me feeling sad, even scared.

The fact was that the worst thing about my previous life was me. I didn't like myself there, my depression or my outbursts of anger. I didn't even know myself. For the first time since moving away from my parents I felt like a whole person, like I made sense without them. Although it hadn't been easy and I'd had my doubts, overall I had found direction on the island. Away from it, back in the real world, I wasn't sure I knew who I was.

There was a lot of time to think in the warm semi-darkness of the tipi. I found myself dwelling more and more on memories of my real life. Thinking about things that had actually happened to me off the island made me feel like I was remembering a film or something. That version of me felt like someone else.

At last Christmas arrived. My time on the island was almost at an end. I planned to celebrate with a dinner of mussels and the last of my butter. Off the island Christmas hadn't been a celebration for me for a while. While living alone it meant watching procedural crime reruns and drinking Irish cream. Now my parents were dead, it'd be even worse, without even a phone call to them to convince me I wasn't completely alone. On Buidseach, though, it felt like a milestone, something to celebrate, even if I did so alone.

I was mending my hiking socks with a little sewing kit when I heard a tap on the frame of the tipi. For a moment I thought it might be the wind, then it came again. A knock. I moved the boots that were weighing down the plastic door curtain and flipped it aside. Zoe, swaddled in knitwear and with a coating of snow on her anorak, stuck her head inside.

'Cosy in here, isn't it?' she said. Her nose was pink and dripping. 'Merry Christmas!'

'Merry Christmas,' I echoed.

'I was wondering if you wanted to come up to camp? We're having a bit of a Christmas party – it's only right that we spend it together, after all, it's the only chance we'll get before we go home.'

Zoe was fairly glowing with delight at the prospect of returning home. I imagined she had whole terabytes' worth of Instagram posts to dream up in advance of the show coming out on TV. For the first time I considered having to go through the interviews again, answering questions I didn't have answers to; about why I'd been kicked out, why I hadn't fought harder or been more willing to compromise. Before it had felt almost like therapy, private, but now I would be on trial in front of hundreds of thousands of viewers. My character, my self, open to dissection.

'I don't really have anything to bring,' I said.

'Just bring yourself! Come on, Maddy, it's Christmas! Good cheer! Forgiveness!' Seeing my face, she sighed. 'Look, we'll all be leaving soon and . . . this is our last chance to make up. After everything, we all did this together. We should be together at the end. Just come and have a good time with us, please?'

I relented. 'All right. Give me a second to get my boots on.'

I stuffed my feet into my darned socks and then into

my wellies. My camera had been spending all its time propped up on a crossbar, filming me, giving me someone to talk to. I strapped it on. On impulse I grabbed the remaining half of a packet of chocolate fudge cake mix – the 'add hot water and wait' kind. It was better than nothing. Together we shuffled off through the thick snow and its icy crust.

'How are you doing?' I asked, as we made our way slowly up hill.

'You mean—' She gestured at her stomach. 'Not sure. I was talking to Gill and she said her period had been late too – so maybe it's just because, you know, the lack of food right now.'

'How are you guys doing on that front?' I asked.

Zoe sniffed but didn't seem in a hurry to answer. I guessed it was getting pretty bad. I was down to my last bits here and there, making up dehydrated meals in quarter batches.

'We're all right. Some of the stuff went manky – not that Maxine's taking responsibility for that. Nothing could possibly be her fault.'

I was starting to think Zoe had only invited me so she had someone to complain to about Maxine. It seemed things hadn't been all togetherness and community since my eviction. Clearly Maxine was still making things difficult. I wondered if she was the new target of everyone's frustrations.

'Everyone else is getting through the rabbits before we leave so that means plenty of seaweed for me,' Zoe said with a grimace. 'It's getting kind of disgusting up at the clearing – I'm glad we're getting away soon. Some of the guys honestly suck at picking up after themselves. We made a bit of an effort today though.' We tramped along in silence for a while, then Zoe clicked her tongue.

'I wanted to say, before we get there . . . I'm sorry, for what I asked you to do, and for, you know, saying that stuff about you, behind your back? That was really shitty of me and I don't want you going home thinking that I was being fake or mean . . . I'm sorry.'

'Thanks, Zoe,' I said, trying to be gracious while at the same time wondering where this was coming from, if it was for my benefit or that of the camera. 'I'm sorry too, if I was harsh that day . . . It's just, it sort of hit me, reminded me of something else. I might have overreacted.'

Zoe frowned. 'Reminded you of what?'

'Mum used to tell me this story . . . she probably only made it up to scare me. Keep me in line. It was about this girl at the big school. Mum said she got pregnant and she didn't want her parents to know, so she bought some dodgy pill or . . . concoction online and it didn't go well for her. She died. It was Mum's favourite cautionary tale even after I got pulled out of school. It's what made me decide on my final dissertation – abortifacient plants. I found it sort of grimly fascinating, what plants can do.'

Zoe nodded and I realised her mind was somewhere else, perhaps thinking about getting back to the mainland, to a doctor. I patted her awkwardly on the shoulder.

'You'll be all right, don't worry.'

'Thanks, Maddy.'

We reached the camp and it looked so different to the last time I'd seen it, I was momentarily stunned. The snow had blanketed over the churned-up dirt and someone had made a crude wreath of pine branches and hung it over the hut's doorway. A snowman leant drunkenly in the middle of the clearing, wearing a bucket as a hat. Smoke rose through the hole in the roof and the smell of roasting meat was evident. From inside the hut came the sounds of raucous singing and laughter.

'Come on, let's get in the warm,' Zoe said.

She pushed in through the plastic curtain and shrugged off her snow-covered coat. I followed and awkwardly did the same, conscious that I'd been sleeping in the clothes underneath for more than a couple of days.

'Look who I found!' Zoe announced, replacing her woolly hat with a crown of pine fronds. Eyes found me and I felt myself blush. Everyone else was wearing similar pine or ivy crowns and Gill had red lipstick on. Zoe's body glitter had clearly done the rounds. Everyone had sparkling cheeks and Duncan had combed some into his beard. A pine branch had been stabbed into a bucket of dirt to approximate a Christmas tree. Someone had clearly tried to decorate it with pinecones, foil-wrapped shells and plaited string.

'Merry Christmas,' I said.

'Merry Christmas,' most of them echoed unenthusiastically. Only Shaun smiled. I wasn't sure if he was happy to see me alive and well, or just supporting Zoe's idea to bring me in from the cold on Christmas. I felt my tentative good cheer waver. Clearly this was a gesture not approved by the whole community. I was here on sufferance. Trapped by Zoe's festive efforts, I decided to stay for a short while, then make my excuses and get back to my tipi.

I took a seat by the fire, noticing with a start that there were bones amongst the embers. Tiny rabbit bones littered the fire hole and flames licked out from the eyes of several charred skulls. There were rabbits cooking over the fire as well, two of them on a rudimentary spit. Juices hissed in the flames, dripping onto those bones already picked clean.

The others were gathered around, watching the rabbits as Shaun turned them over the fire. There were cups around and I saw Andrew passing a sticky bottle of buckthorn wine across to Frank, whose cheeks were red already. I noticed that on what had once been the bookshelf there were now several bottles of varying coloured liquid, ranging from dark purple to light brown. More experiments in brewing most likely.

I dug the crumpled foil packet out of my pocket. 'I brought cake . . . sort of.'

Andrew took it from me with a frown. 'I didn't give that to you.'

'She took it. I told you she'd had stuff out of the box,' Duncan said.

I flushed. 'Well, if I hadn't it would've been eaten long before now so . . . call it a Christmas miracle.'

Shaun took the packet from Andrew. 'Thanks, Maddy,' he said, giving Andrew a 'drop it now' look.

'Who's up for charades?' Zoe asked brightly. Too brightly.

We played charades. Then the playing cards came out and we played sevens and poker. Bets were made with ring pulls, buttons and bottle caps. Shaun served the two roasted rabbits, putting two more on the spit from a bucket. Blood dripped on the dried-out pine boughs that lined the floor. A bottle was passed around.

I had a sip of the wine but declined further offers. The wine smelled ripe as a compost heap and left a thick, furry residue on my tongue. The others were making quick work of it though. Bottle after bottle came down from the shelf to be sloshed into tin cups. Some of it was murky and smelled weirdly familiar, yet unlike wine. Zoe and Gill grew giggly, and Duncan got louder and louder the more he drank. We were eating the rabbit with our fingers from tin plates. More bones rattled into the fire, popping and crackling in the heat. All around the fire were dark, drunk eyes and chins slick with meat juices. I started to feel uneasy, but I wasn't sure why.

'Let's play a drinking game,' Shaun declared, once the meat was done with.

'I think I'm going to go,' I whispered to Zoe. 'It's getting a bit late.'

'You can stay the night,' Zoe said. Her cheeks were

pink with the warmth from the fire and her leafy crown was tilted to one side. 'Don't go, Maddy, we're having fun.'

'What's your problem?' Andrew said, voice suddenly sharp.

'Nothing, I'm just going before it gets too dark.'

'She can stay the night though, right?' Zoe said.

The fire crackled and spat in the silence that followed. No one answered Zoe and no one looked at me. Clearly I wasn't welcome to share the hut I'd helped build for even one night.

'And on that note, I'll call it a night,' I said, standing up. I picked up the nearest bottle to me and held it up. 'Thanks for a year of quality company, guys.'

I turned and snagged my coat, ducking out into the cold before I'd even put it on. I heard Zoe call my name but no one came after me.

I picked my way through the trees, cursing myself for not bringing a torch or even my bag. Cursing myself for being so stupid. The cold of the night was shocking, even through my coat. What little moonlight there was glanced off of the snow, leading me onwards.

Several times my booted foot crashed through the ice crust on a hole and sent me stumbling. Under the snow the ruts and gullies of the path were invisible. I started to worry about hurting my ankle, possibly breaking a leg. I went slower, knowing that no one was going to come looking. If I fell, hurt, I wouldn't be found until they came down to wait for the boat.

I nearly dropped the bottle from the hut a few times

but never considered leaving it. It was Christmas after all; there wasn't much else to do but drink. When the tipi was in sight I twisted off the cap and took a deep swig. As soon as the liquid touched my tongue I spat it out onto the snow, coughing and spluttering. It wasn't wine at all; it was water. Water and fly agaric. Not enough to get them sick. Enough to get high. God only knew how much of the stuff they'd dried and squirrelled away for when the wine ran out.

I washed my mouth with a handful of snow and went to bed. No matter how anxious I was about my return to the mainland, it would at least get me away from the others.

Chapter 20

The day of our departure dawned bright and clear as glass. The sky was a pure, open blue and any scrap of heat was sucked up into it as soon as it was exhaled. The snow was blinding and newly fallen. Every breath was like drowning in a frozen sea. I catalogued each sensation, knowing I would probably never experience this again.

I'd cried on the last night. Alone and thinking of the long journey back to normality, I'd let the tears fall and put my hands on the dirt floor of my tipi, as if to tell the island I would miss it. The previous day I'd found a holed stone on the beach, tumbled smooth as an egg. I wore it now around my neck, on a strand of grey wool pulled from my jumper. A keepsake from Buidseach. A reminder of who I'd been.

We were to be collected around midday at the point at which I and the rest of the women had been deposited. It was strange, remembering how we'd arrived as boys and girls. There were of course still two groups; only I was the entirety of mine.

With no clock I busied myself cleaning up my camp and packing my things, keeping an eye on the sun as it rose higher in the sky. I had considered dismantling my tipi but that hadn't felt right. Instead, I swept out the fire hole and laid a new pile of logs and tinder. I'd read once about Alaskan trappers who left their little shelters ready for anyone who might come along, in need of warmth or food. Although it was unlikely that someone would stumble on my tipi, it felt right to leave it ready.

I took my bags to the beach we'd been set down on, all those months ago. There I lit a small fire to keep me warm and settled myself on my rolled-up bedding, waiting for the boat to come. I was once more wearing my camera. I felt by turns as if I was waiting for rescue, or a prison ship. There was little I could do to change things though. It was time to go.

The others arrived shortly after I'd made my little camp on the beach. I'd not seen or spoken to any of them since Christmas, over a week ago. Even then it had been dark enough that I'd not had a good look at them. In the clear light of day, they were a ragged bunch. I imagined I looked much the same. The men were sporting beards of varying thickness, and had oily, unwashed hair grown overly long, held back in buns or shoved into a hat. All of us had been wearing and re-wearing the same three or four sets of clothing for eleven months, washing them by hand. There were holes and frayed, faded seams all around. We were all thinner, hands calloused with burst blisters and burns, but all of them seemed happier than I'd seen them since we first arrived. Glad to be going home.

We sat around the fire. They ignored me entirely, aside from Zoe, who offered me a quick smile. Maxine sat apart from the others. Zoe and Shaun also seemed to be on the outs; he sat with Andrew and she took a spot a short distance away by Gill. Perhaps it was the thought that they'd soon be at opposite ends of the country. I doubted she'd told him about her suspected pregnancy.

In any event it didn't matter who sat where, no one was really talking. All eyes were trained on the horizon, waiting for the boat. I could almost hear their thoughts of food, heating, electricity and soft beds. I longed for those things too. I just didn't long for the world that accompanied them, for who I was in that world. Not everything I missed would be there when I arrived.

I think after the first hour we all knew something was wrong. Zoe was the one to speak up, asking aloud if we had the wrong day. Maxine got out a little diary and checked for them. It said the same as mine. Unless we'd both independently miscounted, this was the agreed date, our final day on the island. So where was the boat?

We carried on waiting. But there was an edge, an expectant, anxious twist that hadn't been there before. The small fire I'd made started to die out, but I didn't go to fetch more wood. To leave, to re-stoke the fire, would be to admit that we would need that fire. That we would be on that beach another hour, or two. Despite my reluctance to leave I didn't want to think about what that might mean.

Andrew kept checking his watch, our only marker of time. Today was the day according to its tiny digital display. No one asked him how long it had been. Too long was the answer and knowing the actual weight of the time, in minutes and hours, was something I didn't think any of us were ready for.

Finally, the sun, that burning white hole in the blue sky, started to descend. The shadows grew longer, our silhouettes moving up the beach towards the trees. The cold had stolen in under my clothes ages ago. I felt like a statue.

It was Zoe who finally broke our silent vigil with a question that was barely a whisper.

'What should we do?'

No one answered her. Not right away. We just sat there, looking out on the calm, empty sea. Then Duncan stood up.

'Well, I'm going up to that cabin to ask those guys what the fuck is going on.'

I'd not thought about the two camera guys. Surely they were being picked up with us. They'd come on the same boat I had. Where were they? I was about to say as much when Andrew beat me to it.

'Aren't they leaving with us?'

Duncan paused, seemingly at a loss for words.

I took the chance to speak. 'They might be staying

to break down the equipment or something. But we should find out – there might have been a delay with sending the boat over for us. The weather's unpredictable this time of year.'

No one mentioned that it was as clear and crisp a day as we'd yet seen. No one had to. I knew as well as they did that no boat would be having trouble today. Still, what choice did we have but to believe it?

'Get back to camp and get a fire going,' Duncan instructed Gill. 'If we're stuck here for tonight, we'll need to eat. I'll come back when I know what's going on.'

I picked up my day pack and slung it over my shoulder. 'I'm coming too.'

Duncan didn't say anything, just turned and started for the treeline. I followed, the snow crumbling under my boots. At any other time I'd have put his silence down to pig-headedness or his dislike of me. But now it felt more like fear, a fear I felt as well.

We hiked up the hill, picking our way over the steep gullies and around fallen trees. The woods were quiet aside from the crunching of our boots. Our breath made thick white clouds in the gloom. By the time we reached the top of the hill that looked down over the portacabin, it was almost completely dark. I'd got slightly ahead of Duncan on the long walk, and stopped on the rise to let him catch up. I had the sense that I didn't want to face this alone. Together we looked down at the snow-topped cabin.

There were no lights on at all.

I was glad Duncan didn't offer up some excuse, like that they must be asleep already. Something was very wrong. To deny that now would somehow make me feel worse. Without a word we started the descent down to the meadow and on towards the cabin.

I reached the portacabin first and shone my torch around. Everything was quiet and undisturbed. There were no footprints in the snow. No divots or holes where footprints had been filled in with fresh snowfall either. The generator beside the cabin was silent. I turned the beam of the torch to the door and my breath caught in my throat.

When I'd last seen the cabin it had been summer. I'd looked down on the little structure in its tangle of overgrown wilderness and noticed that the door was open to let the breeze in. Now, in sub-zero weather and with small flurries of snow starting to fall once more, the door was still open. I heard Duncan's footsteps come to a halt behind me.

I pushed open the door.

For the first time I was grateful for the cold. I imagined that without it, the smell would have been unbearable.

Inside the portacabin all was dark. The light from my torch flashed back at me from screens and steel fixtures. Against the back wall were bunkbeds, the kind I'd seen in prison films, plain and utilitarian. On the left wall was a door, I presumed to a bathroom. Beside the door was a kitchenette. The right-hand wall was given over to desks and a bank of monitors. All were dark, not a single light blinked. Several things had fallen over: a desk lamp, some books, a mug.

The floor was obscured by drifting snow nearest the door. Then with dried leaves that had blown in. Furthest from the door, around the bunkbeds where a shape distended the blankets, there was a large, brownish pool.

Against every natural impulse, I went closer. My feet crunched in the darkness. I followed the torchlight down and saw a layer of dead flies between the leaves.

The bedding was soaked and frozen with the same brownish effluent that covered the floor, but it did not obscure the face of the man in the bottom bunk. One of the two whose names I'd learnt and forgotten months ago. I could no longer tell which as his face was so warped; empty eye sockets gaped at the ceiling, his mouth hanging open too wide, holes where insects had burrowed into his cheeks. I gagged and turned quickly from the liquefying body, reaching the door before I vomited bile onto the pure snow. I retched and heaved until nothing else would come, then picked up a handful of clean snow to press to my sweating face.

Duncan had come out of the cabin behind me. I saw the saliva in his beard and knew he'd been sick as well, inside.

'How long . . .' He didn't finish the question, but I shook my head.

'I don't know. Months, maybe . . . I think –' I smothered a dry heave '– I think I smelled it . . . him. Before, when I was up there.' I waved a hand towards the hill. 'This door's been open since summer.'

'Christ,' Duncan muttered, glancing at the cabin. 'What, though, I mean . . . how?'

Again I shook my head. 'I don't know. I didn't look.'

Silence stretched out between us as I sluiced my mouth with snow.

'Where's the other one?' Duncan finally murmured.

My stomach churned. 'Bathroom?'

Without a word Duncan strode back into the cabin. I heard the door crash on the inner wall as he threw it open. Then Duncan swore.

As much as I didn't want to, I followed him in. Duncan was in the bathroom doorway, frozen. Peering around him I saw a shape on the floor. A body. Clearly the insects had managed to get at more of this poor bastard. There was barely any flesh to him. He was lying beside the toilet, one claw-like hand reaching up, clinging to the bowl.

Without speaking we left the cabin and stood in the snow.

'What the fuck happened here?' Duncan said. 'They're . . . they can't just be fucking dead.'

Him saying that made it real. There were two dead bodies in the cabin behind us. Bodies of men we had met. We were on an island, with two dead men. The boat had not come for us.

'The phone,' Duncan said suddenly. 'The radio or whatever. Where is it?'

He turned back to the cabin and I went with him,

reluctantly. We shone our torches along the array of screens and computers. At the end nearest the door was a dock with a blocky handset in it. A satellite phone of some kind. Duncan snatched it up and pressed buttons, then swore.

'Dead,' he said.

I felt a cold weight settle in my stomach. 'Generator's not making any noise. Must be out of fuel or something.'

'There has to be some spare,' Duncan said, already shining the light around to look for it.

'I'll check outside.'

We checked, both inside and out. There was no spare fuel, only the tanks hooked up to the generator, whose needles hovered at empty. Obviously when the two men in the cabin had died the generator had wound down, drained by things left on inside. But surely the production team had planned for that fuel to be used. Why had no replacement fuel been delivered?

A loud bang made me jump and I snapped out of my thoughts to find Duncan glaring at a newly made dent in the cabin wall. He cradled his fist in his other hand.

'What the fuck?' he breathed, then louder, 'What the FUCK?' punctuated with another punch and another dent in the wall. He rounded on me. 'What is going on?'

'I don't know,' I said, pointlessly, because how could I know? 'But we should get back to the others and tell them.'

Duncan's eyes widened and I could see him processing what I'd just said. The others had no idea of the horror show we'd discovered up here. They were all back at camp, waiting for news. He cast a helpless look at the cabin door.

'There's nothing we can do for them,' I said, as gently as possible. 'We should tell the others.'

He nodded and turned away without a word. I followed and we made our way slowly back towards the main camp, weighed down with bad news and terrible knowledge. What wore at me more, though, was what we didn't know. Where was our boat? What were the people who'd sent us here doing? How had two healthy young men died so suddenly?

We arrived to a subdued camp. Everyone was inside, bags heaped by the entrance. The place looked bare and stark with no bedrolls or clothes lying around. It looked more like an animal den than a home for eight people. The only nod to domesticity was a pot on the fire, in which a thin gruel of seaweed and rice bubbled. Gill was staring into it as if mesmerised by the bubbling mess.

'We've uh . . . we've got something to tell you,' Duncan said, rubbing his bruised knuckles with his other hand. 'The cameramen, they're um . . . they're dead. For a while. They've . . . been dead a while.'

A wave of shock went through the huddled group.

'What about the phone?' Andrew said. 'The boat?'

'The phone's dead,' I said. 'Generator's out of fuel. Nothing up there works.' I took a breath, weighing up what I was about to say and how it would affect them. 'There wasn't any spare fuel up there, which means they didn't have enough to last this long, because something must have been using power even if they weren't . . . They would have run out long before now, using power . . . and no one's brought more fuel.'

There was silence. Zoe started to cry.

'I think,' I said carefully, 'that both of them had to have died around the same time. They didn't try to get to us for help or, apparently, summon any help from the mainland.'

I didn't add that they could have called for help – and received none. It was an option I didn't want to present right now, not with everyone still in shock.

'How did they . . .' Andrew said, then broke off.

'I don't know. We didn't really . . . examine them. But, from the way one was in bed, the other by the toilet . . . maybe they were ill? Or something made them sick.'

'Poison.'

I looked round and found Gill staring at me, her face an unreadable mix of emotions.

'What?'

'They could have been poisoned,' Gill said.

A chill crept up my spine. 'They might have been affected by carbon monoxide from the generator but . . . I don't think that's likely, given it was outside.'

Gill continued to stare. I turned my attention to the others, telling myself she was just in shock and not thinking clearly. 'We don't know what happened to

213

them, or why the boat didn't come today. But, perhaps there was a good reason for the boat to be delayed and it may well be here tomorrow. In the meantime we need to stay calm.'

Only Zoe's sobs broke the silence that followed.

Chapter 21

'I think it was the thing that hit us the hardest, their deaths. Not the boat not being there. At the start we had so many theories and ideas about why it was late. So many hopes, that it would just turn up. But the bodies . . . We couldn't explain that,' I say, twisting my hands together, callouses grating over each other, rough as rock.

'Being confronted with their deaths must have brought home how serious your situation was,' Rosie, the interviewer, says.

'Strangely, it didn't,' I reply, ignoring her as she snaps her mouth closed, annoyed at my correction. 'After so long there, living as we were . . . it was almost like they were a separate species, certainly a separate community. Their deaths were worrying, but only insofar as they related to us. To our situation. I don't think we spared much thought for them as people, terrible as that is to say. It was a luxury we didn't have room for, mourning people we didn't know. No . . . I *think the worst part of it all, for us, was not having that influence anymore – those representatives of the outside world.' I force myself to put my hands in my lap, to stop fidgeting. 'Without them there we didn't have anyone to go to, no arbiter holding us accountable . . . It was just us, or rather, just them . . . and me.'*

Chapter 22

The next morning we rose and breakfasted on the meagre rations available. I'd spent the night on the hut floor. No one had said anything about me going back to my own shelter. I think we all had bigger concerns and I wasn't going to volunteer to spend the night alone.

I guessed that, much as I had done, they'd used up most of their food in a final farewell meal. The stores of shop-bought goods were basically gone, aside from a few tablespoons of rice. Similarly, from what I could see of the food box, preserved food was getting low as well. They must have had significant spoilage or had been eating a lot more than when I'd been in the community. I told myself not to worry. The boat would come that day.

I wished I was better at lying to myself.

The truth of it was that, from the moment we all trudged down to the beach, I knew no boat would come. Perhaps some of the others did too as, although we all brought our bags, the cooking pots and things were left behind. None of us wore cameras; mine was completely out of charge anyway. My charger, like the rest of my stuff, was still piled where I'd left it on the beach.

Cold dread sat like clay in my stomach as we gathered sticks to make a large fire. We sat around it like crows, hunched against the cold, scanning the flat horizon. Freezing rain had started overnight and now continued to fall, pitting and melting the snow, turning it to ice.

As morning turned to afternoon we all grew restless. Duncan paced up and down the gravelly beach and I noticed Shaun and Frank passing a bottle of murky water back and forth – likely mushroom brew.

'I think,' I said, the silence shattering like so much glass, 'that maybe we should leave a lookout and then . . . get on with finding some supplies.'

Everyone turned to look at Duncan. He'd been thrusting himself into the leadership role since we arrived, but it was still weird to see how they all looked to him for answers. Perhaps the last democratic vote had been the one that turned me out of the community.

Duncan gave a sharp nod. 'You're the one that lives down here so it's a good idea if you keep a lookout.'

I wasn't too shocked by the implication that I was still not welcome in camp. The immediate shock was over. Now we were back to normal, whatever that meant.

'I need to be able to forage and cut firewood too,' I pointed out. 'Unless we're going to pool our resources.'

218

'You can do the mornings. Then one of us will come down and relieve you,' Duncan said, already turning away and picking up his bags.

I didn't bother pointing out that it was currently afternoon and therefore not my 'shift'. It didn't seem worth it and I could forage along the shoreline well enough. What worried me more was his deflection over the supplies. Even now, in this grave situation, I was on my own.

'Should we maybe think about building, like . . . a boat?' Shaun suggested, turning red when Andrew barely suppressed a bitter laugh.

'With what? Given the tools we have, the best we could hope for is a raft. And a raft is not getting us back to the mainland. No rudder to steer. We can't even make proper oars to row with, not with just axes. It's miles and we'd be at the mercy of the current.'

'I was just saying,' Shaun muttered.

'Well, if all you've got is idiot ideas, keep them to yourself. There's a good boy,' Andrew snapped. Duncan laughed. They formed a miserable little line and headed back to the clearing without a backward glance at me.

I went and stashed my things in the tipi. It was strange but somehow the inside of it felt smaller, more ramshackle. I suppose it was the difference between it being a temporary camping shelter and a more permanent dwelling. It was a sobering thought and I hoped against hope that it would not be permanent – only a short extension of my time on the island.

Only a few days before I'd been depressed at the idea

of leaving Buidseach behind, now I was angry at my own stupid whimsy. It was true, I had enjoyed being on the island, at first. Since being ousted from the community, life had been harder but I'd been able to find some comfort in my tipi, knowing that my time there would soon be over. In fact if I had a boatload of supplies at my disposal, the prospect of being stuck on the island would be quite different; I could see myself being able to build a life. But I didn't have a boatload of things to help me. I barely had a bagful. My food was down to a few handfuls of dried mushrooms and nuts. The firewood enough for one or two campfires. For the first time it occurred to me that we might starve before help came. Panic snatched at me, making my heart beat rabbit-fast. I squeezed my eyes shut and forced the sharp whirl of emotions down. Panic wouldn't feed me or keep me warm.

With my bucket in hand, I went down to the shoreline and picked it over. As I turned rocks and lifted clumps of winter-leathered seaweed, I occasionally looked out to sea. There was no boat, no sign of one at all. Just water, stretching on and on. I couldn't see even a shadow of the opposite coastline. Somewhere out there, millions of people were going about their lives; working, shopping, watching TV. Millions of people completely oblivious that on this little island, we sat hungry and afraid.

Before dark I'd found a gratifying number of mussels and a reasonably sized crab. At least we had seafood going for us. I took my bucket up the beach and found a sharp-sided boulder to crack the crab against, killing it. In my hut I boiled water in the billycan and dropped my finds into it. The shellfish weren't enough to replace the calories I'd lost to exercise and cold, but they filled me up a bit and pushed back the edge of panic even further. For today at least, I was fed and warm.

It was only as night closed in that I realised I'd still not charged my camera. None of us had. The little solar chargers we had been given worked with one of two batteries so we charged one by day while using another. I'd not thought to charge mine the previous day – thinking it was the last day on the island. I'd also not done it today when I got back to the beach. I thought back and couldn't remember any of the others putting their batteries out to charge before we left camp. None of us had even been wearing our cameras.

The crab in my stomach suddenly felt alive again, crawling and snapping at my insides. Was that why Duncan had been so quick to bar me from their supplies and turn me out back to my tipi? After all, it had only been my threat of our constant recordings that had made him give me rations the last time I was pushed out. Perhaps he was banking on no one seeing the footage, ever.

That thought scared me more than the food shortage or the missing boat. It was the first time I'd felt truly separate from the world on the other side of the sea. The first time I'd felt like its rules and laws wouldn't be there to protect me. I thought of the times I'd returned to my tipi to find it searched, looted. It was clear that was going to happen again, maybe worse now.

I made a quick decision. My one recourse was to go back to hiding my things and to wear my camera continuously. If I wanted to survive, I had to keep my rations safe from theft. It didn't take long to round up what I had; there wasn't much. The rain had started to worsen and I was grateful for it as it meant there was less snow to betray my tracks.

I found the cave and crawled inside. Everything was much as it had been before, only colder and slightly damper in the outermost section. The inner chamber was as dry as ever and I carefully replaced my few things on the outcrops in the stone. Seeing how little I had, all lined up like that, only worsened my dread. Still, at least my supplies would be safe there. I hoped.

It was then that I thought of the portacabin. Duncan and I had only taken a cursory look around, but surely there had been food stored there, in the kitchenette? It was late now, fully dark, and the others had been out of my sight all day. Had they already taken the supplies? The thought made my heart jump with anxiety. I knew that if they had the food I could whistle for any rations. If they'd been reluctant before when we knew our time on the island was limited, they would surely not be any more generous now we had no idea when rescue would come.

I snatched up my empty bag and quickly left the cave. There was no time to waste. I had to get to the cabin and see if there was anything there I could salvage for myself.

The route was difficult in the dark, but I'd had some practice hiking over ice and snow in the pitch black. I found my way easily enough to the rise and descended it with trembling legs. All the while fear had me turning my head, looking for shadows in the trees. What if the others had already been and gone? Worse, what if they were still there?

I steeled myself before entering the portacabin. I had my torch with me but only turned it on once the door was closed. I kept the beam low, under the windows. Everything seemed to be as I had left it. Still, I went quickly to the cupboards and opened them, one after another.

All were empty.

I could have cried in my disappointment and bitter anger. I shone my torch on the floor and saw the evidence of many footprints. They had been there. They had taken everything. A tiny part of me wanted to believe that tomorrow someone would come down with a share of the supplies. But I knew that part of me belonged to the normal world, not the situation I was currently in. What was fair and good did not apply here, not right now.

Sure that there was something they had to have missed I went into the bathroom to search, as much as I didn't want to go anywhere near the body that lay there. I moved around it carefully, opening cabinets, all of which were empty. I guessed that they had once contained soap, bleach, other cleaning supplies and maybe some first-aid things too. The only thing left was a pair of yellow rubber gloves beneath the sink, balled up behind a pipe.

I opened each cupboard in the kitchenette and felt into every corner hoping to find even a stray stock cube. They were completely cleaned out. There were lockers under the computer consoles and when I opened these they did still have supplies inside. Mostly wires, cables, plastic ties and parts. I went through everything and ended up emptying out some of the plastic storage boxes to take with me, along with some cable ties. There was one useful thing in there, a bottle of seventy-percent isopropyl alcohol. Presumably it had some use in cleaning electrical equipment, but now it was mine.

I sat back on my heels and pressed my hands against my eyes. This was it? How could I survive without extra food and supplies? In desperation I looked around and found myself staring at the bunkbeds. I'd forced myself not to look at them the entire time I'd been in the cabin, desperate not to spend another moment looking at the body there, but now I saw something aside from the horror. Under the bottom bunk, just visible under the fall of the filth-encrusted blanket, was the edge of a plastic crate.

For a few moments I was frozen. There was something under that bed, I was sure. Something that the others had not found because who in their right mind would go under a bed with a decomposing body in it? No one. No one that is, unless they were truly desperate.

I fetched the rubber gloves from the bathroom and removed my coat, tucking the sleeves of my shirt into the gloves. With my scarf wrapped around my mouth and nose, I edged towards the beds.

The smell, though muted by the cold, was still present. Up close, it hung thickly in the air. The bedding on the bunk was crusted and frozen, stiff when I tried to push it aside. In the end I lifted it up, folding it over the body. Underneath, there were new horrors. Things had clearly dripped and pooled during the summer and now stalactites of liquefied fat and flesh hung from the slats of the bed. The floor was greasy under my gloved hands, thick with rancid gunge. My eyes stung with tears of revulsion. Still, I edged the sticky plastic crate out and pried off the lid.

The box was the same kind of clear plastic as the cache boxes. A cheap, large-capacity storage crate. Inside, arranged neatly and as pristine as the day they were packed, sat rows of tins, packets and boxes. Food. Medicine. Soap and luxuries. I started to cry, the tears soaking my scarf. With trembling hands I pulled off the gloves, turning them inside out and throwing them under the bed.

I didn't even look at the labels, just packed everything into my bag as quickly as possible. I found myself glancing over my shoulder at the door as I did so. Once I was done I used my foot to push the box back under the bed out of sight.

Standing there, near the shrunken bodies of the two men I barely knew, I felt a wave of gratitude. If they hadn't shoved that box under the bed, I would have nothing. As unintentional as it might have been, they had saved me.

'Thank you,' I whispered, feeling instantly foolish.

I turned and went out into the night.

It wasn't easy getting the bulging bag of supplies back to the cave. I didn't mind one bit. The entrance into the second chamber was so narrow I had to unpack item by item and push them through. In the darkness I still didn't get a good look at what there was but could feel the shapes of bags of pasta and rice, the slosh of tinned beans, solid little boxes of tablets. Inside I filled the plastic bins and pushed them into a recess in the wall. Hopefully, no one would look there, even if they found this cave within a cave.

As I left the outer cave, I decided I would need to make something to camouflage the entrance. I would come back with a simple wattle and daub panel to wedge a little way into the opening. With plenty of ferns and leaves it could look as if the cave entrance was nothing more than an outcrop of rock.

I would also keep charging and wearing my own camera, so there would be a record of the others' actions, even if just on the internal memory card. Perhaps that would deter them from doing too much to threaten me.

I picked my way back through the woods to my tipi and tried to settle myself for the night. It was hard; although I was exhausted I was also tense with fear and worry over our future, my future. Already the divide between myself and the others had widened. They had taken all they could and didn't appear to have thought of me. I felt ill at ease that after only two days, shocking and frightening as those days had been, they were already closing ranks.

I could only hope that the boat would come, sooner rather than later.

*

Rescue did not come on the third day of waiting, or the fourth, or the fifth. As the first week of our abandonment came to an end, I started to feel that something was deeply wrong.

There was nothing else to think about. My days filled up with creating and discarding theories as to why we were still waiting for rescue. In the mornings I kept watch on the icy beach, gathering what I could from the shoreline and sitting by a campfire, charging my power bank. I turned over the idea that the production company was pulling some kind of stunt. Or perhaps somehow we'd lost track of the date, Andrew's watch was losing time, and we were to be collected in a few days' time. Even that we'd misunderstood how long we were to be on the island in the first place. Maybe everything was running as it was expected to, and we'd just collectively convinced ourselves of incorrect facts.

Brooding on the reasons behind our abandonment kept me awake at night, but it was not the only thing to do so. I found, as the first week came to an end, that I was living a kind of double life.

By day I kept watch, changing places with Maxine at noon. She didn't attempt to speak to me and when I asked how she was or how things were going, she gave one-word answers. In the afternoons I kept busy around the tipi, splitting firewood, foraging and beach-combing. I noticed that Maxine watched me as much as she watched the sea; she wasn't wearing her camera. I didn't want to fall into paranoia, but I had a feeling she was reporting back. For what purpose I had no idea, other than that it gave them something else to focus on – their dislike of me.

At night I was at my most active. Once I was sure that the darkness was total and the others were likely in camp, I hurried to my cave. I'd spent some time securing the place and now had a camouflage panel which went across the entrance, making it look like a small hole choked with foliage. Mostly I went there to hang seaweed from the lines I'd strung, where it could air-dry and be preserved. I also stashed some of my beachcombing finds there: another bucket, ripped netting, a small fishing buoy. Every small thing I could squirrel away felt like so much ballast against an uncertain future.

There was a whisper at the back of my mind, one that grew louder each day, that said I was right to be afraid. Not just that rescue would never come, but that I was trapped with seven people who hated me. Seven increasingly desperate people and limited resources. I was already hiding my supplies from them, but that part of me knew that wasn't enough. The cave had stopped feeling like a storehouse and more like a bunker. A panic room. I was sleeping in my tipi but that was just a front, hiding this place from the others. I told myself that there was no reason to be afraid for myself. I put that anxiety at the back of my mind and worried about bigger things, like why we were still on the island.

After the first week had passed, I expected some kind of meeting. We needed to talk about what was happening and what we were going to do. Even as split communities we were all in the same shit situation. But no such summons came from Maxine as we passed on the beach or any of the others. I waited until night on the seventh day, when the watch was abandoned and everyone would be at camp. Then I made my way up there, determined to come to some agreement.

I found the clearing deserted and smoke rising thickly from the hut. No surprise that they were all hunkered down for the evening. I stopped outside and knocked on the door post. There was muttering inside, then Shaun stuck his head out.

'Maddy, what's up?'

'I came up to talk about what we should do now – it's been a week.'

'Right . . . Uh . . . we were gonna come and see you tomorrow.'

'Oh . . . Can we talk now instead?'

'It's not really the best time right now,' Shaun said,

looking anywhere but in my eyes. 'Everyone's kind of tired and . . . You know how it is.'

'Right, so you want me to go?'

'Sorry,' he said, lamely.

I caught a whiff then, from inside the hut. The smell of cooking meat, but also of spices and tomatoes. I sighed.

'I don't care that you guys are eating the food from the portacabin, OK? So if that's the reason you won't let me in—'

'No, it's not that,' Shaun said quickly, glancing at the camera on my chest. 'It's just that . . . uh . . .' he chewed his lip and lowered his voice. 'Duncan thinks that, I mean, we all think that it would be best if you didn't come around here. Because . . . you know . . . you stole that cake thing before and we don't want any of our food going . . . missing.'

'Are you kidding me? He wasn't that concerned about theft when you were all having secret dinners together, or helping yourselves to what I foraged!' I took a step back and raised my voice further. 'Just admit it, Duncan, you've been stealing with both hands and this is all just bullshit to justify starving me out.'

'Shut the door, Shaun, it's getting cold,' came Andrew's voice.

'Tell the bitch to piss off,' Duncan jeered.

Shaun looked uncomfortable. 'We'll see you tomorrow, yeah?'

Catching his eye for the first time I noticed a glazed look. He was high on something; most likely the others were also drinking mushroom tea. There was no point getting into it now.

'I'll be waiting,' I said, and turned to go, ignoring the catcalls from inside the hut as I retreated from the clearing. I picked my way down to the tipi and got myself warmed through. I was angry and humiliated, but I would handle it tomorrow.

Chapter 23

'Do you think it was mostly his fault? Duncan, I mean,' Rosie asks, as I pause to collect myself.

I frown, not appreciating the interruption. I have a story to tell and an order in which to tell it. This woman knows nothing of what I've gone through, and from her question I see she's not been paying attention.

'Duncan was only one person. He wasn't a good person, at least, not to me, or even the others really. But he couldn't have done what he did alone. If anyone else had said no, had refused to participate, things would have been different. I think he was blinkered. He believed in what he was saying about me, what he was doing to me. But the others, Gill, Maxine, Zoe . . . they knew it was wrong, that they could easily become targets, and so they joined in.'

'You think they made a conscious choice to appease Duncan, rather than be made outsiders as well?'

I shrug. 'I can't speak for them, only what I think, but yes . . . to a certain extent they were afraid, and *they made a calculation for survival. We all did, in our own way.'*

'If things had been different; if, say, there had been more food, better weather, if you'd taken a more passive role, do you think things would have gone the same way?'

I've thought about this, obviously. It took up a great deal of my time as I sat in a police cell, going over and over what had happened. What if I had done things differently? What if the show had ended when it was meant to? What if we'd all gone home to our lives as normal people and not what we became?

'I think . . . there were things we all could have done differently. But, given who was with us and what they had already done . . . I think violence was inevitable.'

Chapter 24

Next morning I built up a campfire in my watch spot on the beach and made myself some elderberry tea to keep myself warm. I'd already found a few things on the beach, including a length of PVC pipe, cracked but useable, and a large crab that I'd trapped in a bucket of water and was leaving for later.

They arrived shortly before midday. It was the first time I'd seen most of them in a week. The change was quite stark. On the day we'd expected to depart they'd seemed ragged and thin, but happy. Now there was an air of depression around all of them. There were dark circles under their eyes. Andrew's jumper had food down the front and all aside from Zoe were squinting in the bright light. I suspected they were hungover. I couldn't tell from Zoe's frame under the bulky hiking coat if she was showing signs of pregnancy. Perhaps even without it the lack of food would have made it hard to tell. Of all of us, I was the only one with my camera around my chest.

'Morning,' I said, gesturing to the fire. 'Feel free to have a seat.'

No one said anything and I felt a pulse of unease. Then Duncan cleared his throat and rubbed a hand over his ragged beard.

'This won't take long,' he said. 'We've been discussing the situation and it seems likely that we're going to be on our own for a while. For whatever reason. So we need to survive as best we can until we know more, or until the situation resolves itself. For all we know the production company's gone bust and they're waiting on the coastguard or the army to come and get us out of here.'

I'd considered this. The entire process of getting to the island; the lack of a real presenter, the small boat, only ever meeting Sasha or Adrian. It all screamed 'low budget'. If the company had discovered they didn't have the money to hire a boat, they'd have to get outside help to rescue us. But if so, why hadn't they realised before the day we were due to leave, and what was taking them so long? After all, not everyone was like me, they had people waiting for them. Surely someone would have tried to contact the camera guys to tell us what was happening? Did they not care that there had been no response? Why had no one sent a boat to check on us? I hoped that Duncan was right, but inside I remained sceptical. Something else was going on.

'Seems sensible,' was all I said, waiting for the other shoe to drop.

'To that end, we've come for the book,' Duncan said, as if I hadn't spoken.

'The book?'

'The foraging book. We want it back. We need it more than you and it belongs to the community – which you left.'

'I didn't exactly leave of my own volition,' I pointed out. 'But you're right, I don't really need it now that I've committed most of it to memory. I can trade it to you for something else.'

'Trade?'

'For some of the rabbits, to breed from,' I said. 'Then you have access to foraged food and I have access to meat. Everyone wins.'

Duncan shook his head. 'We don't have any.'

'You must do, you're not stupid enough to kill all of them.'

It was the wrong thing to say. Duncan's eyes immediately narrowed and he drew himself up taller. I'd pissed him off.

'We weren't exactly planning on needing them,' he said.

'All right, how about access to the rabbit trap instead?'

Duncan held up a hand to stop me. 'I'm not arguing over it. Just hand the book over.'

'I'm not arguing – I'm trying to negotiate. You want the book, fine, but I need things too and it's not like I'm going to use up the trap. You'll get it back.'

'You shouldn't have taken it in the first place. That

book belongs to the community and you're going to hand it over, now,' Duncan insisted.

I was stunned. 'That book belongs to me, because I bought it – and if you want it, you have to trade fairly for it.'

It happened very quickly. One moment I was standing there, trying to explain my side, the next I was lying on my back on the gravel beach. There were twin pains in my chest where Duncan's hands had shoved me. I gasped, mostly out of shock. Above me there was cold silence, punctuated only when Zoe said Duncan's name, quietly, like a question.

'Help me search the shack,' he said, then gestured at Gill, Zoe and Maxine. 'You keep her here.'

He didn't wait for an answer, but walked off in the direction of my tipi. Andrew, Shaun and Frank followed in his wake. I rolled onto my side and started to get up, only to be pushed back down by firm hands.

'Gill!' Zoe exclaimed.

'You heard Duncan. She stays here,' Gill said.

'But she doesn't have to stay on the ground. Jesus!' Zoe offered me her hand and helped me get up.

Gill circled around me to stand between me and the path to my tipi. I glanced at Maxine, but she was already moving to stand beside Gill. Together they formed a barrier and though I knew I could shove past them and run if I wanted to, what could I do against the four guys? Being shoved to the floor had shaken me. I'd expected Duncan to argue, to shout, but not to physically force me out of his way. What scared me most was that no one had said anything. No one had said 'no', or 'stop'. No one had said 'enough'.

I reached for the camera harness, reminding myself it was still there. Even if the others had discarded their cameras I still had mine on and working. If somehow this was all still being captured I had evidence, I had proof. If we ever got away from the island, I could tell my story.

'If' being the operative word.

I stood there in silence, worrying about what would happen when they didn't find what they were looking for. The book was still in the secret cave, where it had been since I'd noticed them stealing from me. In the distance I heard thumps and crashing, knew that my little home was being thoroughly ransacked. After a while I chanced a look at Gill and Maxine; both had relaxed slightly and were looking over towards my tipi, enjoying the show. Zoe was still near me, now seated on a rock.

'I need your help,' she said quietly, glancing over at the others.

I didn't need to ask with what. 'Are you sure now, that you are?'

She nodded. 'I can't be pregnant, not stuck here like this. Is there . . . is there something you can do?'

I could see she'd thought about it. The idea of trying to end her pregnancy with plant remedies just to prolong her time on the island had been unquestionably stupid. But there were risks involved in pregnancy at the best of times and we were definitely not in the best of times. I was worried about the toll pregnancy would take on her already malnourished body and it was clear she was as well.

'Will you help?' she whispered. 'Can you make like, a tea or a potion or something?'

'I can try,' I said.

'Try what?' Gill said.

I jumped a little, having not noticed her as she sidled closer. Zoe looked like a trapped rabbit, her eyes large with panic.

'Nothing,' she said, too quickly.

Gill narrowed her eyes. 'What were you talking to her about?'

'I just . . . wanted some advice,' Zoe said.

In the distance I could see the pack of men returning. Internally I begged Zoe to shut up. I didn't need any more fuel to be thrown on Duncan's fire, not now he knew the book was missing.

'Advice about what? The baby?'

Zoe stiffened. 'How did—'

'Hard to keep secrets when we're all living on top of each other. I noticed you haven't been cleaning that plastic cup thing – haven't used it at all in fact. And the way you were carrying on with Shaun . . . So you are pregnant, is that it?'

Her piercing voice clearly carried, because Shaun broke away from the others and came running. He stopped in front of Zoe, big-eyed and excited as a golden retriever.

'Zo? Did she just say . . .'

Zoe burst into tears, nodding.

The guys rejoined the group and the palpable anger on their faces was momentarily replaced by confusion. Then Duncan pointed at me.

'Where've you hidden it?' he demanded.

I snorted, recklessly showing my contempt. 'Or you'll do what? Push me again? Hit me? Show us what a big man you are?'

For the first time I saw pure hatred replace dislike in his eyes. Duncan loathed me. Fear spiked in me and curdled my adrenalin and anger. For the first time I wasn't just afraid that they'd steal from me or destroy my things – I was afraid they'd hurt me. Physically.

Zoe was still crying, now in Shaun's arms as he looked around helplessly.

'Zoe's pregnant,' he said, stunned, to no one in particular.

'And Maddy's trying to get her to take some kind of abortion potion,' Gill said, like a schoolgirl pertly telling tales.

I felt my face colour. Clearly she had been eaves-dropping. Maxine looked shocked, Frank's drink-bloated face settled in a mask of disgust and Shaun gripped Zoe tighter.

'Is that true, Zoe?'

She looked up and for a second I thought how beautiful she looked, her nose pink from the cold, eyelashes dark and sparkling with tears. Then our eyes met and though hers quickly darted away, I saw in them the instinct of self-preservation. My heart sank.

'Yes,' Zoe whispered, pressing herself further into Shaun's arms and away from the anger of the others. 'It's true. She told me she could give me something to get rid of the baby.'

'Why the fuck would you say something like that to her?' Shaun snapped at me.

I looked only at him, not wanting to invite anyone else from the mob to lay into me.

'Because we don't have access to a hospital, or doctors anymore. She could very well die because of this pregnancy, here, on this island,' I said. Shaun started to shake his head, disbelieving and angry, I continued, relentless. 'There are a thousand things that could go wrong and we have no way of predicting or dealing with complications. The safest thing, the only thing we can do, is end her pregnancy now, in the early stages. It's about minimising risk.'

'Stop it!' Shaun shouted. 'That's . . . You're just scaring her.' He kissed the top of Zoe's head. 'It's OK. I'm not going to let her poison you.'

'If that's what she's getting up to, she shouldn't have that book – for all our sakes,' Gill put in. 'We still don't know what happened to those poor men.'

I felt suddenly unreal. 'Are you suggesting I poisoned the camera crew? Why the hell would I do that? Never mind how.'

'Maybe this is all you – trying to keep us here,' Gill snapped. 'You poisoned us before, didn't you? Maybe you decided you like being here. So you killed them, sabotaged the radio.'

'That's insane,' I said. 'Why on earth would I want to be stuck here with you lot? All you've done for months is try to do me down, steal my food and shut me out.'

'So you tried to poison us with those mushrooms!' Gill said, victorious.

'I never thought you'd take those sodding mushrooms!'

'Enough!' Duncan roared, and Gill fell silent, like a yappy dog hearing its master. Duncan took a deep breath and then jabbed his finger at me once more.

'You're going to tell me where you've hidden that book, right now.'

'I don't have it. I burned it,' I said, unwilling to admit that I had a hiding place. If they knew about it, they'd go looking.

'Bullshit! There's fuck all in that hut but clothes and some shit off the beach. Because you've stashed it somewhere, haven't you? Like the oh-so-clever bitch you are. Where. Is. It?'

I didn't trust myself to speak. Whatever I said would be the wrong thing. So I kept silent. Duncan's eyes bored into me for a long moment, then he shook his head.

'All right, since you want to do this the hard way. Listen up, everyone.' He looked around the group. 'Maddy here got nothing out of the portacabin. So while she's down to her last scrapings of moss or whatever, we've got enough food for months. Not to mention the medicine, the first-aid stuff . . . So we can just wait.

243

And eventually she is going to lead us straight to that book. But until then, she doesn't exist – got it? We don't talk to her, we don't see her, don't help her.'

'And she doesn't come near Zoe,' Shaun put in.

I glanced around at the assembled faces. I'd agreed to trade for the book, but that wasn't what they wanted. No. Duncan's pride meant he wouldn't give me anything and as for the rest of them . . . they needed a distraction. Baiting me, shutting me out, that was the only pastime the island had to offer, other than speculating on our bleak futures. They needed the book, true, but they needed me to withhold it more. They needed an excuse to hate me, to make an enemy of me. If I handed the book over, it would be something else tomorrow. Nothing would be enough, because if they had no one to blame, no one to talk about or stigmatise, they had no outlet for their fear.

I saw all of this in that moment and felt very afraid.

After a few moments Duncan sniffed and turned away. The others followed him, one by one, until I was alone on the beach watching their retreating backs. Zoe still with Shaun's arm around her. I didn't relax or even dare move until long after they'd all vanished into the treeline.

On shaking legs I made my way back to my tipi. It was in a mess, as expected. My clothes and bedding had been pulled out and strewn over the wet ground, trampled. My bags completely turned out and their contents rifled through, wash things mixed with my dirty hiking boots, reusable sanitary pads chucked to one side in disgust. My crab bucket was overturned, the water turning the packed dirt floor to mud. The crab itself was gone. Maybe they'd taken it, or just thrown it somewhere. I slowly put things to rights, then sat, staring at the embers of my fire, and cried.

The shock and helplessness I felt made me sob breathlessly, shaking. I clutched myself and curled up, angry, wronged and, most of all, afraid. Afraid for myself and for Zoe, for what Duncan might do to me and what nature might do to her. I'd been trying for the last week to carry on as normal, but the reality of our helpless situation had hit me full force in the last few hours. We were trapped. I was trapped. I had limited food and no means to grow more, no sign that rescue was imminent. The others were against me. I was alone even amongst my fellow castaways.

At last, face tacky with tears and hiccupping with residual sobs, I asked myself what I was going to do. What could I do? Part of me wanted to just get the book and take it to them. It would solve this most immediate conflict. But I knew that there would be something else after that. They'd demand my map, my food stocks, my tools. Taking from me was the only way they could increase their supplies. It was also the only form of entertainment they had, a sort of group bonding ritual – baiting the outsider. No, handing over the book would ultimately be pointless.

Duncan hadn't known that he'd missed some supplies at the portacabin. He seemed to think they had them all and that I had basically nothing. From what he'd said it looked like his plan was to wait a while, for me to start going hungry, at which point I'd hand over the book. He probably thought that would be in a week or so. I couldn't imagine him waiting longer. After a short while he'd realise that I had resources hidden somewhere and then he'd start looking, or try to force me to reveal them. He wasn't stupid. If I stayed where I was I'd have a visit from them sooner rather than later. I was afraid to see what he'd do under further stress, with more at stake.

That left me with one obvious course of action: not be here when they came back. I could move to the cave. It was hidden, secret and already had most of my belongings in it. The only problem was that my established infrastructure was at the beach. I'd be leaving behind the latrine, fire pit, smoke hut and the sea – my most valuable food source. But I couldn't see a way around it. I had to make it work at the cave, or face the others when they came to act on their threats.

By the time exhaustion carried me off to sleep, I had a plan. One week was all the grace I could hope for. Maybe less. In that time I would transport everything I could to the cave and get it ready as a sort of bunker, to wait out my time on the island until rescue came. I only hoped that Zoe would come to me before I had to disappear.

Chapter 25

'I'm sure our viewers have seen some of the coverage surrounding Buidseach and the events there. But, as a lot of the information has been conflicting and inconsistent from several parties . . . are you able to confirm the number of people who sadly lost their lives there?'

I assess her steadily. This glossy, perfectly poised woman, pulling her sentiments from the autocue scrolling behind me. Like her own brain is empty except for those digitised letters, spooling from a control room somewhere behind the studio lights. It isn't her fault. She isn't the one thinking up these questions, piling on the sugar to hide the bitterness of the truth. Obscuring gleeful thoughts of ratings with well-feigned distaste and journalistic pride, even as the audience at home leans in to catch every horrific detail. Lapping hungrily like wolves at a fresh kill.

I think of everything I could say, the things I could reveal. The many ways I could wipe the brittle-as-icing *smile off her face. But no. Some truths are for me, and me alone.*

'Six people died on Buidseach, that I knew of at the time I left the island,' I say.

'That number has since risen though, hasn't it?' Rosie presses.

'I believe so, yes. The trial, of course, was . . . well, I think the ordeal was too much for some people. Having to face what happened. I don't blame them for not being able to cope.'

That's actually true. I blame them for other, far worse things.

Rosie smiles that same saccharine smile, slick with gloss. Her eyes flick over the lines of text presumably rolling behind me. What horror does she want me to conjure next? Is she going to ask for the causes of death? The full details of every last breath taken? The starvation, cruel accidents and malice that snatched lives away?

'I'm sure I speak for our audience when I say, your bravery is to be commended,' she says, turning away, to smile at the cameras. 'And we'll be right back, with Madeline Holinstead, after the break.'

Chapter 26

I woke early the next morning and went out to take stock of my supplies. Mostly these were in the smoke shed and comprised split logs and some dried seaweed. I also had my clothes, bedroll, sleeping bag, buckets and other tools to think of. As I went about checking things and then lighting the fire for my breakfast, I became increasingly certain that I was being watched.

Without being obvious I scanned my surroundings in quick glances. The woods were dark and hiding places plentiful, but I thought I saw a flash of orange among the pines. Shaun had been sent to spy on me. The least they could have done was lend him a green jacket. I carried on my morning routine as normal, making spruce tea and eating a sparse meal. All the while my mind was working.

Duncan knew I had hidden the book somewhere and was clearly hoping to catch me going to that hiding place. Before I'd always gone to the cave at night in case I was seen, but I'd not seriously thought I was being watched, not constantly anyway. However, as the day went on the feeling of being followed didn't go away. As I foraged along the shore I felt my neck prickling and when I turned around I caught movement in the trees. In the woods sticks snapped behind me and in retracing my route I saw other footprints in the snow patches. They were not very good at being sneaky. But then, they didn't need to be. Even if they were aware that I noticed them, what was I going to do? How could I stop them from following me?

The constant surveillance was weighing on me by the time night started to fall. I had to start moving things to the cave, I had to make it liveable. Most importantly, I needed to fetch some food for the coming days. I went through the motions of preparing for bed, and then lay in my tipi, fully dressed and waiting.

I had no way of marking the passage of time, but it felt like hours. The fire burned down to nothing and I made no move to rekindle it. I didn't want to give any sign that I was still awake. I weighed my chances. If I left now and was followed, I would lose everything. If I simply went to sleep I would lose precious time in setting up my bolthole. Worse, what could I take? There was nothing to stop them searching my tipi again. It would surely raise suspicion if my bedding and clothes vanished.

In the end, as my eyes were prickling with tiredness, I decided to wait. I would go the next night. Hopefully if they were watching tonight they'd be satisfied that I wasn't going anywhere. One night stationed in the cold would more than likely be enough to make them not want to repeat the exercise. Mentally I picked through my possessions. I would have to move them slowly, in small batches.

Over the next few days I started making my night runs again. Only whereas before I'd felt slightly silly creeping around in the dark, now it felt deadly serious. I went to the cave via a meandering route, doubling back and hiding for long stretches in case I was being followed. It took me a long time to get there and back, and I could only take small amounts of stuff with me. Mostly this was wood, carefully split and stashed in my backpack. I had a lot of it and would need even more. Keeping a fire going was the only way to battle the cold, to cook food and purify water. Fire was life.

To that end I needed a way to have a fire lit in the cave without the light or smoke attracting attention. Light was easy; I'd read Andrew's SAS book extensively and knew I could dig a hole to hide my fire from view even in the open. In the cave, with the barrier across the outer entrance, it would be invisible. Smoke was the problem. My first night back at the cave I explored the back wall of the inner chamber thoroughly. There was another crack there, too small to get through. It appeared to lead into another chamber or tunnel, one that went further back under the hill. I dug my fire hole under it. The smoke would be channelled into the crack and find some outlet further on, I hoped. It was the best I could do.

I stacked my wood along the wall, each piece a

guarantee of warmth. I used ripped fishing net and rope to hang my tools and drying plants from the walls and across the ceiling. Being in that cave for a few hours each night was the only time I felt safe. It was no longer a scary reminder of the witch's house, but a protective warren. In comparison my tipi felt about as protective as a child's playhouse.

As the days went past I started to panic a little. The week I had given myself was only an estimate, after all. I had no idea when Duncan would run out of patience and return for the book. I didn't know what he would do, or when he would do it. I still had lots of wood and most of my bulkier things to move. I had to keep up the pretence that I was planning to stay in my tipi. I knew I was being watched and was certain someone had been through my things while I was out. The need to move silently also meant that I couldn't take much with me when I went out to the cave.

Finally, on the fifth night I decided to try and do multiple trips. I was reasonably sure that I wasn't being watched or followed after dark and, as nerve-shredding as it was to navigate the woods evasively, I'd rather be done in one night than chance waiting a few extra days. I could make one trip with my bedding, come back for my clothes and remaining personal things, then the last of the wood and be done. The wood might take more than one trip, but I was going to cross that bridge when I had to.

It was a good night for it. I'd started taking notice of the moon phases as on a full moon it was harder to find shadows to hide in. That night was a new moon and the very air seemed dark around me. I rolled my sleeping bag and foam mat up as one and tied them with string. With a longer piece of string I made a strap to carry them on my back. I waited until the darkness seemed at its most dense, then I set off.

As had become routine I snaked my way towards the cave. I doubled back a few times and hid for a while under some brambles. I didn't hear anyone in the woods aside from me. There was very little sound at all, as most of the animals were hibernating still. The others would have a long wait for their meat.

At last I reached the cave and separated my roll and sleeping bag. Getting them through the crack into the inner cave was a struggle. I had to feed them through bit by bit, one after the other. Inside I made my bed up in an alcove on the left-hand side, out of the draft from the entrance.

I slid out of the cave and pulled the panel into place behind me. I was pleased with how effective it looked; even when I'd passed the cave in daylight it looked like nothing so much as a slight indent, choked with leaves. I made my way back towards my tipi, legs already strained from struggling in all the snowmelt mud.

Inside the tipi I cursed myself for not packing sooner. I'd been preoccupied with keeping up appearances and not wanted to spend too long in the tipi during the day. I now had to feel about in the dark, picking up clothing and stuffing it into my backpack along with soap, towels, clothes and the rest of my daily use items.

A sudden sound made me freeze, hand still in the bag. Was that someone stumbling on the gravel beach? I strained to hear beyond my own heartbeat. Footsteps. Not close, but loud on the gravel as people slithered and tripped on the loose stones.

I was caught, trapped by indecision. If I stayed they'd be on me in a matter of moments. What would they do then? Something told me they weren't here in the middle of the night to negotiate. If I ran now it meant leaving things behind; the remainder of my clothes, my wood store. Would those things be there when, if, I came back? Doubtful.

It was no choice at all, but I made it just the same. With a tight hand on my half-filled rucksack I darted out of the tipi and, using it as cover, made a beeline for the trees. Once hidden under the shadowy pines, I turned, despite my better judgement, to see what they would do. I wiped the camera lens with my sleeve to remove any dirt or water droplets; deep down I think I knew I'd need some kind of witness for what was to come.

Their shadows came out of the greater darkness, carrying torches. They were the battery-operated kind, not flaming, and no pitchforks were evident. But the mood was threatening none the less. I watched as they surrounded the tipi as if by agreement, spaced evenly around it with Duncan at the entrance. He grabbed one of the three supports and shook it.

'Maddy, come out. Now.'

There was silence as they waited for a few moments.

Then Duncan pushed aside the plastic door flap and shone his torch inside.

'She's not here!'

The figures shifted and turned to each other in consternation. I watched their torch beams whirl as they shone them around, looking for me. I was grateful for the position of the tipi; I'd made my escape over packed earth, not sand. There were no prints to betray me. Duncan started to throw things out of the tipi, my clothes splashing onto the ground like ink.

'Her bed's gone. She's done a runner.' He threw down the last piece of clothing in disgust. 'Fuck! I thought you were watching her?'

He turned to one of them – it looked to be Shaun from the height and shape of him. Shaun appeared to hang his head, clearly saying something in his own defence because the next moment Duncan exploded.

'Oh, was it cold? Fucking hell! I didn't know you were such a fucking pussy. Well now we don't know where she is, do we? Her or the book or God only knows what else she's hiding away from us.'

'She'll come back' – this from Gill, her voice clear and sharp as a gull's scream. 'We'll get her then, won't we, Duncan?'

'If she's had her bed out of here she's not coming back tonight, is she?' Duncan snapped. 'Fat chance we've got of catching the sneaky bitch with Shaun here on the case. Gill, get her clothes up, anything else we can use.'

Gill hurried to do this, scooping up my things in her

arms and making a bundle. I watched as another figure approached Duncan. The torchlight rested on him for a moment and I recognised Andrew. I also saw that Duncan had black streaks on his face, as if painted on with charcoal, like he was off on a guerrilla mission. It would have been funny if I'd not been so frightened.

They'd clearly come intending to surprise me. To do what I wasn't sure, but nothing good. I was frozen, afraid to move in case they heard or saw me. I just wanted them to go away so I could make a run for it. It didn't seem like they were in a hurry though.

I watched as Duncan and Andrew put their heads together. Then Andrew ducked into the tipi and emerged with a smouldering branch from my fire. He passed it to Duncan and went back for another. Duncan waved the stick, fanning the embers until the dry wood burned greedily, throwing jagged shadows on his face.

'What are you doing?' I heard Zoe ask, her voice layered with apprehension.

Duncan answered her by throwing his burning stick onto the tipi. The outer layer of pine bough thatch was wet from the day's rain, but under that there was clearly more than enough dry kindling, not to mention the plastic sheeting. After a few moments the flames started to spread and Andrew added his own stick on the other side. Gill clapped and cheered, linking arms with what I assumed to be Maxine. I watched as the home I'd made months before went up like a bonfire. For a moment the figures around it almost looked like revellers waiting for a firework display. It seemed almost normal that they'd be there, on the beach, watching the fire burn. Then light flashed in my eyes and I heard Gill's voice cry out.

'She's over there!'

The torch was like a searchlight, momentarily blinding me. I was frozen in fear, but the sound of people running towards me snapped me out of it. I turned and sprinted into the trees, fleeing from the shouts and cries behind me.

Fear gripped me as the feeling of being chased, being prey, coursed through me. I crashed through the undergrowth I'd previously navigated cautiously. I twisted my ankles sliding in the mud. A branch whipped across my face, stinging my eye and making me cry out.

Their voices hounded me through the trees. I ploughed on, head down. Eventually I looked up and realised I had no idea where I was. Panic was blotting out all my thoughts, making the familiar strange and terrifying. No landmarks came to me out of the darkness. I was completely lost.

I ran on, not daring to stop. My heart was racing, my side seized with cramp. Suddenly the uneven ground was snatched away and I was falling. Plunging down into a gulley. I hit the ground hard and it knocked the wind out of me. My ankle was badly twisted, my clothes soaked and my breath wheezing as I gaped and spluttered like a landed fish. I struggled, trying to stand only for my ankle to stab pain through me.

Then I heard footsteps over me.

I froze, lying still in the mud and water. All thoughts

of pain were swallowed up by the black hole of my terror. Someone was near, almost on top of me. I heard twigs break and pebbles grind under boots.

When a hand grabbed my arm and turned me over, I nearly screamed. Had a second hand not quickly covered my mouth I likely would have given myself away. It was Zoe, and she looked almost as afraid as I was.

'Quiet!' she hissed. 'You need to get out of here – that way.' She pointed to the left of my original path. 'There's no one looking over there yet.'

I struggled to sit up, then to crouch. 'Thank you,' I whispered.

'I don't know what's going on with them,' Zoe said, and I could hear she was almost in tears. 'They're all off their faces . . . I don't know what to do.'

Dread built below my panic. Not only were they out to get me, they were also high on fly agaric, hallucinating and erratic. On the one hand, decreased motor skills and unsteady perception could help me get away. On the other, I had no way of knowing what they might do if they caught me while not operating rationally.

To the right came the sounds of someone crashing through the dead ferns and fallen branches.

'Go, now!' Zoe whispered, pushing me.

'Be careful,' I hissed, even as I ducked away into the surrounding dark.

My ankle screamed at me to slow my pace, but I didn't dare. Half crouching, I limped at speed through the trees. After I'd gone about fifty feet I recognised a fallen log wedged up on a boulder. The cave was north of there. I forced myself on, now dragging my injured leg. My eye was swollen shut by this time and I could hardly see. A low hill caught me by surprise and I fell down it, wrenching my shoulder when my bag caught on something. There was movement in the trees; it seemed like the whole forest was alive and calling for me.

At last I reached the small clearing where the cave entrance was hidden. I was exhausted and shivering by this time with cold and spent adrenalin. I fell to my belly and pushed the panel back, crawled inside. After fumbling the camouflage back in place behind me I shrugged off my bag and fell through the gap into the inner chamber. Breathless and agonised I leant against the wall. With numb fingers I found the handle of my hatchet and held it close. I waited there, ready for attack, until I passed out.

Chapter 27

I woke up with a start when the hatchet slipped off of my leg and jarred my ankle. The pain was sharp and sudden, replaced soon after by a dull ache. I shifted, stiff and cramped from sleeping upright against the wall. The inside of the cave was almost completely dark. Only a little sunlight filtered in through the barrier and the outer chamber. I could tell it was day, but not the time or what condition I was in. As the night's events flooded back to me, I listened for my pursuers. There was nothing. No sounds at all, other than my own breathing and the sighing of the forest.

Slowly I uncoiled my stiff frame and reached for my bag to get my torch. With it I examined myself for injuries. My hands were filthy, mud caked under the nails and all over the sleeves and body of my still wet coat. I shrugged it off and noticed a big rip on the knee of my leggings. Under it was a large smear of dried blood and several grazes from where I'd fallen. I tried to remove my boot and bit my lip as the pain thundered to the surface. My ankle was very swollen, constricted by the tightly laced hiking boot. Bit by bit I eased the laces open and slowly removed the boot, wincing all the while. Under my soaking wet sock my skin was smashed-berry purple. The imprints of my boot were like scars on the skin, angry lines pressed into the livid flesh.

It was only once the pain in my ankle started to subside to a just-bearable ache that I realised how cold it was. Reaching up to feel my throbbing eye, I felt the ends of my hair crackle with frost. I felt mostly fine and that was incredibly worrying. To be that cold and not even be shivering suggested the onset of hypothermia. I needed to get a fire going, quickly.

Grunting quietly with the effort, I dragged myself across the cave floor. I'd not yet laid a fire in the hole and my hands were like those of a mannequin as I fumbled with split wood and dried weeds. I had a push firestarter and jabbed it hard into the materials. The sight of the yellow flames made me tear up in gratitude.

While the fire got going I removed my wet clothes. I pulled items from my rucksack at random and put them on. In cleaner, dry clothes I dried my hair with the filthy T-shirt and pulled my sleeping bag around me for warmth, stretching my filthy hands towards the fire.

The fire mesmerised me and I soon started to doze. It was an effort to rouse myself enough to take stock of my situation and immediate resources. I had in many ways been lucky. I'd not lost any food or important tools in the fire. I had however lost the bulk of my clothes, including thermal underwear, the thickest of my jumpers and various T-shirts and pairs of leggings. I had, to my name, three complete sets of clothes with some extra items of little to no use. These comprised two pairs of fleece-lined sport leggings, a regular pair, two T-shirts, a jumper, underwear (one set thermal) and a pair of shorts. Aside from this I had some odd socks, tank tops and a single glove. One set of clothes was currently plastered in filth.

My everyday washing things had also been in the tipi when it was burned. I no longer had my toothbrush or remnants of toothpaste, shampoo bar or microfibre sanitary pads. There had been some soap in the port-acabin box, so that was at least something.

Water was the immediate worry, aside from getting my body up to temperature. I'd been carrying a bottle of water on me during the day. It was still in my rucksack and about half full. My primitive water purifier was dismantled and in the cave with me, empty. I was nowhere near the stream but there was enough snow around that the lack of water didn't worry me. What did worry me was that I couldn't get to it; I could barely drag myself across the cave floor.

Going outside on my wounded ankle would be begging to be caught. And getting caught meant . . . what? I had run for my life to reach the cave. It had felt like being seen, being captured, meant death. Was that just my paranoia, my fear from being chased screaming in my veins? Would the others really kill me if I strayed outside?

The higher part of my mind, the part that always wanted to give them the benefit of the doubt, remained unconvinced. We had been on the island for just under a fortnight of extra time. Two weeks was not enough to drive sane, normal people to murder. The rest of me, the parts that had brought me through the woods and saved me, knew differently. Two weeks wasn't a lot in a normal life. We were far from that. As quickly as our situation had devolved, so had we all. Dislike into hatred. Passive aggression into physical attack. To top that off with homebrew, hallucinogens and the threat of starvation . . . I could not be sure what the others would do to me. I wasn't even sure they had planned any of this, or if it had simply happened. Mob mentality. A pack chasing me through the woods because that was its nature.

So going outside was, for now, impossible. I had to wait until I could not only stand or walk, but run. How long would that take? I had no idea.

I went through my supplies and found a packet of ibuprofen from the portacabin. I popped two tablets out and took them with a sip of my precious water. It was weird, tasting the bitter dryness of pre-packaged medicine. I only hoped they would bring the swelling down in my ankle.

With my small mirror lost in the fire I used a spoon to try and get a look at my eye. In the tiny upside-down reflection I could see nothing wrong aside from a cut over my eyelid. I could feel how swollen it was. I moistened the corner of a stray sock and cleaned up the area around the cut, then applied a bit of antiseptic cream. I did the same for my knee.

This tiny amount of effort left me exhausted, but I knew I had to eat something. My body needed energy to heal, to heat itself. I opened a tin of peach slices and poured the syrup into a cup. After eating half the fruit I sipped the sickly juice before covering the open tin.

Fed, I lay down beside the fire and let my mind wander into the dancing flames.

I must have slept again because the next moment I was jerking awake. My eyes snapped open and my heart thundered in my chest. It took a few seconds for me to realise what had woken me: footsteps, crashing through the undergrowth.

I strained my ears and tried frantically to gauge how close the footsteps were, if they were coming closer or moving away. I couldn't tell. Frozen, half lying, half upright, I heard Duncan's voice from frighteningly nearby.

'Did you search over there, under the brambles?'

Frank replied from further away. 'She's not there. Maybe she went to the crew cabin?'

'Then the others'll find her. Keep looking.'

I heard slashing sounds, a stick beating at the undergrowth. Was he near the entrance to the cave? I didn't dare move to peer into the outer chamber. The rustle of my sleeping bag seemed impossibly loud.

After a while the slashing stopped. 'Give me that flask,' Duncan said.

Footsteps approached and I heard the rattling of plastic on metal, the sigh as someone drank deeply.

'Keeps the chills off,' Frank said approvingly.

'Tastes like crap though,' Duncan said, smothering a cough.

'Better than nothing.'

'Yeah . . . better than nothing.'

More crashing footsteps. More people entering the clearing.

'Anything?' Duncan demanded.

'No sign.' That was Andrew. 'She's been in there at some point,' he continued. 'The blankets were moved and there's an empty box. She had something out from under the beds.'

Duncan swore. 'So she does have a stash somewhere. Probably sitting there laughing at us, grubbing up all the food.'

I nearly did laugh then, looking at the half-empty tin of peaches and my own filth-encrusted hands. Oh yeah, I was really living it up.

'Anything from Shaun and Zoe?' Gill said. Clearly she'd been partnered with Andrew.

'Haven't seen them,' Frank said.

'Probably got him building a cot or some shit,' Andrew said. 'Boy's pussy-whipped.'

'Can you blame him though? She's a hot little number,' Duncan said. 'You would if you could.'

Gill must've huffed or looked at them a certain way, because there was a smattering of smutty laughter.

'You're not bad yourself, no worries. Nice tits

266

anyway,' Andrew said. 'Better than Maxine. She's a bit too much like Maddy – tight-arsed.'

'You don't like a tight arse, Andy?' Duncan said, and Gill giggled. 'I say Frank takes Maxine, and Gill, you like Andrew, don't you? You two can shack up,' Duncan said.

'If he can keep up with me,' Gill said, prompting a whistle, possibly from Duncan.

'Who says I want Maxine?' Frank complained. 'Just cos I'm old?'

'And what about you, Duncan?' Andrew said. 'You hoping Shaun decides to share his girl?'

'Nah, I'm saving myself for Maddy,' Duncan said, and I heard a nasty edge beneath his humorous tone. 'Give her something to shut her up.'

They laughed. I felt my whole body clench and go hot with mingled humiliation and anger. But under that there was fear, cold, lingering fear. Even as I heard them walk away it didn't dissipate. If anything it grew. When there was nothing but silence to be heard, I slid out of my sleeping bag and sat by the dying fire, hugging myself. By its flickering light I finally checked my camera for damage. There was a scratch on the lens but the tough cover had protected it aside from that. The tiny light on the back still shone. I had the other power pack, not that I could use it in the cave. But I had it, for what that was worth.

I was safe, for the moment. Still, hearing them talk about me had made me feel worse. It was like they weren't talking about a person, not really. They said my name like it belonged to a thing, a thing that was less than human. A thing they might use and break as easily as if I were a can to be emptied and crushed. Any thought that I might have overreacted at the beach left me. If they caught me, I would not be safe.

I thought of Zoe, who'd saved me, endangering herself in the process. As much as I wanted to believe I had one friend on the island, Zoe had proven to be fickle. I worried for her; with her pregnancy advancing she'd be in danger from complications. Not only that but she'd become more reliant on the others. If they really were abusing fly agaric to the extent it seemed, then they wouldn't be that dependable. Hopefully Maxine would be sensible, though it looked like she was on the outs with the rest of them, filling my old role as camp scapegoat. I was something else now – an enemy. Prey. In any event I couldn't help either of them. My only focus had to be keeping myself alive.

I knew that the only way I might survive being on the island was to hide, avoid the others and wait for rescue. Eventually, somehow, the real world would have to reach us. Even if it wasn't the production company, surely a boat would pass. A fisherman would see us, a coastguard helicopter would go searching. The others all had families and those families would not abandon them. I could only hope that when rescue came, I could seize my chance and get myself off the bloody island. In the meantime I needed to be smarter than the others. I had to cover my tracks, keep myself fed and as healthy as possible. An opportunity would come. I just had to be patient.

The next few days passed slowly.

I couldn't walk or do anything much but lie on the ground, resting my ankle and watching the level of water in my bottle go down. It felt like I was constantly thirsty, but I reasoned that this was just my mind dwelling on the water situation. I tried to keep my mind occupied but couldn't focus on reading or on mending my ripped leggings.

Occasionally a search party came close to the cave, but after that first time they didn't hang around long. It seemed as though they were looking elsewhere, for the moment. There was never any activity after dark and I wondered if they'd had as terrible a time as I had running through the woods that first night. I wondered how long they would keep it up for if they didn't find me soon. They had to be worried about their food reserves, rationing to make them last. How much energy could they afford to waste on hunting me? How long before they turned their sights inward and onto their own survival? Not soon enough for me.

At last my bruises faded to yellow and my ankle no longer hurt when I stood or crouched. I had no way to know how it would do under strain until I left the cave.

Going outside again was an experience I was unprepared for. I waited until after nightfall before quietly sneaking out into the clearing. It felt too open, too exposed after being underground for the past few days. The sheer number of directions danger could come from paralysed me. Every swaying branch and rattling stick falling to the ground made my eyes swivel around me. I forced myself to breathe, to regain some control over myself.

My two main aims were to find water and dispose of my waste. I'd been using a bucket for my latrine and the smell was becoming an issue, even with cold ashes layered over the contents. I left the bucket in the cave opening and crept a good distance away. There I dug a hole and then returned for the bucket. Once emptied, I rinsed it with semi-melted snow. With some leaves over the spot it looked untouched.

Water was a different struggle. There was plenty of snow, but camouflaging each patch of scraped-up snow took time. My nerves were fraying all the while and I was starting to worry they'd break entirely before my work was through. The last thing I did was hide the solar pack, hoping to get some charge for my dead camera.

Before returning to the safety of the cave I realised that my footprints were now all over the clearing. I'd crawled into the cave the night of the chase, and that alone had probably saved me. Now though I could see my prints mingling with those of the others. I cursed myself for being so stupid. Would they notice if they came back? Maybe not. But if I continued to leave the cave the prints would quickly build up, giving me away. I had to be careful. I went to the side of the cave to re-enter, hiding my route under the brush. I realised

I'd been holding my breath only when I replaced the panel and a sigh left me in a rush.

I now had water enough for a while, but I knew I had to plan for the snow melting away and for a lack of rain. How would I get water then, without crossing the island to reach the stream?

The cold was also becoming an issue. In my tipi I had been able to keep a fire going merrily and that had, mostly, kept the chill at bay. Now I had to make my fires small, in case the smoke started to escape through the panel, giving away my position. I was also lacking my thermal underclothes and my heavy winter jumper. Although the cave was well insulated above me, there was a creeping through-draft that quickly ate up the heat from the small fire. I needed more layers of clothing and something to block the crack to the outer cave. Continuing as I was would mean losing calories to the cold.

The answer came to me after days spent shivering, as close to the fire as I could get without bursting into flames: the portacabin.

I'd searched it already, true, as had the others, but had any of us found their clothes? I went over what I remembered of the inside. I'd searched the cabinets in the bathroom, the kitchenette, the console; like the others my main concern had been food. Yet I hadn't found any clothes, spare bedding or even towels. Either the others had already found them before I got there, or they were stored somewhere that hadn't been immediately obvious.

I tried to remember if I'd seen the others wearing new clothes when they'd come to the beach to demand the book. After a year I could probably list every item they owned from memory. I didn't think anyone had been wearing anything new. I thought over the storage places I'd searched. None of them had seemed like places bedding would be stored. There had to be a wardrobe or closet somewhere in the cabin.

It was asking for trouble, but I had little choice. I was spending every waking hour trying to keep warm and failing; I needed to remedy that as soon as possible. I couldn't afford to get ill or waste calories on shivering – I needed every ounce of my energy to put into survival. I needed cloth for filtering my water, for bandages, food preservation and any number of other things. Not only that but any resource I could get my hands on was something the others wouldn't have. If I could enrich my own cache while putting them at a disadvantage, I could increase my odds.

If it was to be survival of the fittest, I would play to win.

Chapter 28

The day I crossed the first of February off in my diary, a little part of me died. I was going back over the old year, day by day, reusing the diary. One month. We had waited a month to be rescued. Still, we were on our own. For two weeks I'd been inside my cave, recovering and then waiting for the right time to get to the porta-cabin. Marking the first day of a new month pushed me over the edge. I had to do it. I would never feel ready. There was no being ready for the sensation of being so exposed, so afraid as I was just standing outside the cave. While I waited, the others might well be enjoying the items I desperately needed.

After nightfall I left the cave, replacing the panel behind me. I'd let the fire go out and hoped that this was not the night the others chose to come looking for me. The idea that I might go back inside only to be met by one of them, waiting for me, had been the cause of many a nightmare in the past week. I was carrying only what I needed: a knife, an empty bag and my torch. I wore my camera almost as a talisman. An all-seeing eye to protect me from their anger and violence.

I took the journey slowly, though everything in me wanted to run and get it over with as soon as I could. Every few feet I stopped to listen for footsteps, voices. There were none. The snow was almost completely gone now but an iron-hard frost had taken its place. This was good for me as it meant I left no footprints. Hopefully the intense cold would also keep the others beside their fires and not out in the woods.

With the portacabin in sight I paused, trying to see if anyone had been posted to keep watch on it. I couldn't imagine any of them volunteering to spend the night in a building with no fire and two corpses for company. Still, I took my time and approached carefully. It was only when I got within a few feet that I saw why there was no need to watch the place.

The door, which had hung open, swollen with damp, had been wedged closed. Across it, nailed in place, were two planks taken from a pallet. I went closer and saw the charred edges. These planks were from my tipi. The cruel irony of my ruined home being used as parts to keep me from getting supplies was not lost on me. There was no way I could remove those planks and pry the door open without making a huge amount of noise. I couldn't rule out the possibility that someone was camped near enough to hear. Even if I chanced it, they'd then know I'd been to the cabin. They'd go looking for what I'd taken and possibly carry off anything I had to leave behind. No, I had to get inside without leaving any sign of my presence.

I circled the cabin as quietly as possible. The windows were no good; they were all shut up and locked from inside. Breaking one would be as obvious as getting in through the door. I crouched in the undergrowth, trembling with nerves. I couldn't leave without blankets and warm clothes. I wouldn't last until spring without them. I was about to go back to the door, to hell with thoughts of caution, when an idea struck me.

A lifetime ago I'd gone to a primary school with two portacabin classrooms. I remembered that in the centre of the classroom there had been a little trapdoor, neatly filled in with a square of nylon carpet.

Eyeing up the bottom of the cabin, I circled it again until I found a panel in the wood lattice at the base. I removed it and crawled into the space beneath the floor. I chanced shining my torch around and saw what looked to be a trapdoor at the end of the passage I was in. There was a smell in the crawl space, one of rot and fungus. I held my breath as much as I could, taking sips of air when I absolutely had to.

At the trapdoor I struggled with the aluminium clips holding it in place. The hatch was slick with something brownish and thick. Around it seeped a circle of darker wood, soaked through. I gagged, dropping the torch. Both it and my hands were smeared with the brown grease; the seeping remains of the body above. I lost my nerve, scrubbing my hands on the dirt below me, feeling the grease squish between my fingers. I coughed and retched.

It took a great amount of effort but I forced myself to stop moving, to stop making sound. I had to do this. I had to keep my head together. That didn't stop me flinching as I finally levered open the trapdoor and found myself right beside the bunkbeds, in a corner by the console. I pulled myself up through the hole, trying not to recoil from the feel of the sticky, saturated carpet. I got into a crouch and with effort forced myself to look away from the corpse and instead search for the clothes I hoped to find.

After scrubbing my hands on the cleaner areas of the carpet, I started to scan the walls for more cupboards and storage spaces. I had already checked the bathroom, and a quick look in through the door confirmed there was nowhere for an extra cupboard to be hidden. Under the console was empty of the wires and things I'd left last time. Clearly the others had taken those. Above the computer screens there was a long, shallow cubbyhole, but if there had been something there it too was now gone.

The feeling of defeat was agonising. I'd come this far for nothing. As a last-ditch effort I checked the corner opposite the hatch, on the other side of the beds. There I found a plastic wastepaper bin, half full. I wanted to kick it, but didn't dare. I'd taken enough risks already.

Then I noticed the shine from a chrome stripe, going up the wall. I felt for it, pulled and a floor-to-ceiling cupboard opened up, knocking the bin on its side. I winced at the sound. Behind the narrow door was a small, but packed, wardrobe.

I only narrowly kept myself from shouting out in relief. Inside the wardrobe were several shelves of folded clothes; jeans, T-shirts, hoodies. At the bottom a cloth hamper bulged with worn clothes. The scent of fabric softener wafted out like a memory of another time. I leant forwards and rested my forehead on a heap of folded clothes, inhaling.

I glanced at the bunkbed with its sightless occupant and shivered. I told myself that it didn't matter, not right now. I needed these things and that was all there was to it. How they got there, why they were there, was not my concern.

There was too much for me to take. There was also no guarantee that the others wouldn't come back and find the wardrobe later on. I had to make the most of the opportunity. I packed my bag with several thick jumpers, woollen socks and a cheap fleece blanket to block the cave's draft. I almost cried in frustration when my backpack refused to fit through the hatchway. I had to remove half the stuff and after some thought, dropped it into the crawl space. I would pack it all again once I was outside. I tried not to think about what might soak into it in the meantime.

It broke my heart to close the wardrobe and leave so much stuff behind. I told myself that I could come back for it, though the likelihood of me doing so was low. Once the warmer weather came I would not be able to crawl through the mess under the cabin, no matter how desperate I was. Maybe the others would find the rest and maybe they wouldn't. Hopefully by the time it mattered we'd be off the island.

I was backing away, lost in thought, when my foot crunched down on something. I shone my torch down and saw that it was a ball of paper. Without thinking I picked it up, it was a reflex from a more normal time; see a mess, tidy it. Once I had it in my hand I stuffed it into my pocket. Might as well keep the kindling.

After escaping through the crawl space I repacked my bag. Only then did I truly become aware of the smell that was now on me. My hands were covered in the stink of death and decay. Away from the horror of the bodies I couldn't suppress it any longer. I desperately needed to be clean.

My small store of courage used up for the time being, I hurried back to the cave. As soon as I came across a waterlogged gully I dropped to my knees and scrubbed my hands in the filthy water. I scooped up a handful of silt and scoured under my nails until the skin hurt. With dripping fingers I snatched up my bag and made short work of the trip back to the cave. Inside I built up the fire under my billycan of water. I didn't relax until I'd scrubbed my hands three times with boiling water and plenty of my precious soap. They looked red raw in the firelight, but at least they were clean.

I wasted no time in using my newly acquired clothes. With a thick pair of socks on and a blanket wedged into the opening to the outer cave, I relished the warmth. Rebuilding my fire had left the kindling bucket virtually empty. I scraped up the few dry leaves that lingered in the cave and then pulled the paper from my pocket.

I don't know why I opened it out. Maybe it was simple curiosity. I had after all been reading the same few books since coming to the island. Maybe I was just hungry for new words to run my eyes over. Maybe it was instinct. Perhaps. Either way, I smoothed out the page and was confronted with a familiar image of *amanita muscaria*. Familiar, because it had come from my foraging book.

I stared at it, waiting for the image to make sense. What was the missing page from my book doing in the camera guys' portacabin? There was no way one of the camera crew could have taken my book without someone at camp noticing. Why would they even want to? No, someone from the camp must have taken the page. Then, somehow, it had ended up in the porta-cabin. Had they taken it there to show the camera guys? Why?

It was like a magic eye picture. One moment I was looking at a useless scrap of rubbish, the next I was looking at something quite different. The answer. What better to trade to two bored dudes than some 'magic mushrooms'? One of the islanders had taken the page and used it to identify fly agaric to trade for extra food, or booze. For whatever reason, perhaps to hide what they had done, they had discarded the page at the portacabin.

When had the page been taken? I'd only discovered it was missing after moving to the beach, but it could have been ripped out way before then. Any of them might have taken it at any time. But then . . . why had they all eaten the fly agaric? All of them apart from Zoe anyway. Whoever had the page must have known what the mushrooms were. Had they just not known that yet, or were they stupid enough to think a little soup wouldn't hurt them?

Perhaps I was giving whoever had taken the page too much credit. Clearly they had not known enough to correctly identify fly agaric. To have killed the camera guys so quickly, so violently, it had to have been something else. The reverse of the fly agaric page was a warning on *amanita virosa*: the destroying angel. Even one of those was enough to kill an adult and the resultant liver and kidney damage would have likely been excruciating. There were various other species just as deadly.

Someone on the island was responsible for their deaths. Accidentally, perhaps, but they had poisoned them all the same. Whoever it was had to have some idea that giving the mushrooms to the cameramen might be connected to their deaths. Two healthy men did not just drop dead without help. Still, whoever was responsible hadn't said anything. Were they too afraid, trying to hide what they'd done?

Perhaps the page had not been left behind out of laziness or fear of being caught, but rather to guarantee it would be found. My page, from my book. Beside the dead men. Implicating me. I remembered Gill and her insane accusations that I had poisoned the two men. Was it just that she hated me, or was she trying to throw suspicion my way to protect herself? Or had it been Zoe, who hadn't eaten the soup? Had she tried to trade the mushrooms for something to bring her period on? Was it Frank, always desperate for some booze? He hadn't eaten any of the soup either, I suddenly remembered. He'd been passed out, drunk. Any of them might have done it. Easier to blame me than to risk reprisals themselves.

Not only did I now know that someone had killed the camera crew, I could also imagine their last moments. Perhaps the first had died in his sleep, but the second . . . The realisation that his companion was dead, searing agony as the toxins attacked his organs. Had he called for help? They'd had power. Perhaps he'd been too delusional by then. In too much pain. If he had called, no one had come. No one, it seemed, had even heard. Even if they'd been too late, they still would have tried, if only to collect the bodies. Someone would have told us. But there was no one.

No one had sent a boat. No one had worried that the cameramen hadn't been in touch for months. Why? Something had to be going on. Had the company gone under? What if the project had been abandoned as everyone jumped ship to new companies? Could our current situation be as simple as no one taking responsibility for a failed idea? No one being in charge of retrieving us and all of them just going after the next pitch, the next job? I thought of those interviews, of Sasha and Adrian. The lack of a real presenter, the tiny boat, slapdash video call interviews. What if their shoe-string budget had finally broken? What if we'd been written off as a loss, just like the equipment that still hung in trees all over the island?

If not Adrian or Sasha, what about the families of the other islanders? Zoe's parents, Maxine's husband and daughters? Even Frank had a brother who featured in all his fishing stories. Everyone else had someone to miss them. We were meant to be home by now. There would have been arrangements: people waiting at the train station, calling for coach times, driving up north. So, where was the outcry? Where was our rescue?

Besides, if everyone else was blissfully ignorant of our situation, we were off the coast of Scotland. Why had no one stumbled across us? We'd seen no boats, not even in the distance. Why was the world just pre-tending we didn't exist?

An idea occurred to me then, so frightening that for a moment I forgot to breathe. I was just so horrified to be peering into the deep, dark pit of sudden reali-sation. I felt all hope leach away from me like blood from a mortal wound.

There was no one out there.

The idea felt so paranoid, so preposterous, that I almost laughed. The only thing that stopped me was the feeling that once I started I might not be able to stop. I might laugh until I couldn't breathe and then scream.

Of all the people who knew about us, or who might come across us, we had not seen or heard from a producer, a family member or stranger since we arrived. No one had answered the radio. No one had sent fuel or a rescue team. No one had so much as sailed past looking for fish.

There was no one out there. Something had happened to the world. Something terrible.

I wanted to scream, to run or throw up and punch and kick at everything in sight. I reached out to do just that but the need to stay silent and invisible held me back. Instead, I threw myself down on the dirt floor and dug my fingers into it like claws. I banged my forehead against the earth and cried as silently as I could into it. When I turned my face to the side I saw the bag of clothing and blankets, mocking me. I'd thought I could survive, but for how long? For ever? Trapped here? I shook my head against the dirt, answering some question only I could hear. I couldn't do it. I couldn't live like this without hope of rescue. I couldn't take this new and terrible idea that had blossomed in my head.

'I can't,' I whispered into the dust.

The cave and all its shadows, the yellow flames and the roots twisting through the crumbling dirt, seemed to sigh. The night wind crept its cold fingers into my hovel to chill my wet cheeks. 'You must,' it seemed to say. 'You must.'

Chapter 29

'I knew they'd kill me, if they found me,' I say.

Even under the lights of the studio, tasting lipstick on my mouth and feeling the butter-soft leather of the sofa beneath me, it's all too easy to return to that cave. I go there in my nightmares often enough. The dark and the wet, the insects and the smoke.

'How did you manage, living like that?' Rosie asks.

'I don't know. If someone had proposed it – living in that tiny cave for weeks on end, I'd say, no one could survive that without going mad.' I give a small laugh that comes out all wrong. 'To live like an animal, less than an animal . . . It's beyond anything I thought I could endure. But the alternative was death. I was surprised what I'd do to avoid that, even at my lowest.'

'But at that point no one had done more than chase you, or push you. Nothing to suggest they might have murderous intent,' my interviewer points out, in a way she probably thinks is diplomatic. 'You didn't necessarily know what they'd do, at that time, did you?'

'Ironically, that's what nearly killed me then,' I say, looking her in the eye and watching her instantly regret her words. 'There's this . . . compulsion, bred into us. To be polite, to be civilised, as if by ignoring a threat we're somehow safe from whoever or whatever is out to get us. That as long as we stay silent, as long as no one acknowledges the fear we feel or what might happen . . . it won't.' I allow myself a small sip of water, feeling anger burning into my cheeks. I put the glass down. 'It's bullshit.'

I almost hear the indignant squeaks of some producer. This is live after all. The horror of my ordeal is one thing. Starvation, deprivation, murder and madness are fine, but please, spare us the language.

'There was a moment where I had to choose between everything I'd ever been taught about how to stay safe, and reality. I had to either play the game of appeasement, negotiating just how much I was going to be hurt, or believe my instincts and try to save myself, whatever the cost. And if I hadn't trusted that part of myself . . . I wouldn't be here.'

Chapter 30

When my parents died, it changed me. All at once, the people I'd loved, who knew me the best of everyone, were gone. I'd lost what felt like the only two people who'd cared about me. My world, already small, shrank until it was just me, alone. I carried with me the terrible ache of that loss. Yet I never spoke about it. I didn't look directly into that absence because I didn't dare. If I did, I knew it would consume me.

I dealt with the near certainty that we would never be rescued in much the same way; I refused to acknowledge it. It hung over me, day by day, as blinding and searing as the sun, but I did not look at it directly. Instead I did what I had always done; I found distractions. In my old life that had meant watching inane YouTube videos just to hear a voice until I was too tired to stay awake. On the island it meant trying to find enough food and fuel to keep myself alive. As distractions went, it worked better than anything else. Strangely the knowledge that one of the others had caused the deaths of two people didn't weigh on me as heavily; I was already under no illusions as to their selfishness, their carelessness. They had lied and hidden the truth of many things to make me the bad guy. Why should the deaths of two men be anything other than fuel to the fire of their group hatred?

I never went out during the day. However, I also wasn't able to sleep during daylight hours. The idea of being discovered, asleep and vulnerable, was a constant fear. I had to be awake to listen for approaching footsteps. Equally I couldn't sleep at night because I needed to go out under cover of darkness. I was therefore operating on the little amounts of sleep I could get in the period after sunset but before the darkest part of the night. Then I slept again in the hours around sunrise. Even so I never slept deeply and was for the most part exhausted.

At night I ventured out to fulfil my needs. Firstly to empty my slop bucket and bury the contents. I had another bucket hidden in the undergrowth to gather rainwater and periodically refilled my filtering apparatus from it. This was also how I charged my camera, leaving the solar packs out, hidden as best I could. There wasn't much point other than having something to talk to, that and the hope that if it came to it, the idea of being recorded might save me. An idea that had almost worn away, along with my hope.

I foraged as best I could without light or access to the shoreline. Pickings were slim given the time of the year and the fact that I couldn't go far. I averaged a few mushrooms or handfuls of greenery to add to my ration pile. I did my best not to think of what would happen when those rations ran out. I was already eking them out as much as possible. There was nothing more I could do.

Although there were several long hours in which I could leave the cave, I had to work so slowly that I made little progress on hunting for supplies. In the darkness it was hard to see what I was doing and I also had to move slowly for fear of making noise. Wood, for example, had to be gathered piece by piece from what had fallen on the ground. Each piece had to be pushed through the cave entrance and to the side so I could still get in. Kindling, moss and leaves for cleaning myself, water, food – all took precious time to find and then get into the cave.

Although I now had more clothes to layer and a blanket to keep the draft out, the cave still got very cold at night. I developed swollen, itching chilblains on my hands and feet from going from the freezing cold to the fireside. I'd lost my manicure scissors with the tipi and now had jagged nails, chewed down or cut with my penknife. I was also unable to wash for fear of wasting precious water. Living in a dirt cave made any attempts to keep clean moot anyway. I got used to finding beetles and spiders in my hair, millipedes on my clothes. They crawled over me while I slept and I was too exhausted to bat them away. In the perpetual darkness I lived in I probably ate more than a few by accident.

During the long waking hours spent trapped inside,

I tried to read. At this point I could practically recite every page of my one novel from memory. More often than not I found myself coming out of a kind of trance, just staring into the fire. Sometimes I heard sounds that couldn't possibly be there: a PC booting up, a phone ringing, a car driving past. I decided it was probably birds imitating other sounds. Though it happened even in the dead of night.

There was a relief in getting outside. The fear of discovery and the tension of being as silent as possible were still nerve-shredding, but the feel of fresh air and the openness of the starry sky were my only pleasures. As much as I was afraid of being trapped on the island, I couldn't blame the place itself for that. After all, Buidseach was my only ally, my protector. I sheltered within it, I fuelled my fire and myself with what it provided. Sometimes, when I tried to sleep in the small hours, I found myself talking out loud as if the cave walls could hear me. I whispered my inner thoughts to the roots and the cobwebs and the sighing wind.

Sometimes I wished the walls could talk back as I thought they'd done before, the words coming in on the wind. If I was going to be trapped on Buidseach I could use someone to talk to. Anyone with a friendly face. If just one of the others had been cast out with me, things would be so different. I'd be so much less alone. At times I would have even settled for the fabled witch. Anyone. Anyone at all.

*

One night I chanced heading a little further from camp. It was unavoidable; I needed wood and there was simply none to be found around my cave anymore, save small sticks that burned for mere minutes. I was also in need of more spruce to make into tea. The needles provided crucial vitamin C, something I was desperate for.

I took with me only the essentials: my penknife on a string lanyard, a canvas bag and my rucksack to carry wood home with me. I crept out into the night and took a few breaths of clear, cold air. The ground was frozen hard as iron and the chill cut like glass. Frost furred the trees and rimed the fallen leaves. My breath rose in dense white clouds and the woods were still and quiet. It was as beautiful as it was formidable.

With the cave to my back I started to walk uphill. I went quietly but didn't bother to keep my head down. It had become fairly obvious that no one was looking for me at night. In fact I'd not heard anyone in the woods near me for a while. Perhaps they also felt the teeth in the cold wind. They were looking inwards to their fire and food supplies.

When I reached the top of the hill I rooted around for pieces of fallen branch and log. Most of it was riddled with rot and woodworm but it would burn fine after a bit of drying. I started to fill my rucksack, fixated on my task. Getting it done as soon as possible meant returning to the safety of my cave.

When I had as much wood as possible packed up, I turned to gathering spruce. Using my penknife on the wiry branches I cut sprigs of needles and dropped them into my canvas bag. The scent was lovely, fresh, after the fusty cave and my own unwashed self. I cut as much as I could, until the bag was bristling with sharp-smelling needles.

Through a gap in the trees I saw the moon. It wasn't full, but the thinnest sliver of bone-white in the sky. Around it the stars really did seem to twinkle. A vivid memory came to me of going on holiday, leaving for the six-hour drive in the small hours. As my dad dragged suitcases to the car and Mum asked endless questions in a hushed voice, I had stood in the street and looked up. The stars had been like a show just for me, a secret for those awake when the world slept. I'd spun and spun, looking up, until Mum ushered me into the car. Even inside, I'd pressed my face to the cold glass and looked up until each star was swallowed by dawn.

The stars blurred and I realised I was crying. My eyes welling up as I travelled back so many years to a time when I had been warm and safe and loved. I was lost. So much so that I didn't hear the footsteps until it was too late.

I realised I wasn't alone only when someone said my name, alarmingly close.

'Maddy?'

I whirled around, recognising from the voice that it was Shaun. He was across the clearing, maybe twenty paces away. I struggled to make out more than his outline in the shadows. As if he knew this he took a step forward into the clearing.

Even in the washed-out light of the moon he looked haggard. His cheeks were dark hollows, exaggerated by the shadows. His beard was still patchy but longer and unkempt and there was a rip in his orange jacket that had been crudely sewn up with blue nylon cord. Over his shoulder was a length of string with a rabbit on each end, hanging by the foot. In one hand he carried a folding spade.

'Where were you?' he asked, voice hushed, as if I'd just appeared, like a magic trick.

I was frozen, staring. I'd worried about this moment for weeks and here I was, confronted by another person. I couldn't move, yet when he took a step forwards my body jerked back without my input. It felt like I was two separate things, my mind and my body. While my brain floundered the rest of me acted on instinct.

'Maddy . . . Stop,' Shaun said, holding up one hand. My eyes were on the other though, the one with the sharp-edged shovel.

I shook my head, taking another step back. I saw his hand tighten on the handle, raising the spade.

'Maddy!'

I ran. In the second before I turned around I saw Shaun start to run towards me. Then it was a chase. He thundered after me, crashing through the frosty plants and stumbling over the holes and gullies the rain had left. He was shouting, I didn't know what. I heard my name but the rest I just couldn't process. My blood was deafening me, hammering in my ears.

Halfway back to the cave I realised where I was

heading. Forcing my brain into gear I turned to the left. Shaun was too close behind. I couldn't lead him straight to my shelter. Instead I hurtled downhill. As I approached the treeline I realised my mistake. Beyond it was the rocky beach and the tidal pools, then nothing but sea. A dead end.

Shaun was still behind me, I wasn't sure how close. Had his shouting brought the others running? Were they surrounding me even now? I had no idea. I couldn't get away. I grabbed at my penknife where it bounced against my chest, tugging the string over my head. With it in my hand I flicked it open and prepared to fight. I stood almost no chance but there were no other options.

I was almost at the treeline, sliding down the edge of a sheer drop. The idea came to me to break out into the open and then charge back at Shaun. Perhaps he'd been too surprised to do anything. I could get round him and back into the woods to hide somewhere.

Then from behind me came a yell, a series of thuds and silence.

My legs carried me a few more paces before I could convince them to stop. When I did I realised my legs were shaking and my breath was sawing in and out of my lungs. My chest burnt and I staggered, aware of my own exhaustion.

About a hundred metres behind me, almost hidden in a gully, was Shaun. He was sprawled on the ground, not moving. For a moment I considered running. If he was winded, I could get away. But he wasn't moving at all and that felt wrong. Very wrong. I crept over to him.

I was alert for any sign of movement, but Shaun didn't so much as twitch. Once I was within a few metres I saw why. There was a steep drop on that part of the hill, down into the crater where a tree had been uprooted. I'd come down the slope to the side of it, but Shaun had apparently not seen it and fallen straight down. He was lying in the hole left by the fallen tree, his head and arm the only parts to have landed over the edge. It looked like he'd been knocked out when he fell, hitting his jaw on the raised edge of the hole.

'Shaun?' I whispered. I couldn't leave him unconscious in the freezing night. I knelt and reached out to touch his shoulder, pushing at him. His head rolled on his neck. Something was wrong with the movement, it was too loose, lolling too far. I flinched back.

With careful fingers I found his throat under the layers of coat and scarf. The skin was hot and sweating from the chase, but there was no pulse. I gasped out a plume of icy breath, no answering cloud rose from Shaun's parted lips. He was dead. From the way his head moved when I touched it, I thought his neck was probably broken.

The suddenness of Shaun's death, not to mention the chase itself, sent me reeling. It didn't seem real. I shook him, hoping for a response. His head only rolled sickeningly. I cast about, helpless. Then my fingers brushed the fur of the rabbits he'd carried. They were still slightly warm, recently killed. I looked at Shaun's unmoving form and let a partition snap down in my mind. Shaun was dead. I was still alive. If I wanted to stay alive I needed what he no longer had use for.

I pulled the rabbits free of him and slung the string over my shoulder. He'd dropped the folding shovel but I found it on the ground and stuffed it into my bag of spruce, which I'd kept hold of unconsciously, the handles wrapped around my wrist. I was about to check his coat pockets and take his gloves when I heard voices. They weren't in the woods but to my left, along the beach. I looked at the stretch of open ground between the crater and the dense treeline. I was stuck.

'Sounded like this way!' came Andrew's muted cry, echoing out over the sea.

Crouched in the shadow of the trees I saw the three of them – Duncan, Andrew and Gill – all running towards me. Their torches shook as they jogged, sending crazed beams across the beach. As they came closer I saw that Andrew and Duncan also had shovels and Gill had two more rabbits over her shoulder. They'd been hunting by night, digging into warrens to get at the hibernating animals. I thought all of this in a flash. I felt another wave of adrenalin crash over my exhausted body. How could I get out of this alive?

That's when my body did something stupid. While my mind was still whirling, deciding whether to stay frozen and hope no one saw me, or wait for them to see Shaun and escape in the confusion, I felt myself uncoil, leaping to my feet and pelting off across the open ground. Behind me I heard startled yells, then running. After a few moments, as I forced myself uphill, I heard Gill scream. They'd found Shaun's body.

Behind me I heard swearing, shouting, as Duncan and Andrew followed me up the hill into the denser woods. Gill's screams grew fainter. She was still at the beach. I clawed my way uphill, hauling against trees and grabbing fistfuls of frosty plants to pull myself up the steeper parts. Any thought of keeping them away from my cave had flown from my mind. I was filled to the brim with prey instincts to go to ground and hide away.

I made it to the clearing. Ahead of me was the opening to the cave. I threw myself to the ground and pushed the panel inwards, crawling in after it. I heard the crunch of glass and knew my camera was done for. My rucksack, packed with wood, scraped across the tunnel wall as I twisted to the side to accommodate it. One of the rabbits was crushed beneath me. I'd lost my bag of spruce as I ran.

In the outer cave I threw off my rucksack and was twisting around to replace the panel when a hand grabbed my ankle. I screamed, a bloodcurdling sound that for a moment seemed to come from the cave itself and not from me. Then I kicked out and felt my hiking boot connect with flesh. There was a yell and I twisted away, snatching up my penknife and shuffling backwards until my back hit the cave wall.

In the entrance I saw a shadowy shape and then it started to crawl towards me. I brought the penknife down in a frenzy, stabbing at the hands that appeared on the dirt floor. The shape withdrew with a yell and

I sat, holding the knife and feeling blood drip onto my hand from its blade.

I listened, ears pricked against the rushing of my blood. Outside came footsteps; whoever had caught me was being joined by the other pursuer. Then I heard Andrew swear.

'That bitch fucking stabbed me!'

'Where?' Duncan said.

'Look!'

'Fuck! She in there?'

'Yeah. There's a hole, some kind of burrow down there. Can't get in though, she's like a fucking animal with that knife.'

'And she already killed Shaun.'

'I didn't!' The words flew out of me without thought. 'He fell! I swear to God he fell!'

There were a few seconds of silence. Then, 'Go get the others. They need to know what she did,' Duncan said.

A moan slipped through my lips as despair flooded me. They were going to tell Zoe I'd killed her boyfriend, the father of her baby. Would she believe me if I told her it was an accident? Not with the others there, not once Gill and the rest had poured their poison in her ear the whole way up from camp.

'What about her?' Andrew said.

'We've got her cornered,' Duncan said grimly. 'She's not going anywhere.'

Chapter 31

'Do you feel responsible?'

For the first time, I sense judgement under her tone. Up until now, Rosie has been sweet and conciliatory. Full of appeasing platitudes like 'Oh, how awful for you' and 'That must have been devastating'. But now we are coming to the razorblade under all that coating. Am I responsible?

'I think, out of everything that happened, I feel the worst about Shaun,' I say, truthfully. 'In the moment I was running for my life, I didn't have the luxury of rational thought. It was instinct, and instinct isn't clever. It's not reasoned or logical. It's just what your body tells you to do to keep it safe. Sometimes survival comes at the cost of pain – to you or someone else.'

'Do you think Shaun was trying to catch you then? That he wasn't looking for your help, for Zoe, but to bring you to Duncan?' Rosie asks.

'I don't know. I don't want to make that choice for him, not when he can't defend himself,' I say, feeling her eyes crawling over my face, hungry for something to sink her perfect teeth into. I hold firm against her, answering only what I can live with. What I can honestly believe.

'When I look back, I'm not sure Shaun knew himself what he was going to do. Maybe he needed my help, or he wanted to please Duncan. Maybe he didn't know yet and it was just his instinct that told him to catch me, work the rest out later. When it comes down to it, we'll never know, will we? I'm here, and he's not.'

Chapter 32

I heard Andrew leave. As his footsteps faded away, Duncan sighed and there was a rustling as he sat on the ground. When he spoke, his voice was frighteningly close. Only a few feet separated us. He sounded so normal, just as he had done all those months ago when we first met; friendly, gracious.

'Well, Maddy . . . look where we are now. You led us a merry chase, didn't you?'

My mouth was dry. I said nothing but tightened my hold on the penknife. It seemed ludicrously small and inoffensive. How much good would it do me when the seven of them came with shovels to dig me out? None whatsoever.

'Not so talkative now, are you?' Duncan said, cutting into my thoughts. 'Surprising really, you've always had such a lot to say for yourself.'

'What are you going to do to me?' My voice was a rasp. I sounded like a wizened crone.

'I don't know, Maddy, what were you going to do to

us? I mean you did poison us, maybe even the camera guys too. You steal food, you hoard supplies that we desperately need . . . and now you've killed Shaun. Did you expect to just get away with that?'

'He fell.'

'Or you pushed him, hmm? You expect us to believe he just fell down and died? And what about the generator, huh? The emergency phone? Did you sabotage them as well?'

'I haven't done anything!' My voice cracked like a dead leaf under a boot. 'It was one of you – you poisoned them!'

'I don't think you know what you've been doing. I mean, I only saw you for a second there, but you look mental. Living in this hole out here. Why? Because you thought we were going to kill you?' He laughed, like he was amused by the stupid antics of a child. 'Really? You honestly thought we would kill you – over what? A book? Jesus Christ.'

'You burned down my tipi.'

'You weren't in it, were you? We were blowing off steam. You really pissed us off. What did you expect? Being so difficult. So selfish.'

He sounded so sure, so casually amused. Was he right? Had I just read too much into their actions, seen murderous intent where there was just anger, scared myself with my own paranoia? I thought of the sounds I heard when I was alone, sounds of the mainland. I thought of the voice that had come to me in the cave. Was I losing my mind? My theory about the mainland catastrophe, some kind of event or series of disasters that had wiped out our production team as well as any who cared for us and left us stranded. Was that really something a sane person would come up with? I felt dizzy and sick. The exhaustion from the chase was crashing down on me. For the first time I wasn't sure of my decisions, my course of action.

'Why don't you come out and talk to me properly?' Duncan said softly, like I was a frightened cat to be coaxed from under an armchair. 'This is just silly, isn't it? We can go back to the camp and get some tea, talk about this like adults.'

I reached forwards, shifting my weight and inching closer to the cave entrance. It was almost involuntary. I felt hypnotised, calm for the first time in weeks, months. In my head I saw Duncan as he'd been on that first day, clean and ordinary and sparkling with adventure and excitement. Everything had been all right then. Perhaps it was all right now.

The arrival of the others broke the spell. One moment it was just me and Duncan and his voice, the next came shouts and swearing and Zoe's sobbing voice screaming.

'Maddy! Where are you? Get out here and look what you did, look what you did to him!' She dissolved into noisy wails.

At that moment Duncan's hand appeared in the darkness, snatching at my ankle. I screamed and slashed at it with the knife, felt the blade meet flesh. He swore and snatched his hand away.

'Fucking mad bitch! Gill was right – we should've knocked you out and dumped you in the sea!'

I backed up and held the knife ready. I guessed that Gill had run back for the others as soon as she saw Shaun and they'd met Andrew on the way back. He hadn't been gone long enough to make it all the way to camp. If they'd taken longer, I might have listened to Duncan. I might have left the cave.

'Go away!' I screamed.

'You murdered him!' Zoe wailed, choking and spluttering on tears and snot. 'You killed him. Oh God, oh my God, he's gone . . .'

I heard Maxine muttering something, probably trying to comfort her. Then Gill piped up with a voice sharp and cold as the night.

'How do we get her out of there, Duncan? She needs to pay for this.'

'Could dig her out,' came Frank's voice, too loud and slurred. 'Dig her out like a stump.' He laughed.

'What do we do with her then?' This was Maxine. The words might have made me hope for a rational voice, but she sounded speculative, excited. 'If she killed Shaun we can't just let her walk around free.'

Frightened tears welled in my eyes and I put my hand over my mouth to muffle any sounds that might escape me. What were they going to do to me? An image came to me of a rope slung over a tree branch, my body swaying and twitching as they cheered and drank below. I started to shake uncontrollably.

'Get over there, she's listening,' Duncan said.

I heard their footsteps retreating and then the low murmur of indistinct discussion. If hearing them had been frightening, not knowing what they were planning filled me with terror. I was blinded with it.

Casting about for a way to defend myself I started pushing my rucksack through the gap into the inner cave. My hatchet was in there as well as the larger knife I used for cooking. The opening was smaller. The wall made of stone. I could hold them at bay in there. I was shaking so much that I knocked my head on the wall as I groped my way inside. Once in the inner cave I snatched up my kitchen knife and brought the hatchet close to me. If they wanted to hunt me like a cornered animal I would fight like one.

I heard them return. There was a sound like something being dragged along the ground. Something heavy. I had only a few seconds to wonder what that could mean before a bale of burning weeds was thrust into the cave, filling it with smoke.

Panic ripped at me as my eyes watered and I started to cough. Were they trying to smoke me out? The weeds started to burn and crackle merrily. I had to put them out or risk the fire reaching me and my wood store. I fumbled for a blanket. Getting back into the outer cave the rock scraped my face and arm, I was too afraid to go carefully. I threw the blanket and started slapping at it, smothering the flames. There were sounds outside, voices shouting. I'd dropped my knife in the darkness. Fear flared as the fire died out. I was defenceless.

Then came an impact, right outside the entrance. I

jumped, skittering back. My hands were like blind spiders as I clawed around for something, anything, to use as a weapon. I found nothing.

More sounds from outside, thumping and scraping. Were they digging their way inside? I shrank back against the wall, frozen. Any thought of finding my knife or hiding away had flown. I stared into the pitch black and waited for the stars to replace the earth above me.

Then, all at once, the noises stopped. Outside there were voices, curiously muffled. Zoe was still crying but there was also shouting and cheers. They were pleased about something. Duncan's voice suddenly came out of the darkness. It was muffled, like the others.

'Well, Maddy, I hope you feel safe now.'

There was laughter, even as Zoe wailed in grief.

'Everyone back to camp,' Duncan said. 'Frank, come help me with Shaun.'

'What about her?' Gill said.

'Andrew?' Duncan asked.

'Fine. If someone brings me some breakfast and a flask first thing.'

'Maxine, bring Andrew his breakfast when it gets light.' Duncan yawned. 'Let's get to fucking bed.'

Their footsteps moved away. As soon as they did I shot forwards, feeling for the entrance to the cave. I had to know what they'd done. My hands met rotting wood and soil where there should have been only air. I scrabbled at it, feeling for a space but there was none. With fear choking me I forced myself to feel around

306

the blockage. Most of the barrier was wood. It felt like a log or stump that had been dragged over, pushed into the entryway. Around it was soil. They must have banked dirt over the barrier to hold it in place and seal me in.

I was trapped.

My breathing came quick and shallow. I realised I was hyperventilating and threw myself at the barrier, tearing at it. I had to get out. I'd only been digging with my hands for a few seconds before I heard Andrew's laugh and stopped dead.

'Come on out then. Give me an excuse to bash your skull in.'

I shrank away, covered my mouth with both hands and started to cry. With my back to the wall I laid down, suddenly boneless. The taste of damp, living earth got into my mouth along with the salt of my tears.

They'd buried me alive. I was trapped in the cave, the acrid smoke still lingering around me, burning my throat as it slowly oozed out through the crack into the inner caves I couldn't reach. Even if I could dig my way out, Andrew was there, waiting. There was no escape.

The events of the night pressed down on me like so much rock and soil. The stars, the chase and Shaun, poor Shaun. He was really dead. Dead because of me. If I'd only kept my wits about me he never would have seen me. He never would have chased me off that ledge.

Zoe's heartbroken wails echoed in my mind. At the

time I'd been so afraid I couldn't look past my own immediate survival but in the darkness those cries came to me again and again. I was the reason she'd lost him. I had taken her partner and protector. She was alone now. Endangered by my careless stupidity.

Lying on the ground I felt lower than a worm. Had I not almost given in and gone to Duncan? All this time I'd thought myself capable and strong, but I was weak, weaker than all of them. They were the survivors. They had supplies, shelter and strength in numbers. I was the one lying in a filthy den with snot dripping down my dirty face. They'd beaten me, locked me away and now I was helpless.

I started to sob and dropped my filthy hands from my face. The sounds of my despair filled the cave but if I had hoped for mercy, none was forthcoming. Andrew did not speak again and I wept until I exhausted myself into sleep.

Chapter 33

'How good are you in a crisis?' Sasha had asked. 'How do you manage?'

'I'm not sure I understand,' I'd said, stumped for the first time by one of Sasha's endless questions. 'You mean . . . an emergency? What kind?'

'Well . . . let's say, one of the group gets hurt. You're the only one with them. What would you do?'

'I suppose I'd make sure they weren't in immediate danger and go get some help,' I'd said, remembering a first-aid course I'd attended years before, long since out of date. Sasha had said they were going to send me on a refresher, but parts of it still stuck with me. 'Or, if I can't leave them, I could shout until one of the others came looking.'

Sasha had nodded vaguely. 'OK, now, what if it's you that's hurt? And you're all on your own. What would you do?'

I'd thought about it. I already lived alone, though obviously there was always an ambulance on the other end of the phone if I needed one. But what about those nights when I wasn't injured, but still hurt? When I came in from work feeling so beaten down, so filled with self-loathing that I could only crawl into bed and cry. Who was there to help me when I was hurt, but myself?

'I'd have to rely on myself,' I'd said. 'The things I know how to do, the skills I have. I'd keep myself calm, maybe talk to myself if that helped – and I would get through it.'

'Sounds like you have some experience with life-or-death situations,' Sasha had said.

'Not really,' I'd said, remembering the stilted voice of an anonymous police officer telling me he was very sorry. It was a bad road, icy. That far into the countryside they never gritted, never repaired. The car was old. My parents likely died on impact, didn't suffer. He'd asked if I needed him to contact anyone else. I said no, held myself afterwards and cried out for a mother I was never going to see again.

'I just have a good imagination.'

*

I woke with the taste of mud and smoke in my mouth. Without lifting my head I knew where I was. I wasn't blessed with even a moment of unreality. This was my reality now.

Sitting up, I felt every part of me protest. The chase both up and down hill, followed by the scuffle and a night on the ground in the cold, had stiffened me up. I felt like a wooden dummy. My fingers were raw from clawing my way up slopes and digging at packed soil. One of my nails was torn and hanging off, I felt it trailing on my cheek as I wiped at my sticky eyes. My face was stiff and sore, plastered in dried tears, dirt and mucus. I felt pitiful.

With wakefulness, however, came an awareness of hunger and cold. My body forced me to focus on the present. My situation was no longer new and terrible, merely terrible. I still needed to eat, to warm myself.

Without the small amount of daylight let in by the panel, both caves were now equally dark. At least it wasn't airtight; a faint breeze came from both the smoke hole and through the dirt at the door. I'd let my fire die before venturing out the previous night. Now I struggled to get it going in the pitch blackness. My torch was somewhere but finding it in the chaos I'd made while snatching up weapons and blankets was a task I wasn't equal to. I dragged the half-burnt bale of weeds to my fire hole and got them going again, adding splinters of wood until a merry blaze rose up. With its light I put my living space to rights, found my torch and breakfasted on a half-full tin of plum tomatoes, warmed in the flames.

With some food in me I stripped off the camera harness and found that the lens had indeed been caved in as I crawled into the cave. A stone or something had been forced through by my weight. It was useless now, but then, it had been useless since that day on the beach. I just hadn't known it then; how little a record mattered if we were never found.

With a spare sock and some water, I made the best attempt I could at cleaning my face and hands. My clothes were filthy, but I didn't have the energy to change. My hair, already tangled from doing without a hairbrush for weeks, was matted with twigs and leaves. I scraped the mass up into the semblance of a bun, secured it with an elastic band and picked out the worst of the debris.

That done I was out of distractions. It was time to face my situation, starting with the water. Like wood and foraged food it had to be brought in from outside. Unlike wood and forage, I would die within days if I ran out. In my collapsible water container I had roughly two litres of filtered and boiled water. The collecting bucket I'd brought in yesterday evening had about two inches of rainwater in the bottom. I was not in immediate danger of running out. Still, I was worried. How would I get water now that I was trapped inside? There was no way I could dig down far enough to get at the groundwater.

Wood was less of an issue. I'd been collecting nightly and, counting last night's haul, I had enough to last a while. Hopefully the weather would be getting warmer and I'd not need to have the fire so built up. I laughed, making myself jump; now that the entrance was sealed up the cave would be easier to heat.

The food issue was second to water. I had a bit of food from the portacabin, but my stocks of dried and smoked forage were long gone. Without access to the outside I was stuck eating what I had on hand. Dropping my bag of spruce had been a mistake. I didn't have another source of vitamin C. I would just have to hope I could get by until . . .

I stopped short, mental calculations faltering. Until what? Rescue? Was rescue even coming? If it did how would they ever find me in a hole underground? I tried to picture the boat finally turning up, Adrian skidding on the beach in his ludicrous shoes. The image didn't ring true. No, I couldn't see that happening. I knew deep down that something had gone very wrong. If we were going to be rescued it would be by strangers. Strangers who wouldn't know I was one of the islanders. Would the others tell them about me if help came? No, of course they wouldn't. That would mean admitting that they'd shut me in to starve to death.

Panic started to build in my chest. No one was going to find me if I stayed in the cave. Yet if I could somehow escape the others would get me. They had left Andrew to stand guard, perhaps he'd since been relieved by someone else. I had no idea what time it was or if it was day or night outside. If I dug my way out I would be seen immediately. I couldn't be rescued while in the cave but equally, I couldn't be beaten or murdered either. After last night I had no doubts about what being captured meant. If they could seal me up and leave me to starve, they could kill me directly just as easily.

The cave then was the only option, but I had limited food and water. What happened when that ran out? I would die, obviously. I forced myself to take deep breaths in an attempt to control my rising panic. There seemed to be no way forward, no way out of the mess I was in. I was being watched, escape was impossible, but staying in the cave indefinitely wasn't possible either. I needed a plan as much for my own sanity as anything else. I had to have a course of action to follow, to give me something to hope for.

They'd given up looking for me before. I'd heard them searching for a week or so after I moved into the cave. After that there had been next to nothing. The occasional movement in the woods as someone passed by, nothing at all for a while. They had lost interest. Concerns like hunger and the cold, not to mention looking for rescue, had taken precedence.

Perhaps the same thing would happen again. I couldn't imagine anyone volunteering to spend days out in the woods, keeping watch over a dirt hill in the cold and spring rains. It would be lonely, dull and uncomfortable. Sooner or later they'd decide I wasn't worth guarding and leave me for dead. I just had to outlast their attention.

My panicked heart rate eased. I could do that. All I had to do was make the food I had last and find some way to get a bit of water. A few weeks, that's all it would take. Then I could dig a new way out of the cave and come and go as before. By then spring would be in full swing and forage readily available. I just had to last a few more weeks.

I didn't let myself think further than getting out of

the cave. There was no point in considering rescue or my theories about the mainland. I looked only as far as my next action. I couldn't bear to look further.

I had two immediate concerns; water and what to do with the rabbits. Shortly after I'd cleaned myself I discovered a third problem – the slop bucket. I'd emptied it the night before but now I had nowhere to dispose of the contents of my bucket latrine.

I had enough water for a few days at least so I got started on the latrine issue first. I would have to bury it inside. I lived in the inner cave so the outer cave would have to be my toilet area. With my folding shovel I dug a hole into the matted roots of the floor. The shovel was more suited to hobbyist metal detecting and not very sturdy. Using it for months in the allotment and latrine digging had blunted it. I gouged at the dirt with the dull blade anyway. It took ages but eventually the hole was about two feet deep. The soil went into the toilet bucket, to be dumped on top of the hole after use. Disgusting, but effective.

I tried not to think about how long it would take me to dig my way out of the cave.

Next, the rabbits. I had managed to hang on to both of the ones I'd taken from Shaun, somehow. One was slightly flattened from being under me as I crawled. Both were dirty. They'd still been warm when I'd taken them so I guessed they were fresh enough to eat if I did so quickly.

With my dynamo torch propped up I moved close to the fire so I could see more clearly. Maxine and

Shaun had always been the ones to prepare the rabbits for cooking. My only experience with skinning was cutting the stuff off of chicken thighs. I'd only ever gutted a fish before. Once.

I ended up with a fairly mangled pile of meat. It was piled up in my billycan, glistening in the flames. Some of it was still on the bones; jointing the animals hadn't been easy. In the end I'd settled for cutting pieces of meat free. The guts, organs and skins I'd piled into my latrine hole and covered over with dirt. I wiped the blood from my hands with the damp sock and discarded it into the hole.

Deciding how to cook the meat was the next step. Dimly I was remembering a book I'd read once. Not a guide or anything, just a novel. There had been starving people and they'd poached a deer from somewhere. The rich meat made them sick after so long without proper food. They had to make soup instead and eat slowly. So I made soup, poaching the meat in a little water with salt and juice from the tinned tomatoes. I ate slowly. I barely tasted it.

I ate that soup for the next few days. On one of those days it rained heavily. I could tell because drips started to come through the roof of the cave. Using the torch I found the place where the water was coming through and scraped at it with my shovel. Soon a thin stream of muddy water was pitting the dirt floor. I put my water bucket underneath and draped a cloth over the top to filter out the worst of the soil. As long as there was rain, I would have water.

In between making these little adjustments to my new existence I sat by the blocked entrance and listened. I wanted to know what was going on outside. Not just the other islanders, but anything at all that wasn't my own thoughts, my own breathing. I could only hear the heaviest rain and no birdsong or creaking of the pines could penetrate the dense earth.

After a few days I thought I'd worked out the pattern of my guards. The people on watch seemed to change regularly, I assumed by day and by night. It always seemed to be a pair by day. I could hear them talking. I guessed when day was as that was the period in which someone else visited regularly, presumably to bring food. The voices changed; Andrew and Duncan, Andrew and Frank. Maxine. I couldn't see them delivering meals, so assumed they were the guards and Maxine brought them food.

Night was the quieter time. Although there was talking several times a day when food came, there were no voices at night. I only knew someone was there by the occasional sneeze or the crack of a hatchet as wood was cut for the fire. I had no idea who watched the cave at night. It seemed like only one person from the lack of talking, but it could easily have been two people taking turns to sleep.

I judged the days and nights by this cycle of voices. As each cycle completed, I marked off another day in my old diary, re-crossing our days on the island.

Listening to them was my main occupation. I had to keep track of how closely they were watching me.

Eventually I hoped to hear nothing at all. Once that happened, I could start digging my way out of the cave.

After the first night, when Andrew had threatened me through the blockade, no one spoke to me directly. They spoke about me sometimes, but as if I was an animal that couldn't understand them. Mostly they speculated on what supplies I had and how long they'd last. Other times they whispered and I supposed they were talking about the camp and their own troubles. Or planning on how to get into the cave. Stuff they didn't want me to hear. Sometimes they forgot to whisper, or were too intoxicated to bother. I had no idea how much fly agaric they'd managed to find and dry, but it seemed from the periods of raised voices and merriment they were using it regularly, even when on watch.

One night, five days after I was shut in, I heard Duncan say, 'What are we going to do about Zoe? She's driving me up the fucking wall.'

I'd been filling in the latrine, but I stopped to listen. Talking at night was unusual. The guard had changed only a short while before. I guessed it was dark but not late enough for sleep.

'I know. Christ, she wants to get herself together.' That was Andrew. 'I mean, yeah, it's sad Shaun's dead but we've got bigger shit to be worried about at the moment. Where the fuck is that boat?'

'No fucking clue. But she's not doing herself any favours carrying on like she is. I mean, we're the ones trying to keep everything together. We're the ones making sure there's food and wood and water. What's she doing? Nothing. She just sleeps and cries. She's like a fucking baby.'

'And what about that baby? She doesn't look like she's getting any bigger.'

'Reckon it was a put-on to get Shaun to stay interested in her?'

'Maybe.'

I bit my lip. If they were right and Zoe wasn't showing signs of her advancing condition, it meant one of three things: she'd been mistaken, she'd miscarried – whether by design or by chance – or she was so malnourished things weren't developing as they should. The first didn't seem likely. She'd been so sure the last time we spoke. If she was still pregnant and not getting enough food she'd be in danger of not having enough nutrients for her and the baby. Leaching her strength until she had nothing left, and they both wasted away.

There was silence for a while and I almost left them to it, thinking they were done. Then Duncan spoke again, quietly. 'Do you think Gill's right?'

'About the camera guys, you mean?'

'Yeah.'

There was a short silence. 'Maybe? Gill's got some pretty funny ideas about stuff. Not exactly the brightest bulb, is she?'

'She's a dense fucking cow, but that's not the point,' Duncan said. 'She reckons Maddy did something to those camera guys, poisoned them.'

'Maybe.'

'. . . She said it was one of us.'

'Maddy did?'

'Yeah . . . Before you guys came, she was ranting about how it was one of us, that we gave those blokes poison mushrooms,' Duncan said, slowly, like he was actually thinking about what I'd said. I held my breath, straining to hear what came next.

'Why'd we do that?' Andrew said. 'Makes no sense.'

'Dunno. Probably she was just making stuff up so we'd leave her alone, fight amongst ourselves. I mean, if one of us had given them mushrooms we'd have said so by now, right? I mean, we've all been sitting around trying to work out what's going on. Someone would have said.'

'Probably was her. And now there's Shaun . . . When we do get out of here no one's going to believe a word she says. They'll probably arrest her.'

'Yeah . . . supposing we get out of here.'

I strained my ears in the silence that followed, almost thinking they'd let the conversation lapse. Then Andrew spoke again.

'It has to be something more than just weather or cost delays. They'd have drummed up enough cash to get us by now, or got the authorities in. What if . . .' Andrew continued, then stopped.

'Yeah?'

'What if . . . there's no authorities? What if . . . something's happened out there?'

'Like what?' Duncan said, contemplative. 'A war?'

320

'Maybe.'

'With who?'

'Take your pick. We've been here over a year. We don't know what might have happened back home. What if there's been some kind of regime change or the government's collapsed? The oil could've run out or some kind of superbug—'

'Crackpot.'

'Am I?' Andrew said. 'The world's a fragile fucking place. When I was working at the city farm we did all these campaigns about factory farming. All those chemicals and antibiotics they pump into the animals to keep them from rotting alive in those cages. We eat that shit. Air's polluted, water's poisoned. Sea levels rising, flooding, storms. GMOs and mad cow. It's a race to see what gets us first. What if something has?'

There was a long silence. I had to agree with Andrew, at least in part. There were many things that could have happened in our absence. He did seem way off the mark with some of them though. I thought of biological weapons, nuclear fallout, chemical gas, and shivered. Was that better or worse than what I'd envisioned? Was any of it better than the rest?

'And you reckon she knows what's happened, do you?' Duncan said. 'How?'

'I'm not saying she for sure knows something we don't but . . . she's not stupid. Maybe she's looking at the same things we are and she thinks, hey, something's fucked up out there . . . She's not tried to get out.'

'We're guarding her.'

'All right,' Andrew countered, 'but even before that. She didn't try getting away, swimming for it or . . .'

'That's basically suicide. Do you not remember how long it took us to get here on the boat? Even if we built a bloody raft we'd never reach the shore.'

Andrew made a frustrated sound. 'I know! My point is, she hasn't tried to get away, or signal for help or do anything but sit in that hole.'

'So?'

'So . . . maybe she thinks there's no point. No one to come save her, nowhere to go because there's nothing out there.'

Duncan seemed to have nothing to say to that. There was no more talk and after a while I went to the inner cave to bank the fire and got into my nest of a bed. Sleep was even more elusive than usual.

I kept thinking about what Duncan had said: that whoever was responsible for the poisoning would have said something. I didn't agree, mostly because I knew what it was like to be scared that the whole group would turn on you. But surely if whoever it was had made some kind of trade, the others would have noticed that they suddenly had more food, or illicit booze. Most of them had been stealing from the stash together, sharing their ill-gotten gains. If it was Gill, she'd have gone to Duncan like a loyal dog with her prize in hand.

Something else had been bothering me. Fly agaric was very distinctive, red with white scales, the classic fairy-tale toadstool. There wasn't really anything similar enough to it, to be taken for fly agaric. Certainly not anything like the destroying angel, which was mostly white. To have mixed the two up wouldn't just be a matter of stupidity – it was nearly impossible to do so by accident.

Then there was the accidental poisoning that had hit everyone at camp. Whoever had the page would have known what fly agaric looked like and what it could do, but they had all eaten it anyway, aside from Frank and Zoe. Why allow that to happen unless whoever it was had something to hide, something that made it too dangerous to reveal they knew anything about mushrooms? Like the murder of two people. Had Zoe or Frank been responsible? Shaun had only eaten enough to get a bit high; had he known not to overindulge? Gill was the first to throw up; had she done it on purpose to purge the toxins before they metabolised? My mind swam with explanations and accusations. Was I being paranoid, or was something not adding up?

What if it wasn't some accident by someone too greedy or stupid to pick the right mushrooms? What if it had all been completely intentional? Pass off lethal mushrooms for hallucinogenic ones. They looked much the same when chopped and dried after all. Easy to use one side of the page to find destroying angel, the other side to convince the camera guys that it was fly agaric.

Only there had to be a reason. The cameramen had been killed before we ever even knew the boat wasn't coming. Why kill them? What did it achieve? What could make someone poison two strangers and leave them to die? More importantly, who had done it and what would they do now that they were trapped, fighting for survival? If they were willing to kill seemingly at random, what would they do for the last bit of food? The slim hope of survival?

Andrew's words kept going round and around in my head.

Nowhere to go.

Nothing out there.

What gets us first.

Suicide.

I'd heard someone say once that 'suicide is a permanent solution to a temporary problem'. I was willing to bet that person had not been trapped on an island with a murderer and no hope of escape. It was not the first time that killing myself had occurred to me. There had been moments, fractions of seconds where I'd looked at my penknife and thought about just letting go, throwing the fight for survival. But it was no sure thing. I couldn't think of ending it without picturing myself, hurt but not dead, weakened, easy prey. I didn't want to make myself more vulnerable than I already was.

Whatever Andrew thought, whatever I had imagined, there was still a world out there. My only hope was that it would find us sooner rather than later.

Chapter 34

The time passed, as slowly as I'd ever known it to. My guards didn't seem about to lose interest in me. I heard them come and go every day and at the end of each cycle of changes I crossed the day off in my diary.

On some days it rained. On most it didn't. When the water ran out I sucked a stone to keep my mouth from drying out. When rain came again I had a strange idea that the water was coming out of the dirt itself and not from the outside. I sat and watched it emerge as if it was a miracle.

My stock of wood grew lower each day. I used my blunt shovel to gouge dirt away from the walls and hacked the thicker tree roots with my hatchet. There were only so many but I piled them up and hoped they'd dry out. There was nothing I could do about food except ration it tightly.

I spent the unending hours lying by the entrance, listening. The air in that cave was foul with rotting meat and my own waste, but I had to hear them. I had to hear something. Sometimes I thought they had finally left me alone, but then someone would speak and I'd know they were still out there. The weather would be getting better, no reason not to sit outside and watch me. What else did they have to do?

Without sunlight, fresh air or the sight of stars I felt myself start to close down. While I focused on trying to keep my body fed and warm, my mind began to wander where I could not follow. The noises that I'd heard before – car horns, supermarket tills, dogs barking – were all still there. And the voices. I heard singing, music like from a radio. People talking in the crack at the rear of the cave. A voice telling me to get some rest, that everything would look better in the morning. Sometimes it sounded like my mum. Sometimes it was someone else, the voice from before, telling me I must go on.

I started to see things too. The roof of the cave sparkled with stars or swam with lights like fish in a pond. I saw things mostly when it was fully dark. I tried to keep the fire going as much as possible. Then one night, lying by the small cluster of flames, I saw Shaun's face amongst them.

I recoiled. With the wall of the cave at my back I sat frozen, eyes fixed on his. Shaun peered out at me between the glowing logs and scraps of root fibre. Then he coughed and smoke spiralled upwards.

'Maddy . . .'

'Shaun,' I whispered, voice cracking from disuse. 'What . . .'

'I came to see you,' Shaun said. 'I wanted to ask you why you did this to me?'

'I didn't . . .'

'You ran. If you'd stayed put, I wouldn't have followed you, and I wouldn't be dead.'

'I was scared.'

'You didn't even know what I wanted. How could you be scared?'

'But—'

'I wanted your help, for Zoe. I needed help and you killed me.'

I closed my eyes and shook my head until I felt dizzy. When I opened my eyes again Shaun's nose was an inch from mine, his eyes glowing red as coals.

'You killed me!' he bellowed, making my ears ring.

I screamed and threw myself away from him, crawling to the other side of the cave and curling into a ball. I lay there with my hands over my ears and my eyes squeezed tightly shut. It was a long, long time before the prickling feeling of being watched drove me to look behind me again. For a second, no more than that, I saw someone else by my fire. No more than a shadow, a trick of the flickering fire. It wasn't Shaun, I saw that much. Then the firelight shifted and it was gone.

It was ridiculous, but inside I knew what, or who, I'd seen. The witch from the story, my story. The witch of Buidseach. She was the one speaking to me that night, the one who said I must go on.

I pressed my hands over my eyes and told myself it wasn't real. None of this was real.

But of course the worst parts were.

It occurred to me that the voices outside might be no more real than those in the cave. Perhaps the others had stopped watching me days ago. I spent the next few days listening carefully to reassure myself. They were real. They had to be.

I was in a kind of limbo. As long as I was in the cave they couldn't get me, but eventually I would have to take my chances. To stay was to eventually starve to death. I had to wait. A chance would come, I was certain. What it would look like or when it would arrive, I had no idea. I could only hope that it would be soon and that I would be strong enough to take it.

My food stores grew lower and lower. I was almost used to being tired and hungry all the time. It had been the norm for months. I slept as much as possible and even when awake my mind wandered off for long periods. I could almost ignore the gnawing of my belly, the parch in my throat when the water ran out.

Eventually all I had left was sugar, salt and olive oil. Once I had known the exact amount of calories in white sugar, a product of sharing an office with diet obsessed co-workers. I fell into line with them, popping sweetener tablets into my coffee, eating non-fat yoghurt, cutting doughnuts in half and saying, 'Oh, I really shouldn't . . .' Now the idea of that made me laugh aloud 'til the sound filled the tiny cave and tears rolled down my hollowed cheeks.

When I stopped the walls laughed back, a low cackle. The hair on my neck stood up and I closed my eyes, afraid of what I'd see.

The next day the bulb in my dynamo torch burned out. I shoved the useless bit of plastic in a corner and lost track of it. The walls of the cave were bare of roots and I'd started hacking pieces off of the stump that blocked the door. It was wood after all. I needed to keep the fire going. In the darkness eyes appeared and watched me. Shaun spoke to me. I didn't like the dark. Bit by bit I burned my books as kindling. The forage guide too, not that it mattered anymore. Evidence of some possible crime was worthless. No one was ever going to find us.

When it rained worms wriggled through the dirt roof of the cave. I collected them and crisped them in oil. There weren't enough for a proper meal. I drank sugar-water. I listened and slept. Lifting my head made me dizzy and sick. Voices came and went but the names that went with them wouldn't come to me. I couldn't direct my thoughts anymore, they scurried from me like spiders.

Dimly I realised that I was dying. This idea came to me one day as I watched the lights spin on the ceiling. It should have scared me but instead I felt a kind of relief. The decision was out of my hands now. I didn't have to try and fail at ending my life, nature was going to do it for me.

'Well then, Maddy, looks like I win – doesn't it?'

Of course.

I turned my head slowly to the side. The fire must have gone out, or had been out for days. I couldn't remember the last time I'd had the strength to get up and tend to it. Sitting to the side of me, clean and well-fed, sat Duncan. He held the foraging book and flipped the pages like it was a waiting-room magazine.

I tried to snatch the book before I realised what I was doing. He only laughed and held it away from my weak flailing.

'I have to say I thought you had more in you than' – he waved a hand – 'this.'

'You're not real,' I whispered, partially into the dirt.

'Yes, I am. I'm out there right now, eating and drinking and taking charge. But I'm also in here with you. Because you think this is all my fault.'

'It . . . is.'

'It's not, though. Not really. I mean, I didn't strand us here, did I? And I didn't make the others hate you, blame you. No, you did that with your shitty attitude and by being so fucking inflexible. That's why you're alone in here. It's why you were alone out there – in the real world.'

'No . . .' I muttered.

'Yes. You thought coming here would make you a better person. Less angry, less depressed. But that's all you. You're the one who hates her parents. Bet you were glad when they checked out. But you can't admit that, can you? That you blame them for the way you are. And they were right, weren't they? You have to be protected from everything. Weak little Maddy. Too fragile for school, too sheltered for real life. That's in your head and you brought it here. You can't get away from yourself, Maddy, no matter how hard you try.'

I said nothing, blinked away tears.

'So, like I said, I win. Because I get to be the good guy – the leader, the fucking head honcho and you, you're in here, dying alone like you were always afraid would happen.' He looked up at the ceiling, which was plain dirt again, hidden in shadow. 'You don't deserve this place, how beautiful it can be. And you'll never see it again.'

'No!' It started as a weak denial and ended a shout. I dragged myself into a half-sitting position, glaring at Duncan. He only looked amused.

'I'm not giving up,' I grated out, voice like splintering wood. 'I'm not letting you win.'

'I already have.'

'You can't force me off this island,' I hissed, remembering how I'd promised myself the same thing all those months ago, alone and cast out of the community. 'And you can't force me to die here like an animal.'

'Oh yeah?' He started to fade away like the Cheshire cat, until only his hands were there, waving the book like a child playing keep-away. 'Prove it.'

The words echoed in my head until they were in another voice entirely, raspy as a crow's. I tasted them on my lips.

My hands, like claws, found the dirt wall and I started to dig. I felt sick, my head banging with an intense ache and my limbs shaking, but I dug like it was all I knew how to do. I heard rain as the hole grew. My mud-slick fingers slid over the ragged stump and I carried on. Splattered with dirt I dragged the mud inside, handful by handful, until there was a hole I could wriggle my starved body through.

I slithered onto the ground outside as if being born again. Rain drummed down on me, clean and cold and shocking. I rolled onto my back and let it fall on my face. For a while I could only lie there, drinking down the rain.

All was quiet except the drumming of the water, the patter of leaves.

Slowly, feeling like an old woman, I got to my feet. My legs were shaking and I'd not stood up straight for weeks. There was no room in the cave. Taking a step made me dizzy and I braced myself with a hand on a tree. Although I was under the trees and the sky was cloudy, what little light there was hurt my eyes. In it I could see how filthy I was. My skin was grey with ingrained dirt and newly painted over with mud. My fingernails were black and my hair hung around my shoulders in ratty clumps.

In the small clearing I could see the remnants of a camp. There was a hole with charred wood in it, though green sprouts of grass showed through the wet ashes. A pot hung over it on a tripod of sticks, but one had tipped and the whole thing now hung drunkenly. The pot held only rainwater and leaves from the trees above.

The cold rain cleared my head a little. Being able to see, to hear and smell and feel, chased away the visions.

Everything felt real, more real than anything I'd felt in weeks. I could think and what I thought made bile rise in my throat.

I staggered into the trees. There was a path worn through the undergrowth. My guards had passed this way often enough to leave a trail. I slipped and slid as I made my unsteady way through the forest.

There was an incline down a flinty slope and I stumbled then fell. At the bottom I fought to collect my scattered wits. Getting up took me a few minutes. With the help of a stick from the forest floor I carried on. It was not the last time I fell. My legs seemed not to belong to me and I lost my footing a lot on the slick ground. I could feel my energy leaving me with every step. What little grit I'd mustered to get out of the cave was spent. I knew that before too long I'd fall and not be able to get up. But I couldn't stop. I had to see for myself.

At last, as night began to creep in, I arrived at the camp. I couldn't calculate how long I'd been walking. It felt like a year. Details of my surroundings passed me by. I had eyes only for the hut, which was quiet, and its smoke hole, which was clear. The side wall of the hut had gaps in it, charred sticks stuck up like bones.

Inside the walls were scorched, ashes and charred logs scattered on the floor. All around were discarded clothes, pans crusted in mould, mildewed sleeping bags.

They were gone.

That was when my legs finally gave out. Sprawled

on the ground with their discarded rubbish, I screamed until I laughed and laughed until it turned to sobbing. When my vision turned to dancing pinpricks it was almost a relief. I felt myself blacking out and let it happen.

Only the thought that I might not wake up consoled me.

Chapter 35

By some awful miracle I didn't die in my sleep. Or so I saw it at the time. Had I known how close I was to rescue, I might have fought harder, clung to life. As it was, I had no reason to think I was anything but doomed.

Whatever strength I'd had was spent in reaching the camp. I found I couldn't get to my feet at all. The knowledge that the others were gone hit me again. The injustice of it filled me with a surge of anger so murderous it scared me. While I'd been losing my mind, they'd been saved. While I had starved, they'd been freed from the island. Despair and rage coursed through me. My emotions were as unstable as the rest of me, swinging from one extreme to the next.

Crawling, I searched the hut as best as I was able. I had no real expectation that there would be food around after so long but it was all I could do. In among the abandoned clothes, bedding and tools I eventually came across a jar of Maxine's jam. It was three quarters full and rimed with green mould. I scraped that off with a finger and ate some of the berry jam underneath. After a short rest I crawled out to the clearing. By the fire a tin plate had collected leafy rainwater. I gulped it down and rested my head on the grass.

When I woke again it was getting dark and desperately cold. I was able to get myself into the hut and realised that I was still wearing my fire starter on a string around my neck with my knife. I'd been terrified of losing it in the darkness of the cave. I made a small fire using the fallen sticks from the scorched wall. With a pile of mildewed bedding scraped together as a nest, I fell asleep by the fire pit.

The following morning I finished the jam, feeling an ounce stronger than the day before. It was like coming out of a long illness and getting used to walking around again. I hobbled about the clearing collecting wild greens to eat and taking in the state of things.

It was clear that the others were gone. I assumed they'd been rescued. After all, if they'd moved to another camp, which they had no reason to do, they would have taken their things with them. No, it looked like they'd seen a boat or something, dropped everything and deserted the camp without a backward glance. There were plates and cups around the outdoor fire hole as if for a meal, and washing rotting on a line by the wood store.

I guessed that the partly burned wall of the hut was deliberate sabotage. This was mostly based on knowing what Duncan and Andrew were like: vindictive, selfish.

Just as they'd burned my tipi they'd tried to destroy the hut and its contents. Even though they'd left everything behind, the idea of me using any of it must have been too much. Had everything not been so damp with spring rain, the whole hut would have gone up.

By the fire I racked my brain trying to work out when the others had disappeared. The confusion I'd suffered in the cave made this nearly impossible. Real or imagined voices had blurred together until I'd not known who was really there and who wasn't. From the grass growing in the fire hole at the camp I thought it must have been a while ago. Maybe a week? Two? Really, I had no idea. What month was it? I'd lost track ages ago.

The fact remained that I was alone. The island was now truly deserted and it was unlikely the others would tell their rescuers of the woman they'd buried and left for dead. Not even Zoe, now she thought I'd murdered Shaun. No one was coming back for me. Another boat might come, eventually. Though since it had taken months for the first, I wasn't expecting another for a while. I couldn't do anything about that. I also didn't have to worry about the others. I felt free, safe. After the months of uncertainty and fear that feeling hit me like a drug.

Of course I was still weak. Being on my feet for more than ten minutes at a time was a strain. I gathered what I could close to the camp and stayed in the hut, recuperating. Since coming to the island I'd grown used to assessing my odds. Though improved by being out of the cave, things still looked pretty dire. I had no store of food, no aid and no hope of rescue. I was squatting in a half-ruined hut with no resources and no strength to do anything. I was still in danger, albeit a less obvious kind. The island itself was not my enemy, but if I couldn't recover my strength fast enough it would kill me all the same.

The wild greens would never give me enough calories to live on, but they could give me a little energy and slow my starvation. I spent a few days grazing close to the clearing and then went further. Mushrooms were my reward; dryad's saddle and the dependable jelly ear fungus. Sunlight and fresh air did as much for me as the return of nourishing food. My strength returned, little by little.

As I explored the camp it became obvious that things had been deteriorating before it was abandoned. The latrine was still where it had been last time I'd visited. No new hole had been dug, and the shelter had not been moved. There was a stench rising from it and in the woods I found what looked like human waste in small holes and behind bushes.

The clearing itself was littered with bones. They looked to be rabbit but some were a lot smaller – rat or something similar. It looked like the others had eaten and just dropped the bones when they were done. Before, we'd had a sort of compost heap for our vege-table scraps and other rubbish. We'd turned it regularly so it would rot down rather than moulder. It seemed to have overflowed and gone untended. Now it was a sprawling mound with intestines and rabbits' skins thrown on top, riddled with maggots.

The shower hut was falling down and it looked like they'd been using the wood from it for their fires. The half-finished cabin too. I guessed that they had been starving. Too weak to chop trees and haul logs. From the looks of things they'd been nesting in the hut, letting all work fall by the wayside. Part of me understood. After all, I was in the same position: weak and lacking in food and rest. Yet they'd had more than me. The thought that I'd been shitting in a bucket, forced to bury it where I lived, while they let a perfectly good latrine rot to nothing was infuriating.

With a few days of mushroom-laden meals under my belt, I managed to get down to the beach. I took a rucksack with clothes and a sleeping bag. Getting there and back in one day was not something I was up to. I found the remains of my burnt tipi as well as the fires we'd lit to stay warm as we waited for the boat. In the ruin of my old shelter I found my manicure scissors. They looked like an archaeological find, centuries old. It felt strange, being back there. So much had changed since that first day of fruitless waiting. It had all happened so fast.

The hike wiped me out and I spent that night in my sleeping bag beside a small fire. Each day I harvested blue-black mussels and steamed them, eating well for the first time in months. Judging from the growth in the forest it was late spring. April perhaps, or May. If it was too late in the year, the mussels would be bad, but I didn't get ill. That was something.

On a warmer than average day I stripped off by the sea. My shirt, which I'd worn so long I couldn't remember changing it, had started to rot away under the arms. My leggings were almost stuck to me in places. I was shockingly pale under my clothes. The exposed parts of me were deeply tanned and darkened further by ingrained dirt, but the rest was translucent, greyish and marked with red sores and rashes. I'd not looked at myself for a long time and my body felt like it belonged to someone else. Ribs, hip bones and knees poked out like sticks. My breasts were practically gone, shrunk back into my body, leaving pouchy skin. When I wriggled my toes in the sand the tendons and bones shifted like the hammers in a piano.

After scrubbing myself with handfuls of coarse sand, I took my blackened nail scissors and cut my hair off in chunks. I hardly recognised it as it floated away from me on the waves. The brownish-blonde colour was gone, replaced by a greyish cast of oil and dirt. Tangled into it were sticks, dead insects and webs. I rubbed sand into my shorn scalp until it tingled. With my arms wide I spun in the sea, feeling the sun on my raw, clean skin.

Something brushed against my hip. Thinking it was likely to be seaweed I glanced down to check what kind.

The thing floating in the water was long and thin, white and drifting like a strand of weed. It took a moment for me to realise what I was looking at: a bandage. An unravelled bandage carried by the sea. I floundered backwards and my hand touched something else. Bloodied gauze. I spun and saw that there were other things floating in the water, coming in on the tide. A yellow inflight oxygen mask drifted towards me. Shattered plastic, a charred travel pillow and a chunk of seatbelt floated by. Further off an orange life vest bobbed on a wave.

I thrashed my way back to the beach and shoved a long T-shirt on over my wet body. With my hands rammed under my armpits for warmth I stood there and watched the sea. A shiver passed through me that had nothing to do with the cold. Months ago I'd wondered about the possibility of a catastrophe on the mainland. I had no idea of what kind, but one that had crippled the country, led to a total collapse of any services that might be able to find and help us. Now this stuff was washing up. Had there been a crash? If so, where were the search boats and helicopters? I'd not seen or heard so much as a whisper of an engine. Where was this medical stuff coming from? Had there been some kind of accident, or attack? What was going on out there while I was stuck on Buidseach?

For the first time I wondered if I was safer on the island than off it. I'd assumed that whatever was going on out there could not be as terrible as being trapped on Buidseach with nothing, without civilisation. But what if I was wrong? What if it was worse?

And if it was, would the others return to the island, their last refuge?

The idea filled me with fear. I'd not even considered that they might want to come back to where they'd been trapped. But if things on the mainland were as bad as I thought they might be . . . what other choice would they have?

Looking out to the horizon I tried to tell myself it wasn't possible. It was not the Middle Ages; nothing could wipe out whole countries within months. We had sanitation and electricity, global aid and treaties. I thought of my glib response to Sasha, all those months ago. Zombies. Just as ridiculous as the notion that the mainland had been completely annihilated. Yet the debris floating in the grey sea told another story. I didn't want to look at it.

Turning my back I hurried to my improvised camp and started packing it up. I was tired and desperately wanted to sit by the fire and eat some dinner. I looked at my bucket of mussels and swallowed. The idea of eating anything from the same sea all that stuff floated in turned my stomach. What if there were bodies out there? Part of me wanted to throw the whole lot back into the water. The rest of me knew that I'd starve without that much-needed protein. I'd been eating shellfish from the waters of Buidseach for days and feeling no ill effects.

I set down the things I'd snatched up and lit my fire. If the choices were going hungry or eating food from the sea that touched the troubled mainland, it was no choice at all. Having experienced true starvation for the first time, it was the thing I now feared most.

Still, as I lay down under the stars I found sleep reluctant to visit me. The sea sighed and hissed as it rolled into the beach, bringing its clues to the outside world closer. In the darkness I heard the voices returning, laughing and screaming in the trees. Covering my ears did nothing to keep the sounds out but I tried it anyway. I hummed a half-forgotten song until my nightmares grew tired of waiting and came to find me.

Once warmer weather started to creep in I knew it was time to go back to the clearing. Summer was coming. The shellfish wouldn't be safe to eat again until after the colder weather. For now, though, they'd done me a lot of good. I was stronger, able to walk for longer periods without getting winded. Most importantly, my mind felt sharper. I could focus more easily and think without zoning out.

Clean and with my gnawing hunger sated, I felt calm. I found myself looking at the future head-on for the first time I could remember. I couldn't pretend anymore that rescue was coming any time soon. Another boat might chance on me but how long would that take? Four months? Six? A year? I had to plan or I wouldn't survive that long. I had to keep myself alive.

When I returned to the clearing I stood at its centre. Only a week or so before I'd crawled into it, half-crazed and starved to the edge of death. Now I looked around me and steeled myself for work. Everything we'd built was in disrepair, falling back to the forest. Already counting down the days to winter, I got to work.

Chapter 36

'Let's talk about the end of the world,' Sasha had said blithely. 'Pretend it happened tomorrow. How would you cope, who would you want to be with?'

I imagined that very little would change. My days were fairly uniform. Monday to Friday I got up early, headed in to the office and avoided people until I went home. Weekends I spent alone, either foraging or cleaning my flat. Mostly I just waited for Monday. If I ever got too lonely I'd walk into town and window-shop just to be around other people. If the world ended it'd be a permanent Saturday afternoon, only without the possibility of shopping or going for a walk. I'd just be stuck in my flat, distracting myself in any way I could.

As for who I'd want with me, I knew the answer well enough. Mum and Dad. Only that was now impossible. Because of me.

I remembered with painful clarity the night I'd called them. I'd had a shit day at work, been chewed out by someone higher up. I hadn't been able to keep from crying on the way home, pushing my way through crowds of shoppers. Desperate to get some privacy I'd taken a short cut and been cornered in an alley by a drunk guy. Nothing had happened, not really. He'd followed me, calling names that I desperately ignored. Then he'd grabbed my ponytail, shocking me. I'd screamed and from somewhere a kind of furious confidence had boiled up. I'd shrieked every swearword I could think of at him until he fled. Then I'd broken, sobbing as I practically ran home and locked myself in my flat.

That was when I flicked on the lights and realised that the meter had run down. Unable to face going to the corner shop in the dark, where that man might be lurking, I'd sat on the sofa for hours. No heating, no light, nothing to eat or watch. All the loneliness and fear and humiliation turning my insides to ice.

In that moment of weakness I'd cracked. As soon as Mum's voice came over the phone I started to cry, and when she asked if I wanted them to come and get me, I couldn't help it. I said yes. More than anything I wanted to be far from the loud, dirty city full of strangers, in a warm, well-lit home with two people that loved me.

They promised they'd be there in a matter of hours. I packed, still crying, feeling the lowest I'd ever been. The lowest I thought I could feel. Then I'd fallen asleep on the sofa, under my coat. Waiting.

They never came.

That was the night they had the accident. The last night I spoke to them. When I woke up it was to the police telling me I'd never see my parents again.

*

I didn't find the graves until I started on the allotment.

With the hut mostly patched up and a new latrine dug under the relocated shelter, it was my most pressing concern. I couldn't survive on forage alone. Although the overflowing compost pile was in a state, the lack of proper care had preserved a lot of the discarded vegetable matter, which had dried out. From these I was able to recover seeds, which I planted in rusted tins full of soil. Each one was a precious thing. I carried them into the hut to keep warm at night and took them outside to sit in the sun every day. Soon they got big enough to plant out.

The allotment was almost completely overgrown. It was as if we'd never cleared it to begin with. Only the ramshackle fence showed where it had been in an ocean of weeds, many of which I'd been eating. With a collection of blunt shovels and limited strength I was working on clearing it when I noticed the heaped earth at the back. Two heaps to be exact, each one about a foot wide and six feet long. They were covered in ferns and grass.

Beside one I found a cross of crudely nailed boards with 'Frank' written in faded marker pen on it. There was no cross on the other. Perhaps it had been lost in the greenery, perhaps it had never had a marker. Either way, I knew it was Shaun's body under that mound.

It was a shock to know that Frank was dead. I wondered how it had happened. Perhaps the harsh conditions had been too much for him? Had he had an accident like Shaun, or something worse? I remembered his love of homebrew and agaric tea. It seemed like every time I'd seen him in my rare encounters with the others, he'd been drunk. Maybe a build-up of toxins had finally caught up with him. Perhaps if one of them had poisoned the camera guys, they had killed him as well. I would never know.

Clearing the graves was not a productive use of my limited energy, but I did it anyway. It felt like the right thing to do. Mostly I did it for myself; to reassure myself that I wasn't beyond caring about them, despite what they'd done. I righted Frank's cross and made one for Shaun. It seemed only right that he should have a marker as well.

I was piling up the pulled weeds and sorting out the edible ones when I noticed the third grave. It was easy to miss, being so small. There wasn't much earth heaped on it but someone had outlined the edges with pebbles from the stream and without the surrounding weeds I could see a clear two-by-one-foot patch of bare soil. I stood there and looked down at the little spot. It was too small to be for anyone but Zoe's baby. I knelt and moved the weeds from around a larger stone. If something had been written there it was long gone. I could just make out a 'B' in black marker, mostly washed away and sun-faded. I traced the letter with a fingertip.

Had Zoe's baby drawn a breath or was this a memorial for a stillbirth? I didn't know. Almost didn't want to. From the size of the dirt patch I guessed that the baby had been full term, or close to it. There was no fourth grave. Whatever had happened, Zoe had survived. I was glad. Even if she'd gone along with the rest of them, she had saved my life once. Acid swam in my gut as I looked at Shaun's grave. I was the reason he'd been taken from her. Not a fitting repayment for Zoe's help. I bit the inside of my cheek and looked away.

I tidied B's grave and left a sprig of buttercups on it. There was nothing else I could do. Guilt followed me for the rest of the day. I threw myself into clearing the allotment and didn't stop digging until my muscles burned and I felt close to throwing up on the turned soil.

The sun went down while I was washing the dirt off myself in the stream. Inside the hut I dried myself off on a ragged towel and put on an old T-shirt of Andrew's over a pair of someone's boxer shorts.

I'd worked hard on the inside of the hut. After living in the cave for weeks I wanted to sleep in comfort, not filth. Without having to make space for eight people's beds and belongings there was plenty of room. After washing the mouldering bedding in the stream I'd put together a nice soft bed on a pile of pine boughs and foam rolls. The dirt floor was covered in fresh ferns and I'd cleaned and replaced all the pots and utensils on pegs on the wall.

I'd nailed some pallet planks to a chunk of log and dragged a stump in to use as a stool. It felt downright luxurious to sit and eat meals at a table, instead of crouched in the dark. I'd also been reading the books left behind by the others and relishing each new story.

But that night I couldn't take refuge in my creature comforts. I knew now that Zoe's baby was buried just across the clearing, along with Shaun and Frank. It was a very real reminder of what the island could do to people. I had to be prepared. Tables and books wouldn't keep me fed. Nothing I did would make up for what had happened to Zoe because of my carelessness, but I could survive. That would have to be enough.

There was a lot of work to get done and I filled the days to bursting with gathering, weeding, hauling water, chopping wood and catching rabbits. I reinforced the allotment fence with sticks and branches from thorn bushes and watched my seedlings grow. It wasn't easy. More than once I had to run out in the pelting rain to find plastic sheeting to shelter the young plants. When birds started eating the seedlings, I made hangers to scare them away by stringing together tin lids and rabbit bones. They hung in the trees and their eerie chiming at least cut through the silence, making me feel less alone. I started to think of them as charms or talismans, warding off the voices that whispered at night.

Coming out of the cave and eating semi-well had banished most of the hallucinations, at least during the day. I knew that's what they were. It didn't make them any less frightening. Some remained, though thankfully I was no longer actually seeing things. I only heard voices, sighing and whispering with the wind. Sometimes the voice from the cave, the witch, came to me in the dark. She sang, or whispered nonsense words with the creaking of the pines. Nothing I did seemed to have any effect on hearing these things. All I could do was ignore them and try to be inside before dark, when they began in earnest.

Eventually working with the blunt and rusted tools that the others had left out over the winter started to frustrate me. On a less practical level I also wanted clothes that didn't remind me of Duncan or the rest of them. It was the last place I wanted to go, but I had to go to the cave and get my stuff.

I followed the vague path I'd taken on my way to the clearing. When I came in sight of the cave I felt my skin start to crawl with remembered fear. A smell reached me clear across from the cave. Living in there I must have been mostly deadened to it, but now the reek made my eyes water. The hole I'd escaped through looked impossibly small. I'd not gained a noticeable amount of weight but I found I had to widen the hole to get in. Around it were the marks of my clawing fingers in the dirt. It looked and smelled like the den of an animal; a dead one.

I bundled my things together in the dark. Everything

felt slightly damp and I wondered if it had always been damp there or if it had crept in without my fires to chase it away. With my tools and salvageable clothing I crawled back out and coughed the stink from my lungs.

It was tempting to fill in the hole but I couldn't bring myself to do it. At the back of my mind was the fear that I might need to get back in there. I wondered if I'd ever feel secure enough to visit the clearing without getting shivers. Maybe one day. After all I had nothing but time in which to try.

On the way back I decided to take a shortcut through the trees. The bundle was awkward to carry and I wanted to get everything back and have a rest before chopping some wood. I was kicking my way through some ferns when I raised a hand to push a branch away. My fingers touched wet cloth and I snatched my hand back, surprised.

Tied to the offending branch was a strip of cloth, bleached grey by rain and sun. I dropped my bundle and untied the fabric strip with shaking fingers. Inside the knot, where the cloth was protected, was a seam of bright blue. A cache marker. I stood there stupidly for a moment, then grabbed my shovel and started to dig.

When the end of the spade hit plastic I whooped. Scrabbling on my knees I pulled out a box someone had sealed up with heavy duty tape. It was smaller than the other cache boxes. Those had been large storage crates, but this was barely bigger than a shoebox. I pried off the lid and found a piece of paper wedged underneath. On it was a printed picture of what had once been Father Christmas. Some damp must have got into the box because his red suit had bled out over the page. The message said simply 'Merry Christmas Islanders!' Under the note was a plastic-wrapped Christmas pudding, a bottle of brandy, some mini Christmas crackers and eight party poppers. One for each of us.

I sat and stared at those things long after my eyes blurred and they devolved into colours and shapes. I was thinking about Christmas, the last time we'd all been together properly. After that there'd been the long, fruitless wait for the boat that never came. All right, so that Christmas hadn't been great. I'd left hurt and angry, but we'd all been together, safe and fed. We were still just people living on an island for a lark, for a TV show. The real struggle, the knowledge that it was real, hadn't reached us yet.

With the box under one arm and my bundle in the other I returned to the clearing. Not knowing what to do with it I left the box on my table. It made me feel strange to look at it. I felt almost like it was something from another time entirely. A capsule of memories I didn't want to look at. Instead of resting I went straight out to cut wood and pile it in the store.

It was getting dark by the time I could bring myself to face the box again. I opened it and screwed up the note. It would be useful as kindling at least. The pudding in its bright red cellophane I put on the shelf.

It could be my emergency rations – high in fat, sugar and dried fruit. Perfect. I picked up the bottle of brandy. It wasn't large, the kind of bottle my mum had kept on hand for lighting the pudding and making hot toddies. Not really enough to preserve anything. I weighed it in my hands, turning it over. Perhaps I could make tinctures from it, there was no telling when I might need some form of medicine.

'Useful,' I said, my voice cracking from disuse. For a moment the sound made me uneasy, as if someone else had spoken.

'Getting out of practice,' I muttered, putting the bottle on the table. 'Maybe I should draw a face on something, give myself someone to talk to.'

I built up the fire to heat my stew and sat there, looking into it. The flames were hypnotic, like figures and animals fighting or waves on the sea.

'If it's not too much trouble, maybe you could bring a boat,' I said, addressing the shadows beyond the fire. 'That's your thing, isn't it? Shipwrecks, stranded sailors.' I picked up a stick and started tracing lines and swirls in the ashes around the fire hole. 'Or maybe you could just talk back. Though it makes sense that even my imaginary friend doesn't want to talk to me. That's fine. At least you're a good listener.'

A laugh came, dry, like twigs popping in the flames.

'Glad you think it's funny.'

I ate my meal and by the time I'd finished, the cold was closing in, the fire dying down. I took myself off to bed. The scent of pine rose up from my mattress of boughs and I watched the embers of the fire wink out, one by one.

As I drifted off I heard that dry, creaking voice again, crooning a lullaby.

Chapter 37

Around midsummer, when the days were long and hot, I decamped to the beach.

The move was temporary. I needed salt for preserving. For salt I needed seawater, lots of it. Lugging it up to the clearing was a waste of time and effort. The work was time-consuming but not difficult. I strained buckets of salt water through rags to get the sand out. After that all that was left was the boiling.

After a week or so of harvesting I had a respectable jar of slightly discoloured salt crystals. I needed a lot more but it was a fair start. I'd also amassed a large collection of broken plant pots, plastic bottles, disposable cutlery and rope. What I was hoping for were more buckets and containers to store water.

My search took me to the northern side of the island. I'd been avoiding it as that was where the portacabin was. It was also where the bulk of the craggy rocks were and lots of flotsam got trapped by them. Getting down to the sea was a struggle because in most places the earth had been eaten away leaving a sheer drop. I took my time and used a knotted rope around a tree to help me climb up and down.

I became quite confident in getting down the short cliffs to the beaches. After a while I decided to tackle the steepest climb on the northernmost point of the island. Standing at the top and looking down, I had my doubts. It was at least twenty metres down, maybe more. A fall from the clifftop would injure me badly, if it didn't kill me outright. I almost turned back from it. I would have, had I not spotted something interesting being tossed by the waves below. It looked like a bin; quite large and made of plastic. The kind of flip-top bin I'd had in the kitchen of my tiny flat. Something that size would hold a lot of water.

I tied off my climbing rope. The bin was a useful item and leaving it to be smashed on the rocks would be foolish. I'd be careful. I'd become quite practised at climbing and it wasn't that far. With a second rope trailing down to pull the bin up with, I started the climb.

Around halfway down I realised I'd made a mistake. The drop was further than it had looked from above. The cliff itself was also not as solid as the others I'd scaled. Mostly it was crumbling earth, not rocks and hard chalk. It was also honeycombed with small holes and burrows, maybe from some kind of bird. There was a stiff wind coming in and it made the rope sway. Chunks broke off when I put my feet on the wall. More than once I lost my footing and felt myself rock sickeningly in the air.

When I reached the ground my legs were shaking. After taking a few seconds to catch my breath I looked around for the bin. This was definitely going to be a one-off trip. It had better have been worth it.

Fortunately, the bin was in one piece. The plastic was bleached a little and the edges were a bit jagged, but it would hold water. After a little experimentation I managed to get my belt around it and tie the rope to that. It was tenuous but I thought it would hold until I got it up to ground level. Aware that this was the only time I'd be making the climb down, I looked around for anything else of worth.

There was disappointingly little. The bin was the only large item I could see. The usual collection of bottle caps and lolly sticks bobbed in the water but nothing I could see a use for. I was about to start the long climb back up when I saw a flash of colour almost buried in seaweed. After pulling a few clumps of bladder wrack away I found a piece of pink and purple cloth pinned under a round rock. Curious, I picked the rock up. It was lighter than I'd been expecting for its size. I was momentarily off balance, looked down and dropped it as if bitten.

The skull landed on the pebbles with a crack. It rolled until its empty sockets looked up at me, a tiny crab crawling in the darkness behind them. Looking around me I noticed other shapes. Things I'd thought to be driftwood now showed themselves; bleached bones, strewn on the wet pebbles. Reaching down I picked up the scrap of cloth. It was a length of silk; a headwrap. Under it, half buried in fine grey sand, was a pair of broken glasses. Zoe's glasses.

I looked down at the skull with its skittering crab. This was Zoe's skull, sun-bleached and tumbled by the sea. I was standing in the middle of her bones. Looking up I took in the sheer drop from clifftop to beach. I thought of the tiny headstone, which I'd started to think of as 'Bea's grave'. I remembered how abandoned it had seemed, how odd it was that Shaun's grave was overgrown. Was that because Zoe wasn't there to care for them?

Had she jumped? Or, worse, was this where the others had dumped her after she died giving birth? If they'd been too exhausted and hungry to chop wood, had they forgone digging a hole and just rolled her off a cliff into the sea? The bones seemed too small to be those of the person I'd known. There was so much more to Zoe than those few scraps of her could amount to. I stared at them and the full force of Zoe's death hit me. She was gone and this was all that was left.

I couldn't leave her there.

Under my T-shirt I had on a tank top. It was threadbare but serviceable. I spread the T-shirt on the ground and started gathering the bones. It seemed as though many of them had been washed away. Mostly they were long individual bones. I could look on them as almost fake props. I struggled in picking up the skull and the remains of what appeared to be a hand, though. With those I was acutely aware that they were human remains. In the end I had a bundle tied up and carefully put it in my rucksack.

Climbing back up the rope was harder than coming down. I needed footholds to get up and those that I found crumbled as soon as I stepped on them. My arms started to burn from holding up my weight and I feared they'd give out before I reached the top. When I finally clawed my way onto the grass I laid on my back and felt my heart hammer itself calm again.

After hauling up the bin and collecting my ropes I headed for the clearing. I knew I wouldn't be able to rest until Zoe was properly buried beside her baby and Shaun. There was just enough space next to Shaun's grave to bury Zoe, with Bea at their feet. But when it came time to put Zoe's bones to rest it felt wrong to just put them in the ground. I looked at them and for the first time imagined how the crabs and gulls must have stripped them bare. I flinched from the thought. I didn't want to see that. I wanted to remember something beautiful. It was what she deserved.

I went to the hut and started looking through the stuff I'd piled up furthest from my bed. This was the stuff I had no use for, personal things the others had neglected to take with them. Mostly it was useless: Andrew's watch, which no longer worked, a pack of cards, dried-up pens, broken sunglasses and of course the cameras, all smashed to bits. I searched through all of it until I'd found Zoe's stuff.

There wasn't much; hair wraps, a small pot of dried-up glitter paint, a necklace tarnished black, a compact mirror and some of the clay bowls she'd made. Most of the bowls were broken, but two were still whole. I also found a little clay figure I couldn't remember her making. It was a little clay woman with a curving belly, full breasts and a blank face, sitting cross-legged. The clay was scorched black from the firing. A shiver passed through me.

Outside I lined the hole with blossom from the thorn bushes and placed the items around the outer edge. In the centre I arranged the bones with the skull at the top. It seemed right somehow, to make things as beautiful as possible, for Zoe.

'You deserved better than this . . .' I felt my voice catch. 'I'm so sorry. I'm sorry.' My voice trailed to a whimper and I started to sob. As I wrapped my arms around myself there came a soft shushing sound, like the wind was trying to soothe me. I raised my head. The air was still, no wind to stir the trees.

'She deserved better,' I said, to the pines and the shadows beneath them. 'This place . . . Why did it have to be so cruel?'

The silent trees shifted slightly in a breeze. I could feel something nearby. A sense of being watched. I knew what I'd said wasn't true. The island wasn't cruel. The island was just that, an island.

'What happens to me then, when I die? When there's no one to bury me? Or do I disappear, taken by the witch? Will anyone know?'

A song came from the shadows beneath the woods. It was as though it came from the trees themselves.

Maybe it did. Who knew what kind of things the witch was capable of? Singing trees, faces in the fire, whispers in the dark. But none of it felt cruel. Like the island, she simply was. There was nothing in her that wasn't also of this place. Including me. I was part of the island now. Perhaps that was why I could hear her.

I covered the bones with soil. The petals would turn brown, rot away, but I would remember them as soft and perfect. Beautiful, just like Zoe. I left the clearing and made for the beach to check on my fire.

The next day the clay woman was on the grave. I had no memory of putting it there.

Chapter 38

'Now, Maddy, you're probably aware that most of our audience are desperate to know – how did you get off the island?' Rosie asks, as though hungry for a juicy piece of gossip. She has no idea what she's asking, or that she hasn't really asked the right question at all.

It isn't really a secret. Or at least, the secret isn't in how I did it. That's already fairly common knowledge. The way I managed to get back to the mainland, by boat, isn't so terribly hard to work out. I told everyone at the trial anyway. So it's not a shocking new development. Stop the presses, woman uses boat to travel over water!

No, where the boat came from is more the point. How it reached me, and why. Perhaps the most important question of all: why had I returned to the mainland alone?

Well, I think, looking into Rosie's expectant face. She and her audience will have to live with disappointment.

Some secrets go too deep to ever share.

Chapter 39

Following Zoe's burial, I began to speak to the witch more often. I talked about the plants I collected, the weeds I pulled up. Commented on the sky, the weather and the shapes in the smoke of my fire as if they were portents to be interpreted. The witch was the only friend I had, the only person I could talk to.

I knew she wasn't real. Even though sometimes I found myself looking for her in the shadows of the woods, as if she might step out and help me carry a load of wood. I felt her watching me and was comforted by it. Real or not, having another person around made me feel less alone, which I guessed was why my brain kept conjuring her up. Maybe I was going crazy but, as long as I could keep myself warm and fed, I could deal with having an imaginary friend.

Even if, sometimes, she spoke back.

In terms of survival, my odds were looking pretty good. The inside of the hut was filling up. I'd made new shelves with pieces of log and driftwood planks. They were slightly wonky but held my supplies well enough. I had jars of salt, dried mushrooms and bunches of dried seaweed. The allotment had done well and I was in a frenzy of bottling ripe tomatoes; chopping and salting them, eating them for every meal. The squash would ripen towards the end of summer and I was already excited for some variety.

I'd built myself a new smoke hut and started experimenting with small amounts of rabbit meat. It had taken a while, but I thought I had a method that would preserve meat for several months at least. I'd also cured myself some rabbit skins and was working on a sort of door curtain to keep the cold air out when snow came. They were rough on the inside and smelled, but warmth was worth it in my opinion. Besides, I'd smelled worse.

I was coming home after foraging by the tidal pools when I saw the boat. It was bright white and unmistakeable against the dark, gravelly sand. It was much smaller than the boat that had brought us to the island originally and it looked strange – so artificial and alien. For a moment I couldn't believe that it was real.

Aside from the boat everything else was quiet and normal. There was no one around. It might have fallen from the clear blue sky for all the sense it made to me at the time. It was only when I crept closer that I saw the footprints in the sand. Two sets.

I reached out and touched the smooth white shell of the boat. Cautiously, as if it was a wild animal. The sides were dry. It had been beached for a while.

That boat is like a rock in a river. Around it my story swirls and parts. It goes one way, reality another. There is the truth and then there is the version I tell afterwards. In the one I tell, I climb into the boat, mad with a desire to escape. I sail away without a backward glance. Only later does it occur to me that the boat must have belonged to someone. Only later do I wonder who.

The truth is a slippery thing, a bitterness that can be sweetened away in the telling. Masked with honey, made easier to swallow. I've perfected the mixture and it works on everyone: the police, the jury and now Rosie.

This, then, is the memory I revisit when the nightmares wake me in the dark. The true story. The only thing that reminds me that I am safe. That the only justice I can expect has already come to pass.

'Where have they gone to?' I whispered aloud, then caught myself listening for an answer, as if the wind or the trees might tell me what she saw. What she knew of these strangers.

'If they are strangers at all.'

Unease coiled in my belly like an eel. As soon as I said the words aloud I felt strange. Had I spoken or had she? I pressed my lips together. It was difficult to know anymore when I was talking aloud or when she was speaking. Either way, I had to know who had come to the island.

I followed the footprints, though I didn't need to beyond a certain point. It was clear the two people from the boat had made for the clearing, following the path we had all used the first time we explored the island. These were not strangers. They knew the way.

When I arrived at the hut I could heard voices inside. Arguing. I stood there, taking slow breaths. Two of the other islanders had returned. They were in my home. There was no escape from them. I was frozen.

'Help me,' I whispered. 'Please help me do this.'

Swallowing my fear I took a step towards the hut. The second was easier, the third I barely thought about. I heard her footsteps behind me. I was not alone.

I pushed aside the curtain and went inside.

It was strange, seeing them again up close. Perhaps they felt the same. We stood there just looking at each other for what felt like a solid minute, then Duncan laughed. It was a sharp bark of a laugh and it made me jump at its suddenness.

'Told you,' he said to Andrew. 'Had to be her. Cockroaches and this bitch. Unkillable.'

Andrew was sitting on my stool while Duncan had seated himself in the middle of my bed. They both had freshly cut hair and trimmed beards. Their clothes were new and good quality; thick coats and sturdy hiking boots. The table had been dragged to sit between them, the cups evidence that they had been enjoying the

Christmas brandy. Following my gaze Duncan raised the almost empty bottle.

'A nice welcome home – cheers.'

'Cheers,' Andrew echoed, raising a hunting rifle in a mock salute. My stomach churned; I'd not thought they'd be armed.

'Came prepared this time,' Duncan said seeing the direction of my gaze and making Andrew snort. 'Course, we didn't know we wouldn't be alone here, but if there's one thing I've learnt it's to expect the unexpected.'

'You thought I was dead,' I said. My voice came out strained. I'd wanted it to be strong.

'Seemed a sure thing. When those arseholes stopped chasing their tails and sent a boat I thought you might realise we'd gone and dig yourself out, but there wasn't anything on the island for you so . . . yeah, we thought you'd die.'

'And the others?' I asked. 'Where are they?'

'Back home,' Duncan said. 'Not Shaun though, you killed him.'

I was about to offer a denial, when I heard her. A soft sigh of breath in my ear. Shushing me. She was right, there was no point antagonising them. I bit my cheek and stayed quiet, waiting.

Duncan rolled his eyes as if bored of me. 'Frank's dead too – but you know that. You must've seen the grave over in the garden. Then once we got back to Scotland Maxine went back to her husband. Gill's gone to her sister's. Good riddance.'

371

'What's it like out there?' I said, annoyed at myself for asking.

Duncan's eyebrows shot up, then he laughed. 'Jesus, you have no idea, do you? What, you thought the zombies had come up to kill everyone, or the bombs were coming down? Had a lot of time to make up little fantasies, didn't you?'

I gritted my teeth, unwilling to give myself away. Inside I felt small and very very stupid. He'd said 'they' sent a boat after all. Had I been so wrong all along?

Duncan snorted. 'It was a fucking stunt. They'd always planned to leave us until February. For views, for excitement. They told our families filming was extended. An extra month, what's the big deal? Like they could possibly understand what it was like here.'

'But they didn't come,' I said. 'In February, there was no boat.'

'Yeah, well,' Duncan spat. 'Plane went down up the coast mid-February. Adrian and Sasha —' he said the names like they were curses '— tried radioing the camera guys to check none of the rescue boats were looking around here, interfering with the show. By the time they stopped ass covering and panicking about the plane crash and why those guys weren't radioing back, and actually sent a boat, it was too late. First you kill Shaun, then Frank had some kind of stroke. Now they owe us, big time, and they're paying out as well, trying to keep it all hush-hush. Compensation for the "accident" to Shaun's parents. Cash for us to keep quiet. I'm thinking of relocating to Majorca.'

'What about Zoe?'

'Oh, her,' he sighed. 'Well, she fucking lost her mind. After Shaun she was hard to deal with but then she went into labour and that was a nightmare – hours that took. Screaming and all that. Then it came out all . . . wrong. There was no talking to her. She'd just sit there and not say anything or even look at you. Not what you want when everyone else is doing their bit. Then she went and topped herself.'

My eyes stung and I blinked away the tears as they tried to surface. I had to keep my head.

'It's not our fault,' Duncan was saying. 'We couldn't watch her every second. It wasn't our job to stop her killing herself. Plus, now her family gets a nice payout instead of waiting for her to give up on being an "influencer",' he said, laying the scorn on thick. 'So they're better off.'

'And now you're here,' I said, mind working, trying to figure out why.

'For the server,' Duncan said, smirking.

'But the generator was—'

'For everything in the cabin. The radio was useless, but the server had solar backup. Kept storing everything. They downloaded it, took it when they came for us. But those servers are still there.'

'You came back to destroy the servers,' I said, suddenly understanding. 'They're covering everything up, but you want to make sure everything really was deleted. So it never gets out, what you did. To me.'

All that time after the boat never came, I'd kept my

camera running. Right up until the night Shaun died, the night I'd been entombed. All that was recorded. I'd thought it would save me, but now it seemed the only reason my tormentors had returned. To stop the world seeing them starve me, attack me, hunt me through the woods.

In the silence that followed the fire snickered and Duncan looked me over. I forced myself not to move or blink, just stood there and waited.

'Look, I know there's been bad feeling, on both sides,' he said. 'But, you need to know what really happened. I mean – things were tough there, for a while. Everyone was desperate and looking to me to take charge and lead us through it. But I couldn't stop them once they got an idea in their heads. And Gill, she kept talking about how you were stealing food, that you'd killed the camera guys . . . It got out of hand.'

I nodded, feeling stiff and numb as a doll. Tension filled every part of me like wire, making my joints ache.

'But now it's all back to reality. We're set for life and nothing's going to bring the others back. The producers are keeping their mouths shut on what happened. The only thing left is to destroy the servers in case some journalist comes looking for all that "lost" footage. I'm done trusting Adrian and that bitch Sasha. Can't be sure it's really gone until it's in bits in the sea. You don't want anyone to know what happened, do you? For people to find out what you did to Shaun? So why don't you grab a spade and maybe, when we leave, I'll let you come along.'

He was interrupted by a clatter as the rifle fell to the packed-dirt floor. We both looked at it, then Duncan glared at Andrew.

'What did you do that for?'

'I don't . . .' Andrew blinked, looking at his hand. He started to get up but instead fell flat on his face. He didn't move, but his breath wheezed in the sudden silence. A few laboured gasps, then nothing.

Duncan's eyes met mine over Andrew's body.

'Looks like it's just you and me now,' I said.

Chapter 40

Things had been winding down, I could sense it. Sasha had finished her iced coffee and behind her, in the shadows of the blinding light, I could hear equipment being broken down and put away. The door to the outside world opened and closed, letting in the sounds of traffic and birds.

'What will you do when you get home?' Sasha had asked. 'Do you have any plans for what comes next, after the show?'

I didn't even have plans for once the interviews were over. There was nothing for me to do except go home and wait. What would I do when it was all over, when I had nothing to wait for?

'I don't know, is the honest answer,' I'd said, too tired and stressed to concoct a lie. 'I hope I'll come out of this . . . different, somehow. Maybe I'll learn something about myself. Maybe I'll have made some new friends. I think what I most want is to learn to be kinder – to not judge myself so harshly, to not assume the worst. Mostly, I'm looking to find myself.'

I'd looked away from the camera to find Sasha checking her phone, not listening.

It was over.

*

The day I saw the plane debris and medical stuff wash up on the beach, I'd realised there was a chance the others might return to the island. If the outside world was damaged enough for crash debris and bloody gauze to be bobbing in the sea, the others might start to miss the island, their last refuge. As the idea had taken root, I'd started to imagine what that might mean. The danger that would bring for me.

There was no fighting them, I'd proven that. There were more of them and they were stronger than me. No. I had to remember Auntie Ruth's advice: get back at them, better and smarter than they got at you. I had to be clever. That was the only way to save myself. I had to stop them before they could hurt me.

I don't know which one of us had the idea. I was sitting at the table, eating my evening meal. The firelight made the bottle of brandy glow. I'd not done anything with it. The idea of making tinctures had sort of faded from my mind. But looking at it then, I thought I heard a whisper, a sigh from the shadows.

'There,' I said, and realised I was holding the bottle. 'I said this would be useful.'

I'd accidently poisoned the others once, after all. I could do it again. Purposefully.

I went into the woods the next day to hunt out the plants I habitually ignored. The poisonous cousins and sisters of things I ate every day. I crushed each one with a stone and steeped them in a pot of brandy. A veritable witch's brew: adder's root, avenging angel, deadly nightshade, devil's bread.

After a few days I strained out the wilted plants and funnelled the liquid back into the bottle. Once I'd done that I just kept it on the table. Anyone going into the hut couldn't fail to notice it. I'd trusted greed, luck and the witch to do the rest.

I picked up the fallen rifle and took Andrew's seat with it across my lap. I felt Duncan's eyes on me the whole time. When I looked up I saw he was sweating, eyes bulging. It looked like he was trying to move but his legs weren't obeying him. He was breathing hard, afraid.

I wasn't sure how I'd expected to feel. Perhaps I'd thought the sight of him being scared of me would feel . . . empowering. Mostly I was just tired, now that the danger had lessened somewhat. Tired and oddly sad. I let out a steadying breath.

'We should have some time to talk,' I said. 'Depending on how much you had.'

'What did you do?'

'Not much. Just poisoned a bottle of brandy. Waited.'

'Poisoned it with what?' he asked, voice rising an octave or so.

'A few things.' At the sight of his widened eyes, I relented. 'Principally hemlock. It causes ascending paralysis, among other things. Right now you can't move your legs; soon, your arms and then your respiratory system will shut down and you'll suffocate . . . like Andrew. There's some other stuff in there, should make it pretty quick.'

'You can fix it?'

'. . . No. Even if I wanted to there isn't anything I could do for you here.'

'Why?'

'*Why?*' I was on my feet before I knew it, holding the rifle so tightly it hurt my hands. 'Why? Seriously? Because you tried to kill me. Because you buried me alive. How about because after everything, you thought you could trick me into helping you cover up what you did. And then what? You'd shoot me in the back of the head and bury me too. *Why*,' I scoffed. 'Jesus, do you honestly have no idea?'

'You killed Shaun, that's why we shut you away. You crazy bitch.'

'Do you really believe that I killed him? That he didn't just fall?' It had not occurred to me before that Duncan might seriously believe I had done it deliberately. 'It's just the two of us, and you'll be dead in a few minutes so . . . no point in lying. Not now,' I said, as gently as possible.

His face creased and I watched as his eyes welled with frightened tears. He didn't say anything but shook his head. No, he didn't think I'd murdered Shaun.

'So why? Why did you tell them I did? Why did you do it? Any of it?'

He shook his head harder but said nothing. Whether he could speak I didn't know. Gurgling sobs escaped him, spit bubbles bursting between his lips.

'We didn't really talk much, not as friends, equals. The thing is, I came here, to this island because I didn't like my life. I didn't like myself. Couldn't forgive myself. I wanted to be better, kinder . . . happy.'

Duncan spluttered and tipped over, falling partway off the bed. His head lolled towards the floor.

'For a while I thought nothing would help. I felt all this guilt over one horrible, cruel accident. But . . . the thing is, all the terrible things that happened, all the things you did, the things that happened to me – I know now it wasn't my fault, it was out of my control. And "happy", what is that exactly? There's contentment, safety, comfort. But happiness? I don't think it's real, not like those other things. Or maybe they just matter more. As for kindness . . . Well. There were a lot of things I could have put in that bottle. Things like what one of you gave those camera guys. Things that would have had you liquefying from the inside out. But despite everything you did . . . I made it painless, as painless as it could be.'

His breathing rattled against the dirt floor, stirring the dry ferns. I waited and eventually it stopped entirely. Then everything was still and quiet. I closed my eyes and let out a breath that had been stagnating in my lungs. After setting the rifle aside I got to my feet and found that my legs were shaky. I felt as though I'd taken a few swigs from the brandy bottle myself.

I got my water bottle and drank deeply, suddenly aware of the dryness in my mouth. Slowly it began to sink in that I'd killed two people. Although I told myself that I hadn't made them drink the brandy, it made little difference. I'd poisoned Andrew and Duncan, then watched them die. I would have to carry that. I wondered if I could, if I would crack. Only time would tell. Then again, perhaps I had cracked already.

'Perhaps.'

I turned at once. The voice was not my own, but it was clear, close and very real.

Behind me stood the witch, fully and in the flesh. She wore black for the occasion. With her came the bitter, graveyard smell of yew and ivy. My first feeling on seeing her wasn't fear, or even concern. It was relief. The others were dead, but I wasn't alone. She was with me.

'And so it ends,' she said in her crow-like voice.

'I should bury them.'

'Not with the others.'

'No . . . Somewhere else . . . somewhere hidden,' I said, already knowing exactly where.

She nodded approvingly, knowing my intent. I noticed for the first time that she was wearing a necklace: a holed stone on a length of grey wool. The necklace I'd made to remember the island by, months ago. Where it was now I had no idea. Perhaps I'd lost it when I fled the beach, or it rotted off in the cave.

Wherever it was, I didn't need it. I would never forget the island, or anything that had happened there.

But I was going to leave.

I dragged both bodies outside. They were too heavy to take far but the place I had in mind was workable. It had long since become dark outside. After building a small fire to see by I started to dig a hole. A pit, right under the compost heap.

By the time the sun was fully up I was patting the last shovelful of rotten vegetation and maggoty skins into place. To anyone happening upon the clearing, their graves would be invisible. Any smell or flies seeming to rise from the heap of waste they'd left behind. Anyone looking for them would have to hunt for a long, long time. Much like the second fisherman in my story, they had dined with the witch and vanished without a trace.

'Will you go now?' she asked from behind me.

'I have to. The truth needs to get out, and I'm the only one that can tell it.'

Her cloak was green as the leaves, the hood pushed back. Beneath it her face was comfortingly familiar, and the mouth curved in an approving smile.

It was my own.

Epilogue

I pause to take a sip of water. It tastes of pipes and dead, cold steel. I'd never realised that water had a taste before. Having drunk from streams and rain, from dripping roots and wet rocks, I can now identify water as others do coffee or wine.

Rosie says nothing. Throughout the studio there's no sound at all. At some point all the milling figures paused and then remained rooted. I put the glass down and shift in my seat. As if released from a spell Rosie blinks and glances towards the cameras and their mute, motionless operators.

It felt the same way the first time I told my story, to a policewoman in the back of an ambulance. The same silence, the shock and unnatural stillness of those who don't know how to react or what to say. Then came the stream of meetings with a solicitor, more questions, more interviews.

I kept things vague on the subject of Andrew and Duncan. Though I didn't lie outright. I tempered the truth with ignorance and seasoned it with innocence. I said only that they returned to the island, that I found their boat and escaped. No one asked what happened between those two events; finding the boat and leaving on it. No one thought of them as separate things at all.

They looked for them, obviously. Sent boatloads of police and dogs to Buidseach to sniff them out. I was even slightly worried for a while, but the witch has a grip on that place. A way of keeping her secrets. They found no trace of them. In the end they assumed they'd tried to swim for it and drowned. It was suicide to attempt it, after all.

During the investigation the other bodies on the island were exhumed. Once the police had remains, they set their sights on someone to blame. They're to be buried again, elsewhere, now that the trial is over. I'm glad. They deserve a proper memorial. At least, Zoe and her baby do. Perhaps Shaun too. Frank I'm not too bothered about.

The show runners had copies of all the recordings, taken from the servers, but after viewing them, made sure they were deleted. All except one. The one they kept as insurance. It didn't matter in the end, of course; they'd neglected to destroy the servers themselves, too busy herding half-feral islanders onto the boat. All the recordings were eventually recovered. The cover-up, just like everything else they'd done, was slapdash.

I saw their recording in court, though; the last piece of the puzzle. Gill with Duncan, Andrew and Shaun, drinking the stolen whisky. Heard them wish me gone from the island. Duncan had told me what she'd said, almost. When he'd tried to drag me from the cave. Gill told them, joked, that they should knock me out and leave me to drown in the sea. The part he omitted, was what she said next; 'It worked before.'

I saw the moment Gill realised what she'd said. That she had, at least in her mind, confessed to murdering her mother; those three words the complete story of a supposed stroke and accidental drowning. Why had she done it? Freedom, I suppose; from caring for her, from missing out on a TV show because she was the daughter with no family, no husband. Nothing better to do than take care of her mother.

I understood what she'd done, in a strange way. Had I not lost my parents, I might have ended up like Gill. Hating and resenting them for needing me as I'd needed them. Still, had she not tried and failed to cover up her mistake by passing off deadly mushrooms as a legal high to the camera crew, we might have had the means to call for help. Had she not left their equipment on when she went back to attempt to erase the footage of her confession, the generator wouldn't have been drained. Without the crew to request more fuel, we were stuck without a line to the mainland. That one act condemned us to months of desperate starvation and violence.

When charges were pressed and she was called to testify, Maxine took her own life. I don't think it was guilt so much as shame that drove her. Guilt requires remorse, and I don't think she ever felt that. I think, to her, Zoe and I deserved everything we got. It was other people knowing what she'd done that she couldn't stand.

I was one of two people to survive the island and everything that came after. Not that I got to speak to Gill. She was convicted for the deaths of Ryan and Eric; their names finally brought back to me by the court proceedings. Despite her 'confession' there wasn't enough evidence for a charge on her mother's murder. She'd killed two men and damned us all, for nothing. I saw that knowledge hit home as she stood in the dock, weeping.

In court I hardly recognised her. Gill wasn't as skeletal as I was, having escaped the island before me, but she retained a haunted, skull-like look. Her red hair had grown out and been cut back to its roots, leaving her with grey wisps. She looked like a corpse under the fluorescents in the coolly modern courtroom. I stared at her while giving my testimony; she didn't meet my eyes once.

Those responsible for extending our stay on the island were also found guilty; of false imprisonment, endangerment, manslaughter and a host of other things. I don't suppose any of them had any real idea of what they were condemning us to. To them it was just a show, just one or two extra months that they could pay us off for later if we made a fuss. I was surprised that I didn't blame them. No one outside of that place could have known what it would do to us to be left there. It was beyond imagination.

I heard some interesting things in court. The text chains and emails between Sasha and Adrian where they'd broken down our interviews and decided who to condemn to a year on the island. They'd described Zoe as 'flighty and insubstantial', Duncan as 'bull-headedly competitive' and Frank as 'the perfect balance of racist, sexist and old soak for the Brexit demographic'. I felt it like a slap when they got to me. 'Madeline Holinstead – mousy, stuck-up and awkward. Clearly maladjusted lone wolf trying to fit in. Perfect love-to-hate character.'

All the effort I'd made to convince them I was a good fit, but they'd known all along. Seen it in me. They'd put me on that island to be ostracised, to be my own worst enemy against people chosen to resent me. I almost laughed, right there in the gallery, the shock of it percolating into something near hysteria. It was the final peek behind the curtain at the mechanisms behind the worst year of my life.

Around the studio people begin to move again. They take my mic off and I'm shepherded to a waiting taxi. The space between everyone there and me seems to yawn, full of things they have no response to, no platitudes to cover. I don't mind. I've become used to silence.

I kept my secret and told no one about the witch. The apparition with my face. Away from the island I was certain she was a figment of my imagination. A symptom of the horrors of that place. Still, sometimes I think I see her, briefly, a shadow in the corner of my eye. A friendly face in a crowd of strangers.

At the train station I board and sit, unruffled by the crowds. I look through the dark mirror of the foggy window. Just like Mum wanted, I'm on my way home, at last. Not to stay, but to sell. I've already found a beautiful piece of land and a cottage with a view of the sea.

I suppose it's ironic that of all those involved in the Buidseach disaster, I've escaped with my freedom. If there was any justice in the world, I probably would have been tried for murder. I don't deny that's what it was. Although I acted in self-defence, I still killed two people. Had I not covered it up, I might even have been convicted. No jury of my peers could have understood what it was like, out there, on the island.

Fortunately I have learned that there is no justice, aside from what we make for ourselves. There is only survival, and the victor tells the story.

Acknowledgements

This book would not exist were it not for the constant support of Vander, the best friend any writer could ask for. From answering questions like 'am I perhaps killing off too many characters?' to providing editorial input, cover art and praise for my self-published work, as well as tea, sympathy, therapy, tarot readings and sheer unbridled optimism. You are too good for words. Without your belief in me, I probably would have given up on my dreams a long time ago. I'm so glad I hit you with that desk on the first day of school. It was the start of something truly special.

Likewise, were it not for the unceasing support of my parents, this book would never have been written. Thank you for instilling a love of reading in me and for taking me to so many places that fuelled my imagination. Even though you didn't always understand what I was doing, you always let me get on with it and helped me every step of the way. Without your help and guidance I would never have been able to go back to university, write this novel, or walk out of so many terrible jobs.

To Jack, my long-suffering brother, thank you for always listening to my stories and for putting up with my 'witchy' rubbish and very pungent scented candles. A special thanks for all the cups of coffee you made during this whole process. I couldn't imagine life without you.

I owe my agent, Laura Williams, enormous gratitude for picking my first novel up and giving me a chance. Though it's been an arduous journey, I'm happy to have been on it with you. Whenever I can't quite work out what's off about a scene, you always manage to find what needs changing, and turn even the most insurmountable issues, into easy fixes. Thank you for talking me down from some of my wilder ideas! I don't think *Stranded* would be half the book it is without your input and enthusiasm.

Further thanks goes to Rachel Faulkner-Willcocks for her kindness, determination and insight, without which this novel would have been the poorer. I am so grateful to everyone on the team at Avon for all their hard work in making this book a reality.